Nicola Chalk was born in 1975 and was lucky enough to have been brought up in a loving family atmosphere in Berkshire. Nicola has always had a passion for writing and has fulfilled her lifelong ambition to have a book published.

Nicola still lives in Berkshire, with her partner Tony in their first home together.

For more information on the author, please visit: -

www.nicolachalk.com

BECAUSE OF YOU

NICOLA CHALK

BECAUSE OF YOU

Vanguard Press

A CIP catalogue record for this title is
available from the British Library.

ISBN 978 184386 325 0

*Vanguard Press is an imprint of
Pegasus Elliot MacKenzie Publishers Ltd.*
www.pegasuspublishers.com

First Published in 2007

**Vanguard Press
Sheraton House Castle Park
Cambridge England**

Printed & Bound in Great Britain

DEDICATION

Dedicated to:- Tony, because of you I got this finished.

A special thank you to my family, for all the childhood memories, Roni, for all our "Bridget Jones" moments and Helen, for being a constant for the past 15 years.

ACKNOWLEDGEMENTS

Maida Vale, Thursday evening writing class 2004, for the motivation and criticism.

Pegasus Elliot Mackenzie Publishers, for making a dream come true.

Helen & Roni, for being my personal expert proof-readers.

Nigel, for my very own website.

Emma, for her artistic expertise.

My friends and family for all their support.

Bella's Story

Chapter One

I love Summer. I always have. I'm the girl who always has the great tan in the Summer (it doesn't matter what the health experts say; I know it is unhealthy to have a tan, but you have to agree it does look fab. Yeah, I know I may look like a leather handbag, but I'll worry about that when I'm forty). I moan and whinge my way through the cold Winter months and as soon as June arrives, so does my personality. I am in a great mood and not only because the sun is shining. I'm about to go round to my good friend Emma's for a barbecue. A few people are expected there and it will be good to have a few beers, a gossip and to sit in the sun. It will also be extremely good to get away from my boyfriend. He is, if I am going to be brutally honest, a pillock.

I used to go to school with Emma but never really knew her. It's a sad state of affairs when you are in the same Maths class as someone for five years but you never actually get to know them, but then again I never paid attention to anything in my Math's class so that is hardly surprising. Emma and I only started to get to know each other at college. In fact, she is probably the only person I really got to know at college (well other than Pillock, but then again I still don't really know him all that well, even after all these years). Emma and I became firm friends.

I pick up the beers I have bought, my purse and my car keys and head off towards Emma's house. I don't really know why I'm driving. She doesn't live far from me and I am planning to have a drink or five anyway, so I will have to leave my car there. I am so very lazy! Did I mention that about me?

By the time I arrive at Emma's, I realise driving was a really bad idea because now I am feeling sweaty and downright horrible. My lovely little, blue fiesta is my first car and I do love her apart from the fact she doesn't have air conditioning. I swing my legs out of my car counting my lucky stars that I didn't wear my short, summery dress after all because I just can't seem to balance the beers, keys and my purse whilst exiting the car like a lady. I have an attractive sweat line above my top lip, so I am glad I didn't trowel the makeup on before coming over. I'm also starting to show sweat marks under my arms. Is it only me that has these problems?

Emma lives in a three bedroom ex-council place about five minutes drive away from me (I told you it was close). The décor is old and seriously needs updating but as Emma points out; she just rents a room and has no inclination of living there forever. Jono owns the house and rents out two of his rooms (I am not even sure if that is his real name. He seems to think it makes him quite cool so we can leave it at that). The second room is let to a girl called Amy or Angie, I am not sure which but then we hardly ever see her.

The front door is open and I can hear the music coming from the garden. A few people are mingling inside, but I just make my way straight outside. Emma is sitting at a picnic table with our other friends Marie and Richie. Let me introduce my friends to you.

Marie is one of my best friends. I have known her since primary school and we have been inseparable ever since. We are quite similar, which is one of the reasons we get on so well. Marie lives a few miles away from both Emma and I, sharing a house with a girl she works with.

All my girl nights out have always included Emma and Marie, including one night where I was so drunk I nearly passed out, but hey that's a different story. Actually, my girlie nights out have always included Richie as well.

Richie is also one of my best friends. We once had a snog at school; I am hoping that this is not the reason that Richie is now 100% gay. Not that it matters, he is one of the first people I turn to in times of trouble (my times of trouble being a regular occurrence at the moment thanks to Pillock).

"Hello mate", Emma greets me and shoves a can of beer in my direction. I look around the garden and recognise a few faces from our locals in the area but no-one I would call my friend.

I settle down on one of the white rickety chairs next to Marie. Richie is in the middle of telling us about his previous night's events. He always has a way of making us all laugh with his tales of being drunk, and the amount of knock-backs he has. This never fazes Richie. He is confident enough to approach any man he thinks is attractive, and if the man is not interested, it's his loss. I wish I had the same mentality and approach. This is probably one of the reasons I am stuck with Pillock.

I sit back in my chair and take in my surroundings and the people around me. Jono is standing at the barbecue handing out charred sausages. He's chatting to a girl who has to be his sister as she looks just like him. There are a couple more people sitting on the grass, as well as a few people milling about in the kitchen. Even on sunny days like this, it seems that the kitchen is the place to congregate at a party.

It would never occur to me to invite Pillock to the barbecue. Firstly, he would want to leave after ten minutes, secondly, he would disagree with everything that Emma and Marie said and thirdly, he would keep on at me that Richie secretly fancies him. Richie's actual words when I first told him this were "He wishes. No Bella he is all yours." I guess I'm the lucky one?!

I put my empty beer can on the floor and pick up a fresh can from the bucket of cold water, conveniently located next to me. What is it about Summer that makes beer so much more refreshing?

That is when I notice him.

The tall man walking into the garden with a six pack of beers in his hand. He sits down on the grass near Jono, at the barbecue. I know this man's name, but I don't really know how I do. Just one of those people that you have heard of but have never met. You know how that happens?

"Who is that?" I whisper to Emma and Marie. They both grin and shake their heads at me, knowing why I've asked.

"I think that's one of Jono's old school mates," Emma says. "He goes out with that red headed girl who works at Marc Antoni."

My heart sinks. The redhead who works in Marc Antoni is stunning. She is very petite and small, with apparently a very nice personality to boot. Oh well. I carry on drinking my beer. I'm suddenly very aware of this man sitting on the grass a few feet away from me. He's quite fair with a Celtic band tattoo around the top of his arm. He definitely has the arms to pull it off. He has short hair and looks like he just had a shave because he has a small nick on the side of his cheek. He looks gorgeous in his blue and white tee-shirt and jeans... Yes I was looking hard enough when he came into the garden to notice that he's wearing an extremely well fitting pair of Levi's (give me time and I will tell you the waist measurement)."

Why is it always the nice looking ones that are taken?

It is after I am finishing off my third beer that I hear him say his goodbyes to Jono and friends. I wonder if I could run after him and what would I say anyway?

"I like your tattoo." I don't think so; I would feel like Jennifer 'I carried a Watermelon' Grey in Dirty Dancing!

Oh well too late now... he never noticed me anyway. I put my empty can on the floor and pick up a fresh one and eat the black piece of chicken that I have been handed on a white paper plate.

Chapter Two

Pillock and I ended a week later. It had nothing to do with my lusting after someone else, although I suppose it's not a good sign for any relationship. It probably just gave me the kick up the arse I needed. I simply woke up one morning and realised I had had enough of Pillock. He is dishonest, loves himself more than he could ever love anyone else, and he's a cheat. I think I am probably partly to blame for that, if you let someone get away with it more than once, then you are making a rod for your own back. At my age (I'm 26 by the way) I don't have to put up with that rubbish. I live with my parents about five minutes away from Emma's. I've always lived there. I love my family home. It is a terraced white house with three bedrooms. I love it because it has mountains of childhood memories. The garden is huge and there is a lake that runs along the end of the garden, which my sisters and I used to paddle in when we were younger. In fact, it is the same lake that I saved my sister's life in. She tripped and knocked herself unconscious. My Mum came running out seconds later after hearing me screaming her name and holding my younger sister up by the hair. My Mum loves that story and always tells whoever would listen about her brave daughter, me not my sister. I haven't the heart to tell her I was the one that tripped my sister in the first place. I am sure even at my age now my Dad would still give me a (well deserved) good hiding. We are not the average family. I am one of three, the middle child. I have two sisters, one nephew and, until recently, a dog. My beautiful Labrador had died a month before. She was 15 years old and had been part of the family since she was a puppy. Don't worry, I'm not going to go all soppy and sentimental on you but I can't promise you that throughout my story. I just wanted to include Sandy because she is a very important part of my childhood. Anyone who grew up with a dog in the family will understand exactly what I mean.

I share a room with my younger sister. Not an ideal situation. I am very organised… actually scarily organised (have you seen Monica in Friends?) and my sister Lin (real name Lindsey-Anne, but will not answer to that under any circumstances) is not. In fact she's just downright messy. She's the baby of the family though, so tends to get away with it more. The third bedroom in the house has been made into a nursery for Ben, my nephew. He is the apple of my parent's eyes; actually he is the apple of the whole family's eyes. I can't imagine my life without Ben in it now and he is only two years old.

I think both my parents are extremely pleased that Pillock and I aren't together anymore. Although they remain sceptical that it will all be back on within a week or so. To be honest they never liked him, but just let me get on with it. That is the best way with me… if someone tells me not to do something then I will do it anyway. Lin is exactly the same. She went out with her last boyfriend for six months and that was just to spite our parents. She had confided in me two months into their relationship that she couldn't actually stand him anymore.

You know when you start reading a book and you get a picture in your head of what the characters look like… have you got a picture of me yet? I usually hate it when they make bestselling books into blockbuster films because it never really seems to match up to your expectations. I hope I am not ruining yours, but I am 5ft 4inches tall (I blame my Dad for that as he is the same height), slim with no boobs (I blame my Mum for that), dark blonde hair (it looks lighter just after it has been washed) and bitten fingernails. I don't think I'm ugly and I'm not a stunner, but hey, somewhere in the middle suits me fine. In fact, I was probably a minger at school. I was always one of those girls who suffered from spots, I had a god-awful perm and my teeth stuck out a bit. I did not suffer from acne, I would like to point out, although I wish I did because Lin did. She had this amazing cream, which would literally burn spots off. Amazing. No, I was one of those people who used to get the huge red number at the end of their nose, or in the middle of their forehead. Yes, that was me, Miss Unattractive, but the last few years have been good to me. My teeth don't stick out anymore, my perm has gone, my hair reaches just past my shoulders and is wavy (which is why I tend to straighten it within an inch of its life) and I only suffer from the occasional breakout, usually when I am about to go on a night out or have my photo taken.

I now know that Pillock was never ever going to be good enough for me. I am worth more than that. It just took me a while to wake up to that though.

Pillock and I met at college, even though we didn't start seeing each other until our courses had finished. I was there, embarrassingly enough, re-sitting my GCSE's. I did actually pass all my exams, but my Mum reckons the E and F grades don't count, which is why I was back at college. I had managed to combine my re-sits (English Language, Literature, Science and Maths) with an AS level course in English. I found learning at college a whole lot easier than school. School was too regimented for me. That's my excuse and I am sticking to it.

I thought Pillock was an idiot the first time I saw him. He was wearing a baseball cap with his name emblazoned along the back. He was also very loud and kept calling everyone Sweetheart and "Bro." Emma was in complete agreement with me. It is just a shame I didn't trust my first impression. I actually saw Pillock in a new light when he was my Knight in Shining Armour one afternoon. A couple of the girls at college had taken an instant dislike to me. They would laugh when I walked past and would turn their noses up at me. Emma had offered on many occasions to give them both a slap, but I always refused. I felt this would just antagonise the situation. One afternoon the girls decided to shout a few names at me across the college foyer. Emma was late in arriving as usual. I tried to ignore them both but the girls did not stop, kept asking me if the "cat had got my tongue", which is a stupid saying in my opinion. What does it mean?

Anyway, Pillock arrived in the foyer, just as I was starting to lose my temper. Both girls obviously fancied him as they started smiling coyly and ignoring me as soon as he was in their sights. He ignored them and looked at me.

"You okay?" he said.

"Yep great," I lied. Inside I was shaking with anger and fear.

Pillock turned to the girls who were staring with their mouths agape.

"Why don't you both piss off?!"

That was the first time I was attracted to Pillock and one of the only good things I can remember about our on/off relationship which is a sorry state of affairs. I mean, the relationship, if you can call it that was more off than on most of the time anyway. We would split up and just as I was starting to get over it all, Pillock would resurface and tell me how much he cared and that, this time it would be different. Unfortunately, it never was. To give you a better idea, we split up about seventeen times (but hey who's counting?) and during one of those seventeen times, I was seeing someone else for about six months. All in all we were together for a total of about eighteen months. I thought Pillock was the one you see because he always came back to me and I saw this as a sign. How wrong could I be? I tore up my photographs, put all my old Birthday/Christmas/Valentine cards into the recycling bin and gave most of the gifts he had bought me (guilt gifts as I liked to call them) to charity knowing I would never regret not keeping one memento of our time together.

The day Pillock and I ended was the day I saw Joe again. I am a believer in things happening for a reason, so I took it as a very good sign.

Chapter Three

I like the town that I live in. From what other people say, I am in the minority though and it was one of my pet hates. Emma says the town was a dive, Richie complains there are no decent clubs to go to and Marie reckons there are no shops. On the other hand I like the fact the town we all live in is quiet. It actually used to be a small village years and years ago (before my time), which is hard to imagine now and it has certainly come on leaps and bounds since then. I agree it doesn't have much in the town centre, about ten card shops (I wish I was exaggerating), three mobile phone shops, Topshop (essential shopping), a couple of hairdressers, a couple of travel agencies and that's probably it. But there is a train and bus station in easy access to us all so when we wanted the bigger shops and the good clubbing nights out we caught the train and shared a cab home. What was the big deal? We are also about an hour away from London and an hour away in the other direction to the coast. I can think of worse places to live. In fact Marie should know this first hand as her brother lived in a right old dive (I'm not going to mention the name of which in fear of insulting one of your home towns). This was the town that I had grown up in so I tended to get narky when people insulted the place. I guess I'm patriotic to my home town.

On the morning I bumped into Joe, I had popped into town to pick up some holiday brochures. I had a good cry before going out of the house, mainly because of the amount of time I wasted on a "no-one special." I had scraped my unwashed hair back in a ponytail, put no makeup on my face and was wearing my Reebok gym trousers. If I'd thought about it, I was *bound* to run into Joe again that day!

I was just walking out of the travel agents when I saw him and I thought quickly about running back into the shop, but realised it was too late when Joe raised his hand in recognition to me. I should always follow Marie's example and never leave the house without some blusher and mascara, because you never know who you might meet. I managed to pinch both my cheeks to allow the colour to flow (believe me, I was looking pale and tired) before Joe got to me.

"It's Bella isn't it?"

"Yes it is," I answered. "Hi."

"How's it going?"

"Good thanks."

"Going on holiday?" Joe pointed to the brochures I was carrying.

"Yep."

"Cool. Well it was nice to see you again Bella," Joe smiled and started to walk away.

"Yeah, bye."

What is it about men you find attractive that makes you go all tongue tied so you cannot even string a sentence together? What must he think of me?

I analysed the conversation over and over again on my walk home. I could've talked to Joe about my holiday, let him know where I was thinking of going and who I was going with. I could've told him that it was nice to see him again, instead of agreeing with him that it was nice to see me again.

I telephoned Marie as soon as I got home.

"Did you get the brochures?" Marie asked.

"Never mind about that," I cut her off. "I saw Joe today."

"Joe who?"

"Joe from the barbecue Joe."

"And…?"

"I made a bloody fool of myself as per usual," I admitted it out loud at last. "I couldn't even talk. He must think I have a speech problem or I'm just really unfriendly."

"Don't be daft. It can't have been that bad."

"I was wearing my gym kit for god's sake!"

There was silence on the other end of the telephone.

"Marie, are you there?"

"In that case you are right it is as bad as you thought," Marie started to laugh.

"I know. Oh well, I'm going to kill myself now. I'll talk to you later," I said.

"See you later Bell," Marie was still laughing as she replaced the receiver.

If it was not so funny, I would have cried.

A few days later, my girls' holiday was booked; Emma, Marie, Richie and I were going to Ibiza for some sunshine, booze and, most of all, laughter. We decided on the spur of the moment to book somewhere. I think I was mainly the reason for the "spur of the moment." My friends were worried about me, but that is why they are good friends.

I love the feeling you get before your holiday. The excitement building up, the countdown to the big day (we are currently on nine days) and shopping. Shopping is part and parcel of a holiday. For some reason you have to buy most things new even though you only bought three bikinis, two pairs of shorts, four tee- shirts and some pink dotty flip-flops last year.

I finally felt I had got the essentials after spending two hours in the glass-covered shopping centre in the nearby town. I bought a new bikini, some blue stripy flip-flops, which matched two summery dresses, a going-out top and a pair of shorts. Thinking about it now, I'm not sure if I bought enough?

As I sat on the train coming back with my shopping bags around me I smiled to myself. I hadn't realised how miserable I had been, until I'd finally walked away from Pillock.

I had years ahead of me. Years ahead to make a total fool of myself in front of nice men that I found attractive, for one. I pulled the brochure page from my bag and looked at the holiday resort for the hundredth time that day. "Not an ideal place for those people wanting a quiet holiday." This holiday is just what I needed; time to get away with three important people in my life.

Whoever said shopping is retail therapy was spot-on. I finally felt like my life was on the up.

I just had one important task to do first.

Chapter Four

Curiosity had got the better of me. Okay so technically I didn't need my haircut, but it's always good to feel you've made an effort before you go on your holidays, right?

I had booked an appointment at Marc Antoni's for a haircut the day after my successful shopping trip. I had never been to MA's before in my life and for the life of me I couldn't really understand why I was here now. I was waiting for one of the stylists to call me a fraud and kick me out, not only that but I didn't really have the cash at the moment to waste on getting my hair done. My normal hair-stylist worked in a shop just around the corner and I was worried she would see me and call me a traitor.

It was finally official. I had become neurotic. It was only a matter of time before I ended up like my Mum and her family. They are a family of neurotics. My Mum is one of two and my Uncle Jim has to make sure his towels are lined up in the bathroom; otherwise he can't sleep (Sleeping With The Enemy spring to mind?). He'll go into the bathroom after you have finished in there to double-check. His wife is just as bad. She will never buy an odd number of fruit or vegetables from the supermarket and will never walk to a destination in a straight line for fear it will bring bad luck. Yep, Aunt Jean, as mad a hatter and actually institutionalised once although no-one in the family talks about that "incident" anymore.

My Mum is a calmer neurotic, just likes things to have their place and especially likes rooms to be aired. Unfortunately, this means even in Winter months when the frost is on the cars outside, my Mum has a spring clean and throws all the windows open with such vigour I always feel like she's about to burst into song.

My visit didn't really go according to plan, because if you

27

hadn't guessed already, I went to MA's to check out Joe's girlfriend. I could faintly recall seeing her down the local pub once or twice but I'd never paid that much attention to her, well why would I?

But this time I had a reason and I wanted to see her, if only to notice a flaw or two. It would ease my mind and make me feel better. I mean I had built the woman up in my mind as a perfect, flawless supermodel and that just couldn't be right.

It probably would've helped if I'd planned my visit a bit better because as it turned out the redhead had the day off today. What a complete waste of time and money. As soon as the young, rather patronising receptionist advised me of this I tried to think of ways to head for the exit, but nothing sprang to mind. Anyway they had my telephone number so I knew I would be charged for the cancelled appointment anyway. Maybe my parents wouldn't mind if I changed our phone number?

Kathy was cutting my hair. The first time I have ever met the girl but she introduced herself as "Kathy, here to help" rather enthusiastically so her name stuck. I sulked my way through the haircut and answered Kathy's annoying questions with short sharp answers.

"Going anywhere nice on holiday?" It's not a cliché. Hairdressers do actually ask that question.

"Ibiza."

"That'll be lovely this time of year," Kathy continued snipping away. "With anyone special?"

She was obviously rubbing it in now.

"My friends," I answered.

"Lovely" Kathy continued. "Got everything organised before you go?"

"Yep all sorted."

"Lovely."

According to Kathy everything was lovely. Her boyfriend was exceptionally lovely (he sounded extremely dull to me). I hardly listened as Kathy chattered on until she mentioned that she'd worked in the salon for about two years. It was my chance to find out more.

"Oh really," I sounded interested. "Do you like it here?"

"Oh yes," Kathy said. "The other staff are great. We have such a laugh."

"You all get on then?" Please, please, please say the redhead is a bitch.

"Oh yes like a house on fire," Kathy continued. "Debs is so funny. She is the comical one of the group, Sally is the one you go to in times of trouble, you know the one whose shoulder you can cry on and Milly's life is such a drama. She is like a walking soap opera because she is so caring and lets things get to her."

Would it be too obvious if I asked which one was the redhead?

"Ah right," I replied. There was no way of knowing if Joe's girlfriend was Debs, Sally or Milly but Lovely Kathy didn't have a bad word to say about any of them. I continued to sulk the rest of the way through my haircut in silence.

To top it all off, I didn't like the way Kathy had styled my hair. My hair always fell into a middle parting and I was used to it that way. Kathy had styled it into a slick left side parting which made me feel like I should be in that Robert Palmer video "Addicted to Love" with a guitar in my hand.

I grudgingly paid over the odds for my trendy new haircut and left the shop vowing never to go back.

I couldn't even admit to any of my friends what I had done today, but at least I could admit to myself that it was good that my holiday was just around the corner, because I had finally lost the plot.

Chapter Five

We had been in Ibiza for approximately eleven hours.

"You're the besssssttest mate I've ever had Bell," Marie slurred as I smiled down at her.

I was currently holding Marie's hair away from her face, as she hugged the toilet, which was actually her best mate at this present time. It was such a shame that Marie was being so sick. The dinner we had at a little Spanish Tapas restaurant around the corner from our apartment was really lovely and also very good value for money. It was not a good idea to remind Marie exactly what she had eaten for dinner now for a very obvious and good reason.

"I'm sho shorrrry," Marie managed to slur before throwing up again.

"Don't be daft," I reassured Marie and stroked her long, dark hair. I am not sure if this was helping her but Marie used this fab conditioner (which cost a fortune) and her hair was so soft, it actually felt quite nice. Marie always apologises when she's sick from drinking alcohol. She has no idea why she does it. I don't mind and certainly prefer this to Emma, the drama queen. She always thinks she is about to die and demands that she is taken to the nearest casualty department. There has only been one occasion when we have all given in to Emma's demands and taken her to the hospital; but that is because she got herself into such a state she hyperventilated and had a panic attack. I thought she had brought on a heart attack!

Marie and I had lost Emma and Richie earlier on in the night or should I say in the early hours of the morning. Richie wanted to go to one of the gay clubs and Emma, being the fag-hag that she is wanted to go as well. I wrote our apartment name on Emma's hand before leaving them. I wouldn't be surprised if I never saw them both again (I am joking, I hope!).

Marie and I had ended up in a really trendy and expensive club called Es Paradis (it cost us twenty quid entrance fee). It was an amazing place. It was an open plan, massive, no really MASSIVE hall with a waterfall in the middle of it, podiums scattered all over with scantily-clad dancers on top of them and the bar was glass topped. The music pumping out of the speakers was deafening and the place was heaving with people dancing and drinking.

Marie shakily stood up next to me in the toilet cubicle. Her hair was now stuck to her face and her eyes were blood shot. She had a sick mark down the front of her bandeau yellow top.

"Do I smell bad?" Marie looked like she was about to cry.

"Not at all mate," I lied and put my arm around her to lead her out of the ladies toilets. Thank God I had a strong stomach. My Mum reckons I get this from the good solid food she cooked for me when I was young (I have refused to eat liver since I was eighteen, much to my Mum's disgust). I just get it from my Dad who can pretty much stomach anything. Richie, on the other hand would be a disaster in this situation. As soon as Marie had vomited the first time, Richie would have been pushing her aside and using the toilet bowl himself.

"Can we go back home now?" Marie asked and placed her head on my shoulder.

"Definitely, as soon as I find the exit," I scanned the massive club for a green exit sign and found a green SALIDA sign instead.

Luckily, our apartment was only about ten minutes away so I gently managed to lead a drunken Marie back to our place of rest. Marie had stopped talking as soon as the fresh air had hit her outside. We walked past a family of four whom I can only presume were on their way to the beach as they all had towels under their arms, sunglasses on their faces and bottles of water in their hands. I was just thinking how keen they were when I actually noticed the time. It was seven in the morning!! I was so

31

thankful that I had stopped drinking alcohol and started drinking bottled water about four hours ago. Marie's head would be pounding later.

Our apartment was quite small. We'd managed to book a family room so it consisted of a double bed and two singles with a small kitchenette and bathroom. It had no air conditioning but it was so close to the town, so it worked out cheaper this way. We weren't planning on staying here most of the time anyway. When we all arrived earlier we had dumped our cases, changed into our bikinis and shorts (thankfully Richie changed into his shorts and tee-shirt) and hit the beach. No wasted time for us.

Emma was already in bed when we walked in. The covers had been thrown on the floor and her head was hanging half off the bed. She was still wearing her new lacy beige top, but had her stripy pyjama bottoms on. Her mascara was on her cheeks and her short blonde hair was standing on end. If I'd had the energy I would have taken a photo to remind her in the morning, except it was the morning. Ah, you know what I mean!

I helped Marie get into bed, taking her diamante choker off first. I could just imagine the headlines at home now. "Drunken girl strangled by her £10 Topshop choker on holiday." She could sleep in her clothes, because that is what I was planning to do.

"I've put water beside your bed Marie," I whispered in her ear. Marie mumbled back so I can only presume she understood. I emptied the washing up bowl of the tea cups from yesterday morning and put that beside the bed as well, just in case. I checked Emma was breathing (thankfully she was) and kicked my sandals off, before I finally fell into the empty double bed.

It didn't matter to me that the bed was lumpy, the sheets were a shade of yellow and there were cigarette burn marks in the pillows. You know the feeling when you get into a bed that has just been freshly made? I smiled to myself as I snuggled right down into the bed with my feet.

Why is it on nights out there is always one person that plays

Mum? There is a person who does not get as drunk as everyone else and takes charge. Tonight, our first night in Ibiza was obviously my turn. I don't think I could take on the role or the responsibility every night though. I was knackered and to be honest I'm not normally that sensible.

I had almost dropped off to sleep when it suddenly occurred to me that the other side of the double bed was empty and that could only mean one of two things. Richie had either pulled and would be full of stories later that day, which we would all much prefer he kept to himself or he was curled up asleep on the beach. That was my last thought before blissful sleep finally took over.

Chapter Six

I was deep in thought, following the drip with my eyes, down my torso until it slipped into my belly button, which was filling up with sun creamed coloured sweat. Am I the only one that has noticed that sun cream actually ruins white bikinis? My beautiful white (and expensive) bikini was looking yellowy and I could only hope that it would return to its original colour in the wash, otherwise that was forty quid down the pan. I hated wasting money.

I heard a scream and looked up. Marie was teaching Richie and Emma yoga down by the sea. Richie had just pushed Emma over as she was balancing on one leg and she had fallen straight into the sea. Yoga seemed like too much hard work for a holiday, so I just lay back and enjoyed the sun.

I couldn't believe that this was our last day in Ibiza. The holiday had flown past. It would be good to get home if only to give my liver a reprieve. The last six nights had consisted of drinking to excess, dancing until our legs ached, living on chips and existing on less than four hours sleep every morning.

Richie was in love. He'd pulled one of the waiters on his first night and since then they had been pretty much inseparable every night, and sickening to watch. He reckoned we were all just jealous, which was probably true. Although, it had worked in my favour because I had the double bed to myself every single night as Richie, the dirty stop-out, had his wicked way with Pablo.

Emma had snogged an older gentleman on her second night here. I'm being very polite by calling this man an Older Gentleman. He must have been in his late forties, which is in the same age bracket as my Dad and freaks me out a bit. Did you know that Patrick Swayze is only a year older than my Dad? I only found that out a year or so ago and it put me off the lovely

Mr. Swayze for life. Although, Mr. Swayze, if you are reading this I am open to persuasion. Marie reckons the Older Gentleman was only a few months from having a hearing aid installed, but Emma put that down to the noisy club. This obviously made no sense as to why he kept shouting "What?!" and "Huh?!" when we were out of the club either. Emma ran into her Older Gentleman most nights and always ended up snogging him before coming back to our apartment. She reckons she doesn't fancy him and it would just be rude not to kiss him goodnight.

Marie has been quite content watching the comings and goings with everyone else, although from the third night she didn't have much choice. She loves her dancing and is always the first to hit the dance floor. Unfortunately Marie fell off the podium in the club whilst dancing and sprained her ankle. She had been hobbling around ever since. She says alcohol helps numb the pain, but it has put a halt to her podium, and any other kind of dancing for the time being.

As for me, I spent most of my days lost in my own thoughts. I daydream a lot. I have sat on the beach on a sun-lounger for the past six days, enjoying the warmth of the sun and the company of my friends. As for the evenings, I've dressed up and enjoyed the Mediterranean atmosphere and cocktails. I am pleased to report that I have only been sick once and Marie repaid my kindness on our first night by holding my hair back. Since then, I have been quite sensible with drink, well, sensible enough to avoid tequila shots anyway. I had the hangover from hell the following day. I crawled around the apartment for a couple of hours before Richie came back to "sort me out" and dragged me back down to the beach. I sat under an umbrella for the rest of the afternoon (which as you all know by now, is extremely rare for a sun lover like me) and felt sorry for myself. I could not even manage to go out the next evening. Richie (bless him) brought me some pizza and chips from the nearby restaurant and whilst the rest of them went out for the night I slept. I slept so soundly that I didn't hear Emma and Marie crashing home in the early hours of the morning and I woke feeling extremely refreshed and ready to go, which is more than could be said for the other three.

We had all saved our best outfits for our last night. Richie looked handsome in his black jeans and new grey shirt, Emma looked gorgeous in her short denim skirt and new backless white top and Marie looked extremely tall and sexy in her killer heels and new knee length black dress. I am so envious of Marie's height. She is 5ft 10 and her legs are undeniably her best asset. She must be over 6ft this evening.

I wore my new white cropped trousers and black strappy top. Richie had managed to perform some miracle with my hair and piled it on top of my head with just a few tendrils falling forward towards my face. I managed to get the girls in the apartment next door to take a photo of the four of us before we went out. It would be quite nice to get a "before and after" an alcohol-fuelled night.

We had a late lunch that day so there was no need to waste any time getting dinner that evening, we were obviously on a mission to make our last night count. I was already dreading my hangover tomorrow. Tonight was going to be messy.

Chapter Seven

"I love this song!" Richie exclaimed and shot off onto the dance floor to perform his infamous Steps routine to Tragedy. To look at Richie on a normal day, you would not think for a moment he was gay, but as soon as he starts to dance the word "camp" springs to mind. I never tire of watching Richie strutting his stuff though and he never fails to entertain me. Pablo looked at his new boyfriend from the side of the dance-floor on the verge of tears. He even shouted "I'm so proud!" causing Marie to choke on her drink. Pablo preferred to be called Pab but I felt like I was a cockney saying pub, so I just avoided using his name.

"You are so being checked out mate," Emma shouted in my ear.

"I am? Where?"

"Don't look now, but there is a bloke at the bar totally eyeing you up Bell", Emma smiled.

You should know two things about me. One is I never ever notice when someone is eyeing me up, they could come over and offer me a drink and I would think that I just look thirsty. The second, is I am not very subtle as I now demonstrated by swinging round and catching the man in question looking at me. I felt myself go red but luckily the bar we were in was very dark. The man smiled at me and I smiled back.

"Go and talk to him!" Emma suddenly ordered. Have I mentioned before that Emma is so bossy! (I do actually need to be bossed about sometimes though).

I didn't have to make the decision to go and speak to the man at the bar because he was walking towards me. I felt my stomach turn over and I tried to look as casual as I could in the circumstances. I was extremely pleased that the first couple of drinks had gone down well although I had hoped for a few more to boost my confidence.

The man was wearing a white shirt with blue cut-off trousers. He had obviously been in Ibiza for a while as he had a nice colour to pull the shirt off. His hair was dark and I could see a sprinkling of dark chest hair curling over the top of the shirt, which I found extremely sexy.

"Hi," The man leant over and whispered in my ear.

"Hi," I said back and smiled again.

"You have a great smile," the man said again.

"Why thank you," I blushed. This was the reason why I was glad the first two drinks had gone down so well because if they hadn't my reply to his compliment would have been entirely different. Something like…

"My Mum tells me my two front teeth are slightly crooked but I think they are okay. I did used to have a brace when I was younger and I am sure that sorted out most of my problems. I do brush and floss regularly, twice a day girl me."

You get the idea.

I found out the man was from Derbyshire which I know is somewhere up North. He said it was near Buxton where the water comes from, which helped me understand the word he said (I thought he was calling me buxom) but didn't help me geographically. Simon was on his second week in Ibiza, he was a sales rep for a computer company and he had just moved into his own flat (oh and he is twenty eight years old).

Simon did actually tell me more about himself, but I couldn't hear very well as we were standing right next to the speaker, but I seemed to nod at all the right pauses in our conversation.

Simon followed us all onto the next two bars. He held my hand to the last bar which I found slightly uncomfortable. I found it even more uncomfortable when Simon suggested we go for a dance. Most men cannot dance unless they are gay, or they are some distant relation to John Travolta.

Unfortunately, the DJ put "The Twist" song on, for reasons

unknown to me other than it was a real holiday "toooooonnnnnn." So there, I was on a packed dance floor holding hands with Simon from Derbyshire "doing" the twist. I looked round on a couple of occasions to see Marie sitting on her bar stool laughing at me and I knew I would be reminded about this in the morning.

After the song, thankfully Simon suggested we sit down. I spotted Emma in the corner of the bar sitting on her Older Man's lap, snogging. Marie, on her bar-stool texting on her mobile (I dread to think what the textaholic's phone-bill will be), Richie and Pablo were still dancing on the other side of the bar. Simon and I sat down on a free table with our drinks, next to the snogging couple. He pulled his chair up close to mine and I knew that he was about to move in for the kill.

I would like to tell you that it was a very romantic moment, but this is real life and we were both drunk. Simon still had hold of my hand and sort of lunged at me, so before I knew it his tongue was inside my mouth and his lips were moving in mysterious ways against mine. I closed my eyes and just enjoyed the moment. I thought of the last person I kissed and remembered that I wouldn't be the last person he would have kissed, so put the thought to the back of my mind.

Simon and I ended up kissing for about an hour before he suggested we leave. I knew it had been an hour because the DJ kept announcing the time on the hour, every hour, a bit like the 10'o clock news, but less business like.

Simon had been a gentleman up until this point and had not even tried to touch my boobs, which is a good thing as I was wearing the chicken fillets that Emma had bought me for my birthday. My sister, Lin, calls this false advertising.

When a man suggests you leave a bar, you know deep down what he is suggesting. I have had sex with three people in the whole of my life, which, considering my age, is pretty poor, well compared to some of the girls in my year at school anyway.

They were on double figures by the time they were sixteen. I was in a moral dilemma. The three people before Simon had not been one night stands. I was just not that sort of girl. Would having a one night stand make me a bad person?

"Ok, let's go," I took Simon's hand and pulled him up from the chairs where we were sitting. Alcohol does make you brave.

Marie and Emma were the only ones left in the bar, as Richie and Pablo had some goodbyes to do. (Our flight was at 10:00a.m, which, as it happens, was only eight hours away). I told Marie and Emma that I was going and they both winked at me. Neither of them mentioned anything about what I was about to do, or that I was a slut for doing it.

Simon and I didn't really speak as we walked hand-in-hand towards the beach. His hand was extremely sweaty. We walked down the wooden steps to the beach. There were still a few people on the beach, but Simon led me to where the sun loungers were stacked every evening. Once there he took me round the other side of them so we were out of sight. I felt my heart hammering in my chest and I couldn't say a word, even if I had tried to.

"You're gorgeous," Simon said and pulled me to him. Corny, yes but by this time I didn't care. Simon and I started to kiss again but this time it didn't stop there.

Simon didn't seem to notice my chicken fillets as my bra dropped to the floor. As our kissing became more intense, so did the touching on both our parts. My normal inhibitions were lost and I felt great. I felt desirable and I knew there was no turning back on my part now. I wanted this to happen. So did Simon, as he unwrapped a condom and placed it on himself.

As my knickers fell to my ankles and I wrapped my legs around Simon's waist, I knew I would probably regret this moment of madness when I got home but for right here and now I felt bloody fantastic.

Chapter Eight

I was glad of the way Simon and I said our goodbyes. There was no mention of keeping in contact or seeing each other again. There were no empty promises. Simon walked me back to my apartment still holding my hand and once there he kissed me softly again on my sore and swollen lips and said "see ya." I didn't watch him go. I walked into the apartment and closed the door behind me.

I was faced with Emma and Marie frantically trying to throw clothes into their cases. They both stopped when they heard me walk in.

"Tell us all!" Emma shrieked, sitting down on the edge of the bed and looking up at me expectantly.

"It was a good evening," I smiled.

"Oh my god!" Emma exclaimed again. "What happened to you? Do you realise you have been gone for three hours?"

I had realised this and the only reason I was back now was to make sure Richie, Emma and Marie had all their belongings together for our taxi at 7:00a.m.

"Let's get your cases packed first then I can talk about my evening," I said. My case was already packed and ready waiting in the corner of the room.

"Spoilsport!"

"Where's Rich?" I asked.

"Saying goodbye to Pablo for the hundredth time. He has already been back once but apparently he forgot to tell him something," Marie rolled her eyes.

"Yeah probably wanted to make sure Pablo had his Mum's address, his Grandmother's telephone number and his old school teachers email address, in case he loses any of the contact numbers," Emma joked.

"Excuse me, I was actually giving Pablo a goodbye gift,"

Richie explained as he walked in the apartment door.

"Urgh, keep that to yourself!" Emma said.

"We'll have to make sure he doesn't forget me in a hurry," Richie winked. "Now my work in Ibiza has been done, let's get the hell out of here!"

I filled my friends in on my night with Simon in the airport lounge, at the departure gates.

"Hooray! It's about time you got a shag!" Emma cheered.

"I don't think they whole flight needed to know that Em," Marie said, looking around at the curious and amused faces of people sitting nearby.

"Ah who cares less," Emma threw some girls an evil look and carried on reading her magazine. That is what I like the most about Emma. She doesn't care what people think about her, what you see is what you get. Marie, on the other hand is an extremely private person and tends to only let the very select few know her personal information (me being one of them).

I was lost in my own thoughts again. I had omitted the very personal details of my night with Simon from my friends. They didn't need to hear them. They were private and I wanted them to stay between me, Simon and probably all his mates on holiday and back home. I smiled to myself and I kept smiling throughout the whole flight. It was not Simon that had made me smile but the way he had made me feel about myself. How had my self esteem become so low?

Emma drove us all home once we landed at the airport, after picking up her car from Elephant Parking. Who thinks of these names? We hardly spoke on the way home through exhaustion and sheer tiredness. I don't think it helped that Emma was driving and she gets extremely grouchy when tired, so it is best to keep quiet. I was looking forward to getting home and I would have the house pretty much to myself. It was a Monday afternoon so my parents and Lin would all be at work and I was planning on having a hot bath, a nice cup of English Tea (it is never ever the same abroad) and an early night.

I kissed and hugged my friends before finally waving them off at the bottom of my close. I pulled my suitcase behind me and actually felt relieved the English weather was cool.

"It's good to be home," I said to myself as I turned my front-door key in the lock.

"It's good to have you home, Bella."

I swung round to see Pillock standing beside a fir tree in my front-garden. He looked like he had been standing there all night.

"What... ermm why? What are you doing here?" I stuttered.

"It's obvious Bella"

"It is?!"

"I love you Bella, I want us to get back together."

Chapter Nine

"Oh my God!"

They were the first three words out of my mouth and then I was at a complete loss at what to say next.

"I know I have not always been fair to you in the past but I have changed. You cannot believe how much I have missed you. I think about you all the time," Pillock said. He was still standing beside the tree in my front-garden. This all seemed surreal.

"Oh my god!"

"Is that all you can say?" Pillock asked and his eyes filled up with tears. I actually saw real tears forming in Pillock's normally hard eyes. I could only recall this happening once before and that was when he crashed his blue mini into a tree. It was a complete write-off. Luckily, Pillock and I escaped with just a few minor scratches but he had tears in his eyes and I am not sure if he was more upset about his car being totaled or the fact everyone in the college reception area saw it.

"I'm tired," I sighed.

"We need to talk about this Bella," Pillock said. "We have things to talk about."

"Yep probably," I couldn't think straight. I had to get Pillock away from my house. I didn't need the ear-ache from my parents, if they knew he had been here.

"Are you going to invite me in?" Pillock asked.

"No way," I surprised myself with how forceful my answer was. "Wait here for a minute."

I walked into my house closing the front-door behind me, leaving Pillock outside. I put my suitcase in the hallway and threw my rucksack on top. I could do without this hassle right now. I wanted a hot bath and an early night!

Instead, I took a deep breath and walked back out of the

house. We walked to the local park around the back of the houses.

"How was your holiday?" Pillock asked.

"Great thanks."

"Did you meet anyone?"

Now was my chance to make Pillock suffer to tell him all about my night with Simon and how he made me feel but instead I said...

"What business is it of yours?"

"Okay."

I had never seen Pillock like this before. He looked shattered, even though I could hardly talk at the moment. I had only ever seen him in the past when he had made a huge effort. Pillock liked to preen in front of the mirror every morning and evening without fail. He showered every morning, wore the most expensive aftershave money could buy all day and even when he went to bed. He used to tell me that he wanted to always look his best for me, but sometimes I wanted him to feel like he could really chill out with me. That way it meant I could too. Pillock would never hug me after sex and, no, it is not a typical bloke thing to just roll over and sleep. No matter what time of the night it was, Pillock would jump in the shower after sex and then he would go to bed. I guess, thinking about it now, it was obsessive behaviour.

I listened to Pillock as we sat on the park bench watching two little girls playing on the swings with their Mum keeping a watchful eye on them. The two girls reminded me of my sisters when they were young. The girls were of a similar age to each other and were wearing the same clothes. Lin and our other sister Annie are not twins and not of similar age, but for some reason my parents used to dress them the same anyway. They loved looking like little girls with their new dresses, whereas I was happy with my new pair of trousers or dungarees.

I hardly took in most of what Pillock said.

45

"We owe it to ourselves to try again."

"We must have had something for us to lasted have long as we did."

"I know you still love me."

"Do you miss me?"

"I want us to grow old together."

"I can't sleep without you next to me."

"I need you."

You get the gist of the one-sided conversation.

I had waited years for Pillock to say these things to me, to make me feel like I was special and now it was just too late.

"We lasted as long as we did because of me," I finally said. I didn't look at him; I didn't want to look at him.

"What? I don't understand," Pillock tried to grab my hand but I pushed it away.

"We lasted as long as we did because of me," I repeated. I paused before continuing. "I was prepared to be a door-mat for you and you liked that. I don't even blame you for it all. I forgave you when you apologised and I believed you when you lied. The only reason you need me is because no-one else would put up with as much as I did. You humiliated me and I am tired of letting you."

"How did I humiliate you?"

I started to laugh.

"I am not even going to grace that question with an answer!" Instead, I got up from the bench and looked at Pillock for the first time since we got to the park.

"Don't go." He had tears falling down his cheeks. Would you believe it? A grown man, in broad daylight, crying over a girl!

"You are wrong, I don't love you anymore," I softly said. I was not completely heartless. "But because of this and because of you, I will be a stronger person, so thank you."

"Can we be friends?" Pillock sobbed.

I shook my head.

"How thick skinned are you?!" I was starting to lose my temper.

I walked away from him then, there was nothing else left to say. Pillock didn't call after me, but I knew he watched me go until I rounded the corner.

I hadn't realised I didn't love Pillock anymore until I saw him today. However, it didn't stop me from lying on my bed when I got home and crying my eyes out. Crying because I knew I would never see him again and for, at last, putting myself first and getting my self-respect back.

Chapter Ten

Three major events happened in the next few months. The first happened two weeks later.

I was sitting in the waiting area of the Rainbow Clinic. The Rainbow Clinic was based just outside the town where I lived and it was a place that specialised in Sexually Transmitted Diseases.

I was starting to get bored with staring at the plain, pale pink carpet, so I stared at the clock instead. It's one of those white clocks; you know the ones that were always at the front of your classroom at school. Round, plain and white. The ticking sounds like you have Big Ben in the room and the seconds are ticking by like minutes. How long have I been sitting here? It actually works out I have only been in the waiting room for ten minutes, that is 600 minutes and that is 36000 seconds. It's actually less than that now because it took me a while to work out those sums, as I mentioned before Maths was never really my strong point.

Poor Richie was mortified when he found out he was having problems down below (you didn't think it was me did you?). He spent an hour screaming down the telephone to Pablo, who denied all knowledge. He made the appointment a few days later and I was here to provide moral support.

Richie had been in the Doctor's room for quite a while and my mind could only run wild with what Richie had to go through.

I kept trying to concentrate on the clock rather than stare at the other people in the waiting room. There were three other people there. A woman in her late thirties, a really young looking girl who could not have been more than seventeen and a woman beside her, who must have been her Mother as she had exactly the same nose, unfortunately.

I don't understand why this place is called the Rainbow Clinic. It is not a place for sunshine and smiles. It should have just been called The Clinic and been done with it.

Richie came out of the room twenty minutes later and told me that he had been asked to wait for half an hour for the results.

"That's a good thing, at least you will know," I whispered to Richie and put my hand over his.

"Oh yeah, great. I'm really pleased to know I am about to die from a nasty disease given to me by a slimy Spaniard," Richie whispered back.

Now was not the time to point out to Richie that the "slimy Spaniard" had actually been the love of his life only fifteen days ago.

Richie was nervous. He did not look at me but gripped my hand tightly. His hand was extremely sweaty and he kept shaking his leg, which he only does when he is extremely excited or nervous. I'm guessing it is the latter causing the shakes this time.

"Do you want me to come in with you?" I asked.

"No. I think I need to find out myself first, but you will be here when I come out won't you Bell?" For the first time Richie looked at me and I saw him as I did the first time I ever met him. We had met when we were sat together in our form room when we were both eleven years old. Richie had his blonde hair parted to the left, his school trousers had been pressed so the crease was right up the centre and he had a small, pale blue rucksack that he clutched to his chest tightly. He was a small, lost, little boy who wanted to be anywhere but there.

"I am not going anywhere," I firmly said and my voice wobbled slightly. I was beginning to feel frightened for Richie.

We did not say a word to each other for the next half an hour. If I started to speak now, I would not have been able to shut up and could have babbled on for ages, either that or I might have cried. I didn't think that was what Richie needed right now. I would be the best friend to Richie if the news was as bad as he thought. I had seen the film Philadelphia with Tom Hanks and Antonio Banderos many times, so I knew what to expect. I wondered if I had time now to pop to HMV and get some classical music. This was the first time I had ever been in the Rainbow Clinic and my chest felt heavy, as if I was having trouble breathing. I hoped this would be the last time I would have to come to this place, but some bad experiences either break you or make you stronger, right?

"Mr Cunningham," The Doctor poked his head out of the room.

I should have mentioned before that Richie's parents are huge *Happy Days* fans. His sister is called Joanie. As you can imagine, they both received a lot of stick for it at school. Richie's parents said that their names made them unique and who wanted to have a boring old name for the rest of their lives. Richie always called himself Rich until he reached secondary school, but finally succumbed to his parents wishes and became Richie. Joanie, on the other hand hasn't and will not answer to anything else other than Jo.

"That's me then," Richie said, but made no attempt to get up from his seat.

"You will be fine," I reassured him. Richie got up from the chair slowly and walked into the Doctor's office. It was like I was watching him in slow motion.

I decided the best thing for me to do would be to get some fresh air. I wanted to have all my senses and be fully alert by the time Richie came out of the Doctor's office.

I walked out of the Rainbow Clinic, closed my eyes and took a deep breath. I opened my eyes to see Joe and his gorgeous girlfriend standing in front of me.

"Hi Bella, how are you?"

I wanted the ground to open up and swallow me as Joe and his girlfriend looked from me to the reception door of the

Rainbow Clinic, which had emblazoned across the front, "The Rainbow Clinic – for Sexual Related Problems."

Chapter Eleven

As it turns out Richie was not going to die from some horrible disease that the Love of his Life gave to him. Pablo had given Richie good old fashioned crabs, which is easily cured with a dose of antibiotics.

Marie, Emma and Richie had to comfort me in the end because, when Joe asked me why I was outside the Rainbow Clinic, I said the first thing that came into my head.

"I don't have a Sexually Transmitted Disease."

Joe started to laugh. Luckily, his girlfriend has just picked up a call on her mobile so had walked away from us slightly.

"Glad to hear it. I don't either. Do you think we should start a club?" Joe joked and I smiled painfully.

"Well it is just you saw me coming out of the place and I didn't want you to put two and two together and make four, I mean five." Oh my god, why couldn't I stop talking?

"I didn't think anything at first," Joe said. "I do now." Joe winked.

"Oh, okay. Well, we have agreed then. You know and I know I don't have herpes or anything," I needed saving. The hole I was digging for myself was gradually getting bigger and bigger. Shut up Bella!

"How was the holiday?" Joe changed the subject (thank god).

I told Joe that our holiday was good and the weather was great, then he said he had to shoot off which was a real shame because other than the fact I was outside the Rainbow Clinic, I was actually enjoying just looking at him.

"He thinks I was a patient at the Clinic doesn't he?" I asked my friends a few hours later, over lunch.

"Yep!" Emma said matter-of-factly.

"Emma!" I cried.

"I'm not going to lie to you Bella," Emma said. "Your denial made you look guilty."

I wanted the ground to open up and swallow me again. Actually, I wanted Richie to go round to Joe's and tell him that he was the one with crabs, not me. Richie must have guessed what I was thinking.

"No chance Bella!" Richie said.

"Okay, okay worth a try."

My mobile rang saving me from going over and over my conversation with Joe in my head anymore. I had only got my mobile about eighteen months ago, because until then I was adamant that I didn't need or that I would use one. It was my sister Annie.

Annie is six years older than me and lives a few miles away from the rest of the family with her long-term boyfriend and their son Ben. Annie and I have never really been that close. We are just completely different people. Annie is what you might call a Hippy Chick. Her family live on organic meals, grow their own vegetables, go strawberry picking on sunny days and don't allow chocolate in the house. Annie also has dread-locked hair (in my opinion not a good look unless you are a Rastafarian), six piercings (two in each ear, one in her belly button and a nipple ring) and a tattoo on the small of her back which simply says "peace" in black scrawly ink. So I guess you can see why we never confide in each other and never really make the effort to see each other except at family get-togethers for someone's birthday. We have probably become a lot closer since Ben was born. He is worth making more of an effort for.

"Hi Bell, it's Annie," Annie says. "I need a favour if possible please?"

"Sure, what do you need?" I ask. I said Annie and I were not close, but at the end of the day we are sisters.

"Could you take me to the hospital please?"

"What?! Are you okay?" I suddenly shriek.

"Calm down, it's not me, it's Ben," Annie said. "He has stuck an orange pip up his nose again and I can't get it out."

It never rains but it pours.

Chapter Twelve

The next major thing to happen was my falling sick. Don't panic, I only have a bad case of laryngitis, which caused my family no end of joy, because I couldn't speak. The major thing happened because I was in my sick bed and it gave me time to think, but I will get to that point in a minute. I only like to go and see my Doctor when absolutely necessary, so I felt on death's door when he gave me a prescription of penicillin and told me to have a weeks rest.

I look terrible. I'm sleeping for England (which I can only presume means if sleeping was an Olympic sport then I would be a strong contender), but I still look like I'm struggling on only two hours a night. Unfortunately, as I share a room with Lin, she is also suffering as well. I spend most of the night tossing and turning, coughing and blowing my nose. Lin likes to have peace and quiet when she sleeps, so I am also being constantly woken up in the night with Lin standing over my bed after digging me in the ribs (let me tell you it is a scary vision when you are half asleep) and Lin asking me not so nicely, through gritted teeth to shut up. I'm thinking of slipping a dose of my penicillin in her tea just to see her face swell up like a balloon. That would teach her not to have any sympathy for her big sister. My Mum is a godsend, although her answer to all problems is always the same.

"Cup of tea, hot water bottle and early night"

It doesn't matter what problem you have gone to see my Mum about, it is the same response whether it is my Dad, Annie or Lin asking.

"Mum, I have bad period pains."

"Cup of tea, hot water bottle and early night."

"Oh love, I have chronic back-ache."

"Cup of tea, hot water bottle and early night."

"Mum, I've had a fight with Kelly at school."

"Cup of tea, hot water bottle and early night."

I find the response extremely comforting now. It's even more comforting when my Mum brings the cup of tea to my sick bed with my hot water bottle.

"Thanks," I say hoarsely to my Mother.

"Don't speak love; you sound like you smoke fifty a day." My Mum stroked my hair, which made it all better.

My Dad, on the other hand, has no sympathy whatsoever, although it is a completely different story when he is ill. My Dad is a quiet man, tends to let my Mum rule the house and steps in as and when he needs to. For example, my Mum telling him I needed a slap for telling lies and me getting one across my backside when I was twelve.

The house is extremely quiet during the day, so I manage to catch up on my sleep then. The only downside is hauling myself from my bed to get my drinks, antibiotics and food.

You can also tell how ill I am by the fact I don't even care that my bedroom is such a mess, caused by Lin.

At the moment, work consists of temping as a receptionist for a local computer company down the road. The money's not bad and the job has been ongoing for the last eighteen months, but it is leading nowhere. I'm good at my receptionist's job, but then how hard can it be?

However, some people just don't have the knack. One of the new girls was covering for me whilst I went to lunch and spent the whole hour chatting to her mates on the phone. The Sales people went mad as important calls were missed. Apparently, I have a great telephone manner and I "sing" to the customers when I greet them with a good morning, the company name and how could I possibly assist them today. I have made myself indispensable on reception, which means I am never going to get moved on. I have changed my job title on my CV to Client Services Specialist, which sounds much more suited to me, and not far off the truth.

I wake up when I hear the rest of my family come home. When I say the rest of my family, I mean my Dad, Mum, Lin and Ben.

"You look bad."

"You don't look so good."

"I hope it's okay that I borrowed one of your tops this morning whilst you were sleeping."

I didn't have much choice as the top in question is now being worn by Lin.

I think she's told me that now because she knows I cannot have a go at her with my voice so croaky and hoarse. Ben crawls up into my arms. Ben is Annie's son and my parents love any excuse to look after him. He's two years old and I love him to pieces. It is like looking at a younger Annie at times. He has her soft features and long eyelashes. I give Ben a huge cuddle and he starts talking about his "ball" which I know is his fluffy football. A fluffy football that when you throw it makes a big jingling noise. Annie bought it for him and it drives my parents mad.

"Dinner!" My Dad shouts up the stairs.

"Come on Ben." My Mum holds her arms out for Ben who immediately throws himself into her arms, literally.

As I get to the table I want to hug my Dad. He has made me my favourite meal, which is bangers and mash. It's as good as I remember it as well. I am starting to feel so much better already. Lin is telling us all about her latest boyfriend. She is one of the lucky ones. She always has someone interested and never seems to go looking for them. Her latest boyfriend is called Luke. The only Luke I can think of is Luke Perry from Beverley Hills 90210, but I doubt it's him. I would have to try stealing him from my sister if that really was her boyfriend. He was extremely gorgeous in his day. He probably has a pot belly and a grey beard by now. Scary thought. Ben is not very interested in Lin's stories though. He has a lot more fun blowing raspberries just as he has put his food in his mouth.

After dinner, I offer to wash up but my Mum tells me I should go back to bed.

"Thanks Mum," I smile pathetically. I am worse than a man when I am ill. I don't think I need to explain that comment. Most of you with brothers, Dads, boyfriends or husbands will understand.

Lin just rolls her eyes as I plant a kiss on my Mum's cheek and proceed back upstairs. Now is not the time to let my parents know that I am handing in my notice at Daley Systems, well for one it hurts my throat too much, and I just don't have the energy to fight with my Dad at the moment. I had made the momentous decision that I had finally had enough of temporary work. It was time to live my dream and follow my heart (I had read a few self-help books whilst I was off sick).

"Bella," my Mum shouts up the stairs just as I have got to the top of them. I poke my head over the banister. "Give me five minutes and I'll bring you up a cup of tea and a hot water bottle."

Chapter Thirteen

I didn't have that much to worry about with my Dad, it was my Manager Karen, who took the news the hardest.

Karen had been a secretary when I had first started at Daley Systems, so we were on equal levels but after my first six weeks Karen was promoted to my Manager and that is when the trouble started.

The power went directly to Karen's head. You actually saw the current hitting the top of her mousy brown scalp.

"This is a letter of resignation," I placed the envelope in front of Karen in her office. She looked at me and started to laugh. What was so funny?

"Oh Bella, I am not in the mood today." She started to laugh.

"I am being serious," I said. "I'm leaving."

"You can't leave," Karen said looking shocked, which is a ridiculous thing to say because as it happens I can and I am.

Once Karen realised I was being serious there was no holding back. I was letting the company down, I was letting myself down and, most of all, I was letting her down and she thought we were friends (that was the first I had heard about it). How can you be friends with someone who talks down to you every single minute for eight hours a day every day?

Karen finally accepted that her attempts at emotional blackmail were not going to work and even the offer of more money did not sway me (although that made it tough). As I was a temporary member of staff it meant I could leave in a week and I couldn't wait.

After my 27th birthday, which passed extremely quietly with a few drinks, a meal and some Topshop vouchers, my first point of call after handing in my resignation was the new book-store that had opened in the High Street. When I first saw the new building being refurbished in town I thought we were in for another card shop.

I had always enjoyed reading. It was actually a passion of mine. It didn't matter who the author was or what the book was about, I would read it. According to my Mum, I had always been this way. She was always asking me when I was going to give all my old books to charity, but I just could not bear to be parted from them. I had a great big holdall in my parents' attic that contained all my old Enid Blytons, Nancy Drews and Judy Blumes. If I got rid of those, I would feel like I was losing part of my childhood. Annie saw no point in reading books unless there was an exam at the end of it. Annie was the brainy one of the family, got a first in her degree and didn't even try, although she would beg to differ on that.

The new book store was aptly named "The Book Store", which I felt made it sound quaint, a bit like the bookstore that featured in that Meg Ryan film.

It was situated at the end of the High Street on the corner right next to Topshop, which is probably a bad thing as I would have no excuse not to pop in.

The Book Store was my idea of paradise. It had two floors which were filled with shelves that reached the ceiling containing all genres of books. It had a refreshment area at the back of the store on the second floor, which had a couple of brown leather sofas with a coffee bar alongside to give customers the chance to have a read of the first couple of pages of their novel before venturing home. I found the whole place homely and the décor, with its welcoming creams and browns were just perfect. The store itself fitted really well into the quiet town. I managed to secure an interview a few days after my initial visit with the Manager of the store, Stella.

Stella was an extremely friendly older lady with shocking white hair which she had tied tightly back in a bun at the nape of her neck. Stella actually owned the store and told me she was looking for an Assistant Manager as she just could not cope with the forty hour weeks any longer. Stella had moved her book store to accommodate the fast expanding business.

Stella was looking to inject young blood into the store and she felt someone of my age would be the ideal candidate. There were only three other people that worked in the store. One was the Shop Assistant who worked part time hours throughout the week, the second was the Saturday Assistant, who was a sixteen year old girl who funnily enough only worked Saturdays and the third person was Jody.

Jody ran the coffee refreshment area. It was her role to make sure all customers who sat in that area had a coffee, a Belgian bun and were comfortable. Stella took me around to meet the Shop Assistant and Jody on my interview. I knew as soon as I was introduced to Jody that we would get on. She must have been about four years older than me and had a really welcoming face.

I could read a novel in the space of a couple of days, so I tended to visit the Book Store every week since its opening four months ago.

My interview with Stella went well, but to be honest, you can never really tell about these things. I could only keep my fingers crossed. It had been a while since I was last at a job interview, there is normally no need for one for temporary work. Stella called me a day later, on the Friday.

"Hello Bella, it's Stella. How are you?"

"Good thank you, how are you?"

"Very well," Stella paused. "I am just phoning to offer you the trainee Assistant Manager's job, if you are still interested?"

My heart leapt with joy.

"Yes I am," I managed to say. I was sure Stella could tell from the other end of the phone that my smile was spreading across my face. "Thank you so much!"

"Don't thank me my love," Stella chuckled. "You deserve

it. I am sure it was a sign that our names rhymed for a start."

I couldn't think what to say to that, so I just laughed along with her.

"Come in on Monday and we can get you started," Stella said.

I thanked her again before hanging up the phone. I stood staring at the receiver for a few seconds before whooping with joy, bringing my Mum out of the kitchen. I hugged her tightly.

"I got it Mum," I shrieked. "I got the job!"

My Mum hugged me back and congratulated me, told me that she knew I was in no danger of not getting it. Mum always knew the right thing to say.

"Celebrating tonight then?" Mum added.

"Definitely," I let go of her and picked up the handset again. "It would be rude not to have a celebratory drink tonight."

Chapter Fourteen

I was meeting Emma and Marie in the pub. I arrived first which is not surprising, as Emma and Marie's timekeeping can be appalling.

I sat on one of the bar stools and ordered a pint of beer from the barmaid.

I know a pint of beer is not exactly ladylike, but it makes no sense buying two halves as it costs more. I may have the job I wanted, but it does not mean I am now rolling in it. As the advert says, every little helps.

I sip my pint and look around the pub, which is when I notice Joe.

Joe is sitting at a corner table on his own sitting staring at his half empty pint glass. He looks deep in his troubled thoughts and seems oblivious to anyone around him. I look to the bar again and notice that there is no-one else with him. If it was a girl sitting and drinking on her own she would be classed as an alcoholic, but men can get away with popping into the pub for a quick one after work.

Joe obviously works outdoors as he is still in his daytime attire. He's wearing dirty, black jogging bottoms, black steel toe-capped boots and a yellow tee-shirt which has a rip along the back. He has flecks of paint in his hair and his hands look dusty.

I am contemplating going over to say hello when Marie and Emma both arrive together.

"Sorry we're late," Emma announces as she walks up to the bar. I smile at my friends and notice Joe from the corner of my eye look up. I catch his eye and smile. He lifts his pint glass in recognition and winks.

"My stomach feels like my throat has been cut," Emma says. "Two Budweiser's and three packets of cheese and onion crisps please."

"Well done about the job mate," Marie puts her arm around me.

"I'm so pleased," I say. "It is exactly what I've been looking for."

"Could you get me the new Jackie Collins novel when it comes out then?" Emma says as she hands one of the Budweisers to Marie.

"I don't think Stella would appreciate stealing on my first week!"

"I didn't want you to steal it, just get me a knock-down price," Emma explains.

"Emma how much do you earn?!"

Emma works for a Design company and has done since leaving university. She earns treble the amount of money that I take home each month so it's a standing joke that she's always trying to find the best bargain or find ways to get money off. Emma is the person who always holds the queue up in the supermarket because she's counting her pennies to pay rather than use a note and she also sorts through the money off coupons she has, in the hope she can save fifty pence off a twelve pack of toilet roll.

"Where's Richie?" Marie asks.

"He's finishing once and for all with Pablo tonight," I explain.

"About time. He should have finished with him when he gave him crabs!" Emma frowned.

"I think it is more to do with the fact that Richie can't afford his phone bills anymore and has decided this long distance relationship stuff will not work." Emma and Marie laugh.

"Sounds about right," Marie agreed.

I tell the girls all about my new job and how Stella seems like a really nice person. I notice Joe go up to the bar and get another drink whilst we are all talking. He is too far away for me to be able to hear what he's ordered but he downs a shot of something which causes his face to screw up and takes his beer back to the corner table.

"Who are you staring at?" Emma swings round and that is when she notices Joe sitting in the corner. "Ah, now it all falls into place"

"Do you think we should say hello?" I ask.

"I think the man needs to be on his own. He looks like he has the weight of the world on his shoulders," Unfortunately on this occasion I know Emma is right. Emma, Marie and I enjoy the rest of the evening. We stop drinking beers after our third and get started on the white wine. This is something I don't recommend.

Marie admits that she's been seeing someone for the past three months. This leaves both Emma and I completely gob-smacked. It turns out that one of Jono's friends is a courier at the company where Marie works. Anyway, they exchanged pleasantries and one day Baz (full name Barry) asked her out for a drink.

"I was not sure it was going to go anywhere, so I just kept it to myself," Marie said. "I didn't want it turned into a huge deal."

I could understand Marie's reasoning especially with Emma (the analyst) and Richie (who has to know every little detail of our lives), but it still hurt all the same that my best friend had not confided in me.

"I did want to tell you though," Marie looked directly at me.

"I know you did," I say back. This is true. Marie and I have shared many secrets in the past and I know how hard I would find it to keep to myself.

"You are not angry with me are you?" Marie asks.

"Not at all." I give her a hug. "Now tell me all about him and when do we get to meet him?" I'm not at all angry with Marie but I still can't help feeling slightly disappointed that she felt she couldn't share this news with me.

The last part of our evening was spent talking about Baz and Marie. Marie was in love. I had never ever seen her like this before. There is the girl who tends to hold back with men, never shows her real feelings. She has had boyfriends in the past but no-one she's ever really cared about, this time I know it is different. Marie's eyes actually shine when she talks about him. I know Baz is important.

The bell rings for closing time and we attempt to get off our bar-stools with as much dignity as possible, which is quite hard considering the amount of drinks we have had.

"Hello ladies." We swing round to see Joe in front of us.

"Hello," We all say in unison. We start to giggle. A sure sign of a drunken group of girls.

"Good evening?" Joe asks. I can tell he is drunk. His eyes are bloodshot and his cheeks are rosy.

"Yep really good thanks," Marie says. "You?"

"I have had better." Joe's eyes look sad and I withhold the urge to hug him tightly. "That's a shame," I manage to say and Joe looks directly at me.

"Yes it is Bella."

Just the way Joe said my name was enough to make me shiver and I thought that only happened in cheesy, romantic novels.

"Well, nice to see you again, Joe," Emma says and starts to lead us towards the exit.

"Yep," Joe continues. "Hold on!"

We stop and look back round at Joe.

"Which one of you lovely girls wants to take me home tonight then?"

Chapter Fifteen

My first day at the Book Store went extremely well. I enjoyed myself and how many people do you know can actually say that about their work?

I spent my lunch hour in the coffee area with a sandwich and a coffee, which is where my thoughts travelled to Joe again.

I had thought many times of the moment when Joe would ask me to take him home, but unfortunately that was not one of them. Joe was obviously in a bad way about something and I could only guess it was to do with his girlfriend, so we had all laughed off his request and made sure he got in a taxi to take him home alone.

Once Joe was safely in a taxi, we could only assume he would eventually find his home safely. Marie, Emma and I bundled into a taxi five minutes later.

"I don't think I fancy Joe anymore," I said.

"Yeah right!" Emma looked at me disbelievingly.

"Well, he obviously has a drink problem and he must be so in love with his girlfriend to be in that state," I said, noticing that the taxi driver was taking us the long way to my house.

"I'm sorry mate, but I don't buy that for second," Emma grabbed my hand. "You fancy the pants off him, but it's okay you can stay in denial for a while."

I hated it when Emma was right. I had tried several times to come up with excuses as to why I didn't fancy Joe anymore but they were all, in a word, crap.

He had a girlfriend (which is a good reason not to make a move, but not to actually fancy someone).

He smoked (I had seen him with a packet of Marlborough Lights on two occasions, although I had never seen him smoke one).

I don't usually go for fair headed men (maybe now is the

time to live dangerously). He could have a drink problem (although I had no real proof of this).

As I just said, my reasonings were crap. I had thought long and hard about what it would have been like to go home with Joe for the night, but I knew I would never have said yes, even if the situation happened again. For one, being on holiday and having a one night stand is one thing but I am not in the business of making a habit out of it and two, I wanted to be more than that to Joe.

"Penny for them?" My thoughts were interrupted by Jody taking a seat next to me at the coffee table.

"Sorry, I was miles away," I said.

"Mind if I join you?" Jody asked.

"Of course not, I would appreciate the company," anything to get my mind off Joe. It was one of the quiet periods in the Book Store, just after the lunchtime rush. This was when we could all take our breaks, although obviously not all together. Stella was downstairs manning the tills. I never understood why more businesses didn't stagger their lunch hours. Banks, for example, their busiest time has to be between midday and two o'clock, so why then do they all take their lunch-breaks during that time? It is just not good customer service.

It was nice to talk to Jody. I found out that she lived with her boyfriend Jez (didn't anyone have normal names anymore?) in Chertsey, which was about half an hour away. They had moved into their own little cottage about six months ago and were in the process of doing it up. Jez worked in the City, something to do with investments or something. Anyway, as it turned out Jody did not even have to work because of the amount of money Jez brought in every month, but she said it just wouldn't feel right being a lady of leisure every day. I could understand that but it brought a smile to my face when I thought about what Marie would say to that.

Marie's ideal career would be a lady of leisure.

"So what about you? Are you seeing anyone?" Jody asked.

"Nope, young free and single," I answered.

"Cool," she said. "Better go, a customer has just walked in."

Jody got up from the table and went behind the coffee counter to serve a lady with the new John Grisham Thriller in her hand.

I was right about Jody. We were going to be friends. There are very few people that you actually click with in real life but Jody was one of them. It had taken a while for Richie and Emma to become friends, which is the case for most people.

Friendship takes a while, but with Marie and Jody, well it just feels natural. Oops there I go being all deep again.

My first week at the Book Store flew past. Stella was there all week showing me the ropes, but pretty much giving me free reign for my ideas. I decided the new bestsellers should be at the front of the shop so that was the first thing that caught the customer's eyes. Stella immediately told me to implement this. I felt important, I knew Stella trusted me and I didn't want to let her down.

I was pleased that my first week was so busy as it took my mind off you know who. Do you think if I stopped mentioning his name it would help?

I had to move on from fancying Joe. There was no future in it and it was taking up too much of my time thinking about it. It didn't stop me from thinking about him just before I went to sleep though. I would just picture his face in my head and imagine a normal conversation happening between us, not one where I can't even string a sentence together but one where I sound witty and funny.

Hopefully I will stop running into Joe that often and my little "obsession" (I use this term loosely as I am not going to start boiling his bunnies or stalking his girlfriend), will pass.

Unfortunately, that was easier said than done.

Chapter Sixteen

Marie was holding a dinner party. Her flat-mate was staying at her parents for the weekend so she had the place to herself and now was the ideal time for us all to meet Baz.

It was also the ideal time for a couple of Baz's mates to meet Marie. This made me feel better, as their secret relationship had obviously been kept from everyone and not just me, Richie and Emma.

Marie doesn't like to cook. I am sure she wouldn't mind me telling you that she's both lazy and impatient, so she normally serves us bloody chicken or beans on toast when we have gone round for dinner in the past.

However, this time Marie had completely surpassed herself. I noticed the table first. I didn't even know Marie had a table in her flat (we always had dinner on lap trays before), but apparently there was always one there hidden in the corner, folded down with lots of photos on.

The table was set for eight people, with placemats set out with cutlery next to them. There were also coasters with empty wine glasses on top and a white serviette on each placemat. There was a scented orange candle burning away in the middle of the table and the lights had been dimmed to make the setting more relaxed. The stereo was on a very low volume but I recognised it as the most recent Robbie Williams album.

I noticed Baz second. He was standing in the kitchen leaning against the doorway. He was wearing blue faded jeans with a blue Ben Sherman tee-shirt. He had a shaved head and a really nice smile.

"Everyone this is Baz," Marie put her arm around Baz's shoulders.

"Hello everyone," Baz said. "I've heard lots about you all."

"Uh oh!" Richie smirked. "I think we had better leave

now!"

The intercom went again and Baz excused himself to let his friends in. You have probably guessed who his two mates are already, Jono and of course, Joe.

"Guys, this is Marie," Baz introduced her. Marie blushed and said hello to Jono, who she already knew and Joe.

Dammit, just as I started to forget what Joe looked like. He turned up at my friend's flat with still slightly damp hair (I have a thing for the "just out of the shower look") and a really nice soapy aftershave on.

Baz was really easy to get on with and he made an effort to speak to Richie, Emma and I. He actually seemed interested in our life stories, although I did feel the need to save him when Richie started talking about his recent bad experience. I just didn't feel that Baz needed to know Richie's intimate sexual problems just yet. Baz was also really at ease at Marie's place. He made sure everyone had a drink before Marie served up dinner. Dinner was takeaway pizzas and garlic bread, although it was nicely served on white dinner plates.

I was sat between Joe and Richie at dinner and this was the first time since Joe's arrival that we managed to say hello.

"How are you Bella?" Joe asked.

"Yeah, good thanks," I replied. "You?"

"Yep not bad although nowhere near as bad as the other night", Joe said. "Sorry, I was bit drunk."

"You weren't too bad at all," I reassured him.

"Just had a bit of a rough day that's all," Joe explained although he didn't meet my eye when he said this so I had the inclination he was probably holding back on me.

"We all have them. Everything okay now?"

"Yep fine. This is a surprise about Baz and Marie eh?" Shame I thought. I was hoping Joe had a massive break-up and was looking for a shoulder to cry on.

The conversation moved onto our friends. Dinner went

71

really smoothly and I sat talking to Joe for most of the evening. I think the wine was helping me loosen up a bit so we ended up talking about my new job and my holiday, which seemed just a distant memory now.

When I got up to pop to the toilet I noticed Baz squeezing Marie's hand under the table and she looked up at him and smiled. That moment nearly brought tears to my eyes. I've known Marie for so many years and I have never ever seen her so relaxed and happy before. I knew Emma had noticed this too as we caught each others eyes and smiled.

Once dinner and dessert, which was Carte D'or strawberry ice-cream, had been finished, we turned up the stereo, opened another couple of bottles of wine and Richie got Twister out. Yes Twister, you know, the game where you spin the board and you have to put your left arm on the yellow spot and your right leg on the green spot. After Emma had beaten all of us three times, Richie got us all playing musical statues and chairs. I was out first on both games.

Joe and I actually had a lot in common. And no, I was not reading too much into it. He had two sisters, although both his were older and were twins. He currently lived at home, but was keeping his options open. He was stuck in a job that he didn't particularly like very much and had dreamt many times of jacking it all in and trying out for the Police force, but Joe admitted that he never had the bottle. He was currently classed as self employed painter and decorator and earnt good money for it, but Joe said it was a hard graft and he would be extremely disappointed with himself if that was his lifelong role.

Joe told me his girlfriend Sally worked at the Marc Antoni hairdressers in town (although, as you know, I already knew this information). I didn't ask too much about Sally because I guess deep down I didn't want to know how lovely she was. It was hard enough now putting a name to the face. Was Sally the comical or dizzy one?

"Six months. Cool," was my reply to Joe letting me know the length of time he had been seeing Sally for.

"That'll be nice", was my reply to Joe letting me know they were going on holiday together in a week or so. He must have thought I was so rude because I just couldn't bring myself to ask where they were going and for how long. I didn't want to know. The relationship must be serious.

"Yeah we'll see how it goes I guess," Joe smiled. He had such a nice smile. Marie and I always liked a nice smile in a man, which is probably one of the attributes that attracted her to Baz.

All too soon the evening was over, in the early hours of the morning. I told Marie that her neighbours must be extremely understanding as her flat was on the second and top floor. It turns out her neighbours were in their eighties, were always in bed by eight and both took their hearing aids out.

Richie had exhausted himself being our Games Master for the evening and had actually been asleep for the last hour on Marie's sofa. Emma had finally finished interrogating Baz, although he had seemed to pass with flying colours as we had to prise Emma off him when we all went to say goodbye to everyone.

"What do you think then mate?" Marie whispered to me as I hugged her goodbye.

"Perfect," I whispered back. It felt all right again that Marie had not told me that she was seeing someone for three months because she still wanted my approval and that counted for a lot in my book.

We left Joe at the top of the road as he was going in the other direction.

"We should all meet up again soon," Joe suggested. "It's been a good laugh."

"Yeah it definitely has," I agreed. "See you soon."

I watched as Joe walked away sighing to myself. If anything, Joe and I would make good friends.

Jono and Emma walked me back to mine before heading

off to their house. We had left Richie sleeping on Marie's sofa.

I knew I would be having nice relaxed dreams tonight after such a happy evening. Well, as soon as I stopped trying to unlock my next door neighbour's house with my key and got to my own bed anyway. I was obviously drunker than I first thought and my poor head was starting to hurt already.

Little was I to know the third major event was just around the corner.

Chapter Seventeen

"I'm pregnant."

There was complete and utter silence in the room and I went to try and say something but ended up opening and closing my mouth like a goldfish.

At least I wasn't the only one, we were all opening and closing our mouths like goldfish.

"Say something then!"

Again, there was just silence.

"How?"

"What a daft question!"

"Sorry" Again there was just silence.

"Oh my god you lot are bloody useless!"

That was a pretty fair comment in the circumstances. I could only imagine what I would feel after announcing the above and there being a silence, which seemed to be lasting forever. Marie looked at me and I looked at Richie, who always knew the right thing to say in bad circumstances. One of our friends at school lost her Mum in a car accident and Richie was great. He hugged the girl, told her he was so sorry and he would be there for her if she wanted to talk. I, on the other hand was useless, had no idea what to say to the girl and ended up avoiding her at all costs. But even now Richie had no idea what to say.

"Let's make this easy for you then. Ask me questions one by one ok?"

Phew, thank goodness! When Emma had told us she was pregnant I thought for one brief second she had been taken over by aliens, which in a sense is correct, if you think about it. There is an alien being growing inside her. But now Emma was just being Emma, taking control and sorting us all out before herself.

"When on earth did you get laid?" Richie asked the first

question, which caused us all to smile, but we all wanted to know the answer. As far as we were all concerned Emma hadn't slept with anyone for over a year since a disastrous two month relationship with the aptly nicknamed "the Confused One." The Confused One now lived in Australia as a Hare Krisna but before he went he did ask Richie out, so you see what I mean about being confused.

"On holiday," Emma said and we all still look confused. "With the older man."

"Urgh Em!!" Richie looked disgusted.

"Richard Cunningham, at least I didn't get crabs!"

"Yeah okay, fair point," Richie sulked and played with the plain silver band on his thumb.

"I didn't tell you because it only happened once."

"But you didn't even fancy him!" Marie said. "It was pity snogs."

"It was also a pity shag," Emma said. "Although more for me than him."

"Huh?" I was lost.

Emma could be scary sometimes with her loud opinionated voice, but she was beautiful and generous. Why would the older, deaf man pity her?

"It has been such a long time since I had been with someone," Emma explained. "I thought I might have closed up."

"Safety measures?" Richie asked.

"I thought it would ruin the moment," Emma looked sad. "How naïve am I?"

For the first time since I've known Emma, I could see how scared and angry she was with herself. She was no longer in control and I could tell she didn't like it, not for one minute. This was not supposed to happen to her. It would be more likely to happen to Richie, so you get the point about it being a complete and utter shock to us all.

Emma has never been maternal. She is an only child and is

happy to be spoilt by both her parents, who live in Spain, and for us all to have kids eventually, so she can be surrogate Auntie. Children smile at her in supermarkets and she wants to know what they are smiling at checking her teeth in her compact mirror to make sure she has no remains of her lunch there. Emma thinks all kids should be banned from public places because they are a nuisance to society, and the idea of being pregnant in the past has disgusted her.

This certainly does not make Emma a bad person. After all she is only twenty-six years old, which is young in this day and age to have kids. Not all women are designed to have children and Emma certainly fits the mould of one of these women.

Richie went to sit next to Emma on her bed and hugged her tightly. This is what Richie did when he ran out of words to say. Marie and I could only watch as Emma wrapped her arms around Richie and buried her head in his shoulder.

Then something extraordinary happened. Something that neither Marie, Richie nor I have seen in our lifetime but we have proof that it happened from an old baby photo of Emma when she was two.

Emma started to sob. Her shoulders started to shake and the sobs were muffled by Richie's shoulders. He just held her tighter and even though we could not see his face, we knew he would be as shocked as we were at Emma falling apart.

Finally, Emma pulled away and looked up at both Marie and I, still clutching Richie's hand for support. Her eyes were swollen and red and her nose was running.

Emma sniffed and attempted a smile.

"So girls, what the bloody hell am I going to do?"

Chapter Eighteen

Marie spoke to Emma for hours, Richie spoke to Emma for hours and I spoke to Emma for hours. We all talked about the same thing. The baby, or the sproglet, as Richie called it.

We talked through all the options with Emma. A termination, adoption or keeping it. Emma shuddered at the thought of all three, but one of them she would have to go through.

On one particular bad day, Emma said she could just drink lots of whisky and flush the baby out. She was just upset and I know she didn't mean it. It was extremely un-nerving to see Emma like this.

On other days, Emma thought about keeping the child and bringing it up on her own. She had no idea how to get hold of the man from holiday and even if she could, I doubt she would have. Emma is an extremely independent person and I knew it took a lot of courage for her to talk about this with us all. No-one else knew, so it was a discussion that only the four of us would be having, but ultimately the decision would lie with Em.

Emma hated being pregnant and blamed it on her emotional outbursts. I had to agree that is was probably the hormones causing the outbursts, as it was so unlike her to have them. Emma had stopped drinking alcohol as soon as she had found out she was pregnant, which was a couple of days before she told us. She woke up in the early hours of every morning and craved cheese and pickled onion sandwiches, so on many occasions Emma had to try and explain to Jono and her other housemate why she was raiding the fridge at three o'clock in the morning. They just accepted the fact she was hungry and stressed out with work, well, they wouldn't think anything else. As I said before, Emma was always in control of every situation. She loved fresh coffee every morning before starting work, but just the smell of the percolator bubbling away was enough to cause her to heave. Luckily Emma had not had any morning sickness yet but we all knew it was just around the corner.

She was beginning to resent the baby more and more every day for the change in her life-style (Emma was in bed asleep by nine o' clock every night), the change in her eating habits (she couldn't stop eating and was always hungry) and for not being allowed the things she loved like alcohol and mayonnaise (I never knew you were not allowed mayonnaise but apparently it's because of the ingredient of raw eggs).

Every day for the past week Emma had asked us all if we thought she was getting fat and we always replied no, which was the truth, but she thought we were just trying to be nice.

Emma was only eight weeks pregnant and no closer to making a decision. She had even toyed with the idea of going to Spain to see her parents and talk this through with them but Marie and I agreed this was a bad idea. Emma's parents would see this as a great idea and would persuade Emma into keeping a child she might not particularly want to raise herself. After all, this might be the only chance they had of a grandchild.

"Do you think I would be punished for having a termination?" Emma asked me one day.

"Why do you think that?" I asked.

"It goes against nature, doesn't it?"

I could see where Emma was going with this one, but it was ironic this was coming from the girl who waxed every part of the body that needed waxing and had regular sun-beds.

"I don't think you will be punished Em," I soothed down the telephone. "I think if it is meant to be, then it will be."

"I am glad I have such a hippy as a friend," Emma said.

"Blimey, I am more like Annie than I thought," I smiled. Emma contemplated the idea of adoption with Marie but quickly discarded that idea as she realised she would still have to go through childbirth. Childbirth scared the hell out of all of us, not including Richie.

"Why would I want to go through all the pain and not even have a prize at the end of it?" So that put paid to the adoption idea.

I spoke to Marie and Richie separately about Emma's situation and we were all extremely worried about her. I was continuously being asked if I was okay at the Book Store because Em was constantly on my mind. I wanted to take the pain away from her and make it all better with a giant band-aid but I couldn't. I felt like a useless friend.

Emma was six days away from being ten weeks pregnant and had just started to throw up the morning before when the decision was taken out of her hands.

Emma had taken the day off sick and was sitting in her own bed at two o' clock in the afternoon when she lost the baby.

Chapter Nineteen

Emma fell apart. Marie, Richie and I took it in turns to go over and see her every spare moment we had. I would jump into my car on a lunch break and shoot over to see her, just to make her a cup of tea and a sandwich. I have no idea if Emma was eating the countless number of sandwiches I brought her, but she thanked me anyway.

Emma felt she was being punished for even contemplating "murdering" her child. No matter how many times we told her that it was not murder, Emma seemed content enough to beat herself up at every opportunity.

The physical pain subsided in a day or two. It was the mental pain that was causing us all concern. I think what upset Emma the most was that the decision had been taken out of her hands and fate had decided for her. Emma wanted to control her own destiny and yes, it was a complete shock being pregnant in the first place but she wanted to be the one to decide what happened next.

I was actually quite proud of myself. Instead of being the cowardly friend who walks away not knowing the right thing to say or do, I have been there for Emma as much as I could be, even when I haven't known what to say or do. I had just been there.

It took Emma nearly a week to stop crying and then she threw herself back into work. The baby subject was now taboo.

"I am all talked out," Emma said to us all. "I just want to move on now."

"It's only been a week, so you can still talk about it," Marie said.

"No, I want to get on."

"Do you fancy getting pissed this weekend then?" Richie suggested.

We all smiled at him. Richie's cure was either lots of hugs or drinking to excess. "Excellent idea," Emma smiled. "Nothing to stop me now."

The weekend was a few days away, so we all agreed to give Em some space on her own until then. I just couldn't stand the thought of my friend sitting on her own every evening going over the events of the last few weeks again and again.

Emma actually phoned me two days later.

"I have an idea," Emma said, as soon as I picked up the phone and she recognised my voice.

"Hi Em."

"Okay, are you listening?"

"Yep, I'm sitting comfortably and everything," I sat myself down at the foot of my stairs.

"I am going to invest in property."

"What?" I ermm… was confused.

"I have savings and my parents want to give me the deposit, so I am going to buy a place of my own, instead of frittering away my money every month," Emma sounded certain.

"That's a great idea," I certainly hoped she was not rushing into anything. The old Emma, before baby Emma would not have rushed into anything like this without giving it serious thought and seeing a financial advisor ten times. The new Emma, after baby, may be a different story entirely.

"So do you want to be my flat mate then?" Emma asked.

"Eh?"

"I want you to be my lodger. You have to admit, you would love your freedom away from your parents and it is about time you got it," Emma's idea sounded so appealing.

"Are you serious?"

"Deadly. I promise I would be a good landlord, so how about it?"

It sounded brilliant. I loved my family dearly but it was time for me to move out, if only to have a room of my own again. Emma and I could be the female equivalent of Men Behaving Badly. I already had the girly night's image in my head. There was no other answer to give Emma.

"I would love to Em," I said. "It sounds perfect."

"Excellent, we can go house hunting at the weekend. I need someone's opinion anyway."

"No problem at all," I agreed. "Are you okay about you know what?"

"Bella, we've agreed not to talk about it anymore," Emma said.

"I know you did but why?"

"Oh Bells," Emma sighed on the other end of the phone. "It's cos I can't talk about it anymore, okay?"

"Okay"

Emma and I agreed to firm up our plans when we saw each other on Friday night, but it was a date. We would be viewing potential properties for Emma to buy on Saturday. How very grown up!

I sighed as I replaced the receiver. I knew what Emma was doing and I knew that I would probably be doing the same in her situation. She was throwing herself into a new project, something to make her forget.

I knew this was something that Emma would never forget.

If I had a crystal ball, I could have reassured Emma that she would be a Mother one day and that there was a reason, a very good reason, for this miscarriage to happen but I'm not a psychic and that is a different story, one for Emma to tell. I was just glad that things happened in threes so things could finally settle down and become normal again.

Chapter Twenty

The Book Store was thriving, well actually I was thriving in the Book Store.

The Book Store was one of my favourite places to be. I loved being one of the first to read the new bestseller and I was in awe when we finally had a writer come to an evening signing session. I had read this woman's work on many occasions. The picture in the back of her books did her no justice. She is a lot prettier in real life. Stella let me meet the writer to show her where to set herself up for the signings. The evening was a huge success and we sold out of her books by the end of the two hour session. A bonus of the whole evening was that I only managed to embarrass myself once, when I first met the writer and said, "I'm a huge fan. I love your work."

Luckily the Writer took it as a compliment and smiled at me. I just went red and willed the ground to swallow me up. She must have felt like blinking Madonna!

I actually woke up every morning and apart from wishing I could stay in bed for another half an hour at least, I was out of bed and smiling as I made my way into work. The store was a twenty minute walk from my house and it would be a lot easier for me to get into my car and be parked up and in work for five minutes, but this saved me a fortune on parking in the town centre every day and I also felt better for doing some exercise.

I was starting to feel lethargic from no exercise and I never had any energy in the evenings. My parents were lucky if I washed up of an evening, that is how lazy I had become.

My parents and I were getting on extremely well at the moment. Ever since I told them I would be moving out once Emma found a place to buy. Lin was ecstatic, as she could finally have a bedroom of her own and how she wanted it... messy!

My parents and I did not argue very much, but living in such close proximity every day can make most people lose their patience and my Dad has none to lose. I certainly wouldn't miss his muttering to himself because I was taking too long in the shower. It could only be a good thing moving out and claiming some independence. I was trying not to get my hopes up, Emma might not find anywhere for ages and even then she may change her mind about renting a room to me. I always look on the pessimistic side, that way it leaves no room for disappointment. I should have known better because, thank goodness, Emma is decisive. It took her two months and eleven viewings to find her new home.

I had no idea which one Emma had her heart set on until she made an offer. I went out to view most of the places with Emma, with Richie and Marie accompanying us as well. Richie and I asked the impractical questions.

"Is there room for a snooker table?"

"Would you have to buy a lawnmower?"

"What day are you going to have your house-warming?"

Whereas, Emma asked the practical ones.

"Can that tree in the front-garden be taken down as it overshadows the lounge?"

"How many allocated parking spaces do I have?"

"What appliances are being left behind?"

Emma was on a mission to find the perfect property and I was along for the ride. I felt like I was on that programme with Kirsty and Phil, but to be honest in real life it is not as much fun as it looks on tele.

Emma made an offer on a two bedroom flat about five miles away from where she lives at the moment. They were new flats and had only one previous owner before Emma. That person, a man in his mid thirties was moving out to move in with his girlfriend which was ideal for Em as there was no chain. The flat inside was cream throughout with cream carpets and it was spotless, it looked like a show home. The furniture was old and tatty but that was going with the owner, although he did try to palm this off onto Emma, who was having none of it. She had her own ideas for the place. There were two good sized bedrooms and a bathroom in between. The lounge and kitchen were all open planned and the view from the window was of the nearby park. Emma's current view from her bedroom window is of the busy road, so this was a bonus for her.

Her first offer was accepted and after that it was all systems go. I had never realised buying a place could be so easy. I thought it was one of the most stressful things you would do in life!

I was so excited for both Em and myself. I was moving out of home for the first time and it was scary. I knew the minute I left I would never be moving back, even if Emma and I didn't get on.

"I can't believe you are moving into your own home. You are such a grown up!" Richie gave Emma a friendly dig in her arm.

"Well it is the bank's at the moment but hey give me twenty five years," Emma laughed.

It had been a while since we had all seen Emma laugh and it was noted. We were all sat in the local pub enjoying a celebratory drink.

"Do you have much more to get?" Marie asked, sipping her white wine.

"Nope I've pretty much sorted it all out," Emma said. "Sofas are being delivered in twelve weeks, my new bed in about six weeks, I've got all the kitchen stuff… ermm I think that's it."

It was true, since Emma had her offer accepted she had been out late every evening and most of the weekends looking for the best buy for her new home.

"What if it all falls through? What is going to happen to the stuff?"

"Richie!" I gave him a stare for trying to burst Emma's bubble.

"What? I'm only being practical," Richie excused himself.

"If that happens," Emma said. "Then I will put the things in storage and find another property."

Baz, Jono and Joe joined us later on that evening. My heart still skipped a beat every time I saw Joe. I know that sounds corny but it must have happened to you right? You actually feel like your heart did a jump. Anyway enough about that. All I am saying is it was good to see him.

"Hello mate," Joe sat on a stool next to me.

"Hello. How are you doing?" I asked.

"Not bad. Glad it's the weekend. Had a pretty rough few weeks really."

"Sorry to hear that, anything I can do?" I asked.

"Do you have a time machine?" Joe asked.

"As a matter of fact I do," I laughed.

Everyone else around the table was absorbed in their own conversations.

"Excellent, lets go then," Joe picked his pint glass up and started to swirl the liquid around the half-empty glass.

"You okay?"

"Well let's put it this way, if you had a time machine we could go back to a month ago and then I could try and stop my girlfriend from sleeping with another bloke," Joe attempted to smile at me. He looked straight at me waiting for my reaction.

I had lost the power of speech. A million thoughts raced through my mind all at the same time. His girlfriend was a bitch, how did Joe find out? He must really be hurting, is he going to forgive her? Who was the other man?

"Lost for words?" Joe's voice brought me back to reality.

"Yeah somewhat. I am so sorry," I reached out and touched Joe's arm which seemed the most natural thing in the world to do even though I have never been one of those touchy feely people. Marie on the other hand would always greet people with a hug or a kiss.

"Don't be silly. These things happen for a reason right?"

I nodded.

I wanted to shake Joe and tell him his girlfriend was not good enough for him and to take me instead. Thankfully, I was still quite sober and I would hope one of my friends would have saved me from embarrassing myself to that extent.

One of the main (and somewhat selfish) thoughts still going through my head over and over again was that Joe, the lovely, kind, gorgeous Joe was finally single.

Chapter Twenty One

"How can you have so much stuff?" Joe was taking one of my suitcases to his van, which was parked outside my parent's home.

"A girl needs stuff," I shouted back.

"That is very true Bella, but why do you still have your school tie?" Richie pulled my old school tie from one of the holdalls.

"Sentimental reasons!" I reasoned.

"You hated school." Richie was right.

"I was wearing this tie when I met you," I grinned.

"Right answer Bellerina," Richie picked the holdall back up and took it down to the van, whistling as he went. As long as Richie felt important and loved then the world was okay by him.

Joe and I had spent most of the evening at the pub talking and having a laugh. Joe hadn't mentioned anymore about his girlfriend and I hadn't wanted to pry. Actually I had wanted to pry but I felt it was too rude to.

I had told Joe that I was moving out into Emma's new place and he had offered his services. It was really going to save multiple trips as I could fit everything into Joe's van (which he had borrowed from his mate at work). I hadn't realised I had so much stuff until I came to pack it all up. I thought my packing would be easy, just a few clothes, toiletries and shoes. Who was I trying to kid?

I had four suitcases full of clothes, two holdalls full of shoes (I felt like Sarah Jessica Parker, well a part from the fact they were not Manolos), a holdall full of old books, another suitcase full of toiletries, a storage box full of photos and last of all my bed and wardrobe which my parents said I could take.

It hadn't taken me long to pack. I had to root around in Lin's wardrobe before leaving the house to claim my clothes back. Lin had already started to rearrange the bedroom the minute the last case was taken from the room and I noticed she had a pair of my jeans stuffed under her pillow but she could keep them, call it a going away present. Marie, Baz and Jono were all helping Emma move. It was a big day for us.

"Right that's it," Joe closed up the van. "Are you following in your car then?"

"Yep I'll be right behind you," I said.

"You lucky thing," Richie whispered in my ear before getting into the passenger side of Joe's van.

"Aren't you coming with me Rich?" I asked.

"No my lovely," Richie said as he closed the door and poked his head out of the van's window. "I think you need to say goodbye."

I looked round to see my parents watching me from the front room window and I got a lump in my throat.

"Okay I'll see you there," I waved Joe and Richie off before walking back indoors. My parents smiled at me as I walked in the front door. My Dad had his arm around my Mum's shoulders and they both smiled at me.

"So that is all your stuff gone then?" Mum asked.

"Yep all done."

"We have a present for you, just in case there's anything you need," my Mum gave me a white envelope. "Don't open it now, wait until you are settled later on. It's just a little something."

"Thank you Mum."

I knew my Mum and Dad's little something would be a substantial sum of cash to help me on my way.

I gave my Mum and Dad a hug then and walked out of the front door. I felt like I was emigrating to New Zealand, not moving a few miles down the road. I would miss not seeing my parents every day, I would miss arguing with Lin about the state of the bedroom, I would miss waking up and chatting to my

Mum at the breakfast table. I looked back at the house before I got into my car. The house that held a mountain of childhood memories, where I grew up, the place where no matter where I was, would always be my home. I don't know how I would feel if my parents ever thought about moving.

This was the house that I lost my virginity in. I was sixteen years old, had been with my boyfriend for seven and three quarter months and we both decided it was time. I had read too many slushy novels, because my first time held no romance and I certainly did not gasp in pleasure (quite the opposite). It was over in thirty seconds and we had our school uniforms back on within ten minutes. His name was Danny and I cried for about a month when he told me that now school was ending so were we. I thought my heart would never get over him.

It's funny how your mind wanders back when you least expect it. I hadn't thought about Danny for years. Leaving this house was the end of an era. I wouldn't be living here anymore.

As I drove to Emma's new place and my new home, the lump in my throat disappeared and an excited feeling bubbled away in the pit of stomach. I felt like I was going on a really long holiday and this would be an adventure.

I arrived at Emma's to see Joe and Richie struggling with my holdalls into the building, but other than that, the van looked empty.

I was in.

Chapter Twenty Two

Emma decided to have a party three months after we moved in. I expressed a concern about the neighbours, but I'm a person who always wants everyone to be happy. Our walls are quite thin. We compromised in the end and said we would have a few of our friends over to celebrate us moving in to our bachelorette pad. In other words, a party.

"Do you think I shouldn't have done food?" I asked Richie who was helping me put pineapple and cheese on sticks and not because I told him that he had to. I'd made a few snacks to put on the long table that Joe had set up along the wall. I look around at all the food Richie and I had prepared.

"I think everyone would like something to nibble on sweetie," Richie winked and picked up one of the sausages on a stick. "I personally can't resist a small sausage."

"Richie!" I exclaimed, although I couldn't help but giggle. Richie and I have the same sense of humour. We both got stopped in town the other day by someone petitioning to stop a new block of flats being built near a children's playground. He had kept referring to it as a "monstrous erection." The man had realised he was fighting a losing battle when Richie and I kept dissolving into tears of laughter. Have you got a picture of Richie in your head yet? Well if not he is tall, very tall with spiky blonde (bleached) hair and he always wears his very small round spectacles, although I have an inkling he does not even need them but thinks he looks intelligent. Did I mention that I met Richie at school? We pretty much hung around together since day one. Richie was my only ally at school and no matter what would always stick up for what he believed in, like when he saw one of the older girls making fun of me, came to my rescue and got a punch on the nose for his efforts. Richie and I both had our first snog with each other. We knew everyone else in the year were already snogging and felt left out so we decided to try it. We couldn't stop laughing afterwards and there is only one word to describe it "wet." I think both our parents thought we were childhood sweethearts, until Richie announced he was gay at sixteen.

"I can't wait to meet Craig," I told Richie.

"You will love him Bella," Richie practically swooned. "He is so gorgeous!"

Craig was Richie's new boyfriend, well actually his first boyfriend for about three years so I could not wait to see the man who had stolen my Richie's heart. He was quite tough on the outside, but I know from experience on the inside he's just a gooey mess. It took him a few weeks to get over Pablo even though Richie knew deep down that he wasn't the one. His face positively lights up when he talks about Craig, so I am hoping that I will like him and I won't have to bash him if he hurts my best friend.

An hour later I was wallowing in the bath surrounded by Radox bubbles. I had a candle burning away on the toilet seat and a CD playing in the bedroom, which I could just hear. This certainly was the life. Emma was supposed to help me set everything up for the party this evening, but she seemed to have disappeared. It was Emma's idea to have the party and it was up to me to buy all the alcohol and food. I was starting to feel like I'd been had.

I had bought enough alcohol to last a few months, beer, vodka, red wine, white wine, whisky and soft drinks. I was starting to feel slightly drunk just looking at it all, although that may be down to the couple of glasses of wine that I had whilst relaxing in the bath.

I was just thinking about getting out of the bath when I heard Emma's key in the front door.

"Hi honey I'm home!" she called.

"In the bath," I call back and I hear Emma walk into the

lounge.

"Fab job mate!" Emma shouts back. "Get out of the bath. I want you to see my outfit."

It turns out Emma had been at the shops for the last few hours buying a new outfit for her party and having her hair done. I had to admit her outfit was lovely. The floor length black dress looks lovely on her.

"Right, what do you need me to do?" Emma rubs her hand and I shake my head.

"Richie and I finished it about an hour ago," I said. "Thanks for your help."

"Sorry!" Emma said and she did look sorry. "Time got away with me. Where is Richie?"

"He went home half hour ago to get ready. It's okay, you can clear up tomorrow," I laugh as Emma's face falls and I walk into my bedroom closing the door behind me.

People will start arriving in the next hour or so, so it is time to get ready. I decide to wear my slim fitting black trousers (Richie calls them my disco trousers, maybe because I always wear them for any drinking/dancing event) and a lilac strappy top. I put my hair up on the top of my head so that just a few tendrils have fallen down over my face. I have to use nearly all my foundation to cover the huge spot that is threatening to rear its ugly white head on my chin. Typical.

I hear the doorbell ring just as I am deciding whether or not to change. There is no time now. Let the party begin.

Chapter Twenty Three

By the time I get into the front-room Richie is already drinking some of the beer and eating the nibbles.

Within forty-five minutes, everyone we were expecting had arrived. The drink was flowing and the nibbles had practically gone. The music was blaring out and everyone seems to be having a great time. The bonus being most people had brought little house warming gifts for us. Emma said this was my home as much as hers so we could share the gifts. We got three bouquets of flowers (which were now looking very elegant in pint glasses), a few bottles of wine, some sort of basil plant (from Richie, of course who said it was to put flavour in our lives) and a large scented candle, which was now happily burning away on the dining table. Craig, Richie's boyfriend was gorgeous. My first thought if I am to be brutally honest was what a waste! But as I watched them throughout the evening I could see how well suited they both were. Craig was definitely the wife in the relationship. Richie was practically running back and forth to the kitchen throughout the evening getting drinks for him, even when it looked like he didn't even need a refill. Richie looked like he may burst with happiness. I was bursting with happiness for him.

Jono was trying to chat Lin up who was showing no interest at all. In fact, Lin had brought her new boyfriend Charlie (an apt name for a man that seemed to sniff a hell of a lot considering he didn't have a cold) along to the party and you could tell he was starting to get annoyed with Jono hanging around. Poor Jono, never seems to have much luck. He just needs the love of a good woman (I am not about to offer my services I hope you understand).

I'd told Joe to invite his sisters to the party. Jez (Jody's Jez) had actually gone out with one of Joe's sisters when he was younger although he can't remember which one because they look so alike now. Small world. I liked Joe's sisters straight away. They were identical, deep blue eyes and medium length blonde hair. Emma took to them straight away, but I am not sure if that was because they gave her a bottle of champagne as soon as they met. I watched Joe from afar interacting with his siblings. He really cared about them, made sure they were both okay and had drinks in their hands. On a couple of occasions Joe caught me looking at him and I didn't look away, just smiled (the confidence inducing alcohol was working).

Overall, the party went really well but I think it would be the last time that Emma would have a party at home. She just could not relax knowing people were eating and drinking on her own cream carpet. Luckily the sofa was chocolate brown leather, so the white wine that Marie spilt could be easily wiped up and without Emma noticing. I kept turning the music down a couple of notches when I thought people were not looking. I just felt it was not a good idea to get on the neighbour's bad side just yet. We're on the top floor so luckily there's no-one above, but there is a young couple below. I hope they both didn't fancy an early night. Emma had toyed with the idea of inviting them but decided against it, stating she couldn't invite strangers into her home. What if they stole something? It takes a lot for Emma to trust someone.

I read this book once that said that everyone has a slight compulsive disorder. One of mine is that I worry about silly little things (like loud stereos) and switches. When I have finished using something I always switch it off at the plug. Why do you think this is? (that may be down to my Mum's neurotic syndrome). For example, Marie always has to listen to the flight's safety information when going on holiday because she feels that she would be jinxed if she didn't. Would you say that is the classic signs of someone with a compulsive disorder? Maybe I just read too much. The last of the guests started to leave after the massive fry up that Joe and Baz cooked the next morning. People just seemed to have slept where they fell.

Thankfully I woke up lying on top of my own bed fully-clothed, with Richie and Craig huddled next to me. I hadn't thought I was that drunk the night before but when I woke with my head pounding away I knew I should not have drunk so much wine.

I groaned when I first saw the front room and kitchen. It was a bomb site. There were empty cans strewn all over the floor, a smell of stale smoke in the air and peanuts trod into the carpet. The clean-up operation didn't take long between the six of us and it wasn't long before we were all thanking Joe and Baz for saving our lives with the joy that is a good old fashioned fry-up.

Joe and Baz left the washing up for Emma and me saying it was only fair, as they had cooked the fry-up. I wasn't in the mood to do any more cleaning but didn't have the energy to argue about it. I just wanted to go back to bed, which is exactly what I did two hours later after eating a fry-up, washing up, drinking two pints of water, running the hoover over the carpet, taking out the rubbish and spraying air freshener in every room (another one of my disorders I think). Emma had got back in bed straight after breakfast. There was no way I could leave the mess for a minute longer, even though Emma kept shouting at me to leave it until the next morning. She knows me well enough to know that when she woke later on her flat would be immaculate again. Whatever happened to her making the effort today?

I saw everyone home and walked down the stairs with Marie, Baz and Joe.

"Thanks for the invite Bell," Joe said, as we walked down the stairs.

"Did you have a good time?" I asked.

"Yes, as per usual," Joe smiled at me. "My sisters enjoyed themselves as well."

97

"I'm glad."

"Are you coming our way Joe?" Baz asked.

"Nah popping to my Mums for a bit," Joe explained so we waved off Baz and Marie, who could only muster a small wave of her hand as she was feeling extremely hungover.

"Well have a nice rest of day," I said to Joe.

"Yep you too," Joe suddenly turned and was facing me. He looked like he was about to say something but then thought better of it.

Say it! My mind was screaming. But he just looked at me intently and I thought for one millisecond that he was going to kiss me.

"I have an idea," Joe said, grinning at me so I could see why I loved his smile so much.

"You do?" My heart stopped beating as I waited for the immortal words to come out of Joe's mouth, letting me know that he had always cared for me and we would be perfect together.

"I think my friend Gav would adore you. Do you want me to set you up?"

Chapter Twenty Four

"What about us?" I had wanted to say. I actually said "huh" and my mouth fell open.

Instead, I found myself agreeing that I was willing to try anything once, which is not altogether strictly true (you wouldn't catch me bungee jumping).

Joe thought it was a great idea. He told me that he hadn't really kept in contact with Gav just recently but they spoke to each other on the phone every now and then. He was a fitness instructor, owned his own home and was twenty-seven years old.

I agreed with Joe that, yes it was a great idea. After he had left looking extremely pleased with himself for thinking up this terrific idea before, I curled back up in bed in my warm winter comfortable pyjamas (every girl must have a pair) and that is pretty much where I stayed for the whole of Sunday afternoon, only waking every now and again when I heard Emma get up to make coffee every hour.

I couldn't understand how I could have got it so wrong with Joe. We both got on so well. I was not the same timid girl in front of him, I would even class Joe as one of my friends. In my opinion, friendship being one of the most important attributes to a relationship. Emma, Richie, Marie and I had listed the top three attributes potential suitors had to have.

"Sex, fit bod and has to like Chinese food," Richie said.

"Trust, loyalty and commitment," Marie said.

"Money, looks and independence," Emma said.

"Friendship, attraction and trust," I had said.

It seemed only Marie and I had taken the three attributes seriously. Although I'm not sure how Richie would get on with a partner who didn't like Chinese food. He didn't even have to introduce himself when on the telephone to the Jade Garden on the High Street. They were immediately aware who it was.

"Ah, hello Mr Cunningham. Usual is it?"

I think it's time for me to move on and realise Joe is not the one for me after all. Why else would he be setting me up with one of his friends? Joe had probably noticed me looking at him like a love sick puppy and had decided to take matters into his own hands without hurting my feelings.

"He does flirt with you Bella and he obviously likes you," Richie was telling me later on that day on the telephone. He was not helping.

"Yeah, but not enough though," I sighed. "Let's talk about something else?"

"Okay, more importantly, what did you think of Craig?"

"He's perfect Rich," I could almost hear Richie grinning down the other end of the telephone at my words.

"He is, isn't he?" Richie gushed. My predicament with Joe was lost as Richie told me all about how Craig and he met (on an internet chat room), their first date being dinner at Craig's (no point beating around the bush) and how they celebrated their first week together (you don't want to know).

Emma agreed with me later as we munched our way through a large deep-pan Hawaiian pizza.

"If he hasn't noticed you and is setting you up with his friends then he's not interested Bella," Emma told it to me straight. I hated it that she was so honest sometimes.

"I know, but we get on so well Em," I took another bite of the pizza.

"Bella if he doesn't realise what an angel you are then he's not worth it," Emma smiled at me. Now was not the time to let her know about the tomato stain she had on her pyjama top.

As I lay wide awake later that night (I don't know why I thought sleeping in the day was a good idea), I knew Emma was right. After all, this date could be a good thing, the start of something special and I owed it to myself to give Jim, Gerry or was it Gav my full attention on our date. I finally fell asleep at two o'clock in the morning picturing myself on my first date with Gav, Gerry or Jim and only seeing Joe's face.

Chapter Twenty Five

I was a nervous wreck. It had been a really long time since a first date.

"I have not got a thing to wear!" I shrieked. I was on the verge of becoming hysterical. "Dammit, I need the loo again."

This was the third time in thirty minutes I had been to the toilet. Richie called them "jitter wees", I just called them a "blinking nuisance."

"I don't want to point out the obvious Bellerina," Richie opened my wardrobe doors. "But you have shed loads of clothes."

I walked out of the bathroom and stood in my doorway wondering if Richie had indeed gone mad.

"Like what?!"

"Ok, you have to stop shouting and calm down," Richie soothed and put his arm around me.

"I'm not hysterical!"

Richie ignored me and proceeded to get his idea of suitable garments from my cupboards and spread them out on the bed. I could appreciate that Richie was just trying to help, but all his ideas were vetoed.

"I haven't worn that frock since I was seventeen."

"Too old."

"Unfashionable."

"No shoes to match."

"Colour doesn't suit me anymore."

"How can the colour not suit you anymore?" Richie asked. "You are still the same person who wore these years ago."

"My idea of what colours suit me has changed," I explained. Was Richie being purposely stupid?

"I will never understand women, but that is why god made me a homosexual," Richie laughed. "Actually, didn't you wear this top to our last school disco?"

It was true. I was a hoarder. I kept clothes for the same reasons I kept photos and cards from people, I was a sentimental old soul. I had to get Richie away from my wardrobe before he spotted my school uniform.

The decision was made twenty minutes later. I was going for the smart casual look, which translates to "I don't want to appear like I am trying too hard, but want to look nice." I wore a pair of jeans with a bandeau top (although I did change my top three times before finally deciding on this one and only because Richie threatened to never speak to me again unless I chose a top in the next thirty seconds).

"Okay I've changed my mind. This is a bad idea," I said. "I don't even know what this man looks like."

"If you don't want to give it a go then don't go Bell," Richie said.

"Really?" Oh no Richie was giving me a get-out clause.

"It's not fair on him otherwise," Richie started to admire his nails and then start to chew them. A very disgusting habit (even though I do it too), because he grinds the nails in his mouth when has finished (I don't do that part).

"No I have to give it a go," I decided. "I mean, if I stand him up, what would Joe think?"

I arrive at the cinema on time, much to the disgust of Emma and Richie, who are both in agreement that I should be at least ten minutes late and Gav (I did confirm his name) would expect that. It was a woman's prerogative after all. I didn't know what film Gav had booked to see so I wanted to make sure I was there on time, I always like to watch the trailers.

I saw Gav before he saw me. He was quite short for a man, about the same height as me with brown hair but quite stocky with it. He had really broad shoulders. He was wearing a pair of jeans and a plain blue shirt which suited him. He had gone for the whole smart but casual look as well.

103

Gav was standing by the box office booth with two tickets in his hands looking around constantly, so I knew it was him. He was the only male looking slightly lost.

"Hi, Gav isn't it?" I walked in front of him and smiled.

"Yes it is," Gav smiled. He had a wonky front tooth.

"I'm Bella," I introduced myself. There was an awkward pause and I wasn't sure whether I should peck him on the cheek, but the moment passed and I decided against it.

"You look really nice," Gav complimented and I blushed.

"Thanks, so what film are we going to see?"

"Ah, that is a surprise," Gav said. "But I bought the tickets because I arrived early so you owe me six pounds and seventy five pence."

The date was a disaster. I knew it was going to be as soon as he asked me for the cash for the cinema ticket. What sort of man does that on the first date? I would have understood going halves if we had gone for a drink for the evening but a measly six pounds and seventy five pence?!

I was prepared to overlook this. Maybe Gav was just very careful with his money and that was a good attribute, right? I continued to tell myself to keep an open mind even when Gav waited for me to get change to give him his cinema money back and when he bought himself a large popcorn and large fizzy orange and asked me what I was going to get myself.

The film was French with English subtitles and I lost the plot halfway through. Gav kept looking at me and all I kept hoping in my head was that he would not even think about moving in for the kill. Thankfully, he didn't but he did put his arm around my shoulders a quarter of the way through, which just made me feel uncomfortable. I just felt like I couldn't move or slouch down in my chair because his arm was resting along the top of my back.

After two and a half hours I was looking forward to going home, but Gav suggested we get a drink somewhere. This was the best thing he had said all evening. It was probably a silly idea for two people who didn't know each other to go to the cinema on their first date anyway. How would they get to know each other?

Gav took me to Burger King. Yes you can laugh, he actually walked past a couple of the pubs on the way and I mustered all my willpower not to duck into one and down a glass of wine.

Unfortunately, because I had presumed we were just going to the cinema that evening, I had not brought any extra money out with me and I didn't have my cash card. I explained to Gav that I had forgotten to bring my bank card and he actually sympathised with me, before ordering himself a large coffee, a whopper with cheese and large fries.

I sat and watched Gav eat his food and drink his coffee, wondering if there was a window in the bathroom that I could jump out of.

"It's official, I am now full," Gav said as he wiped a napkin around his face. I was not sure now if he was actually taking the mick or rubbing it in, but it was certainly time to go.

Gav walked me to the taxi rank, with his arm still hanging loosely over my shoulders.

"Do you want me to come back?" Gav asked.

I nearly started to laugh. "No, thank you."

It was as polite as I could muster and I could tell that Gav was waiting until I was directly facing him again so he could kiss me. There was no way his burger breath was coming anywhere near me.

I clambered into the passenger seat of the taxi, muttered goodbye and closed the door. I then wound the window down, but only because Gav started tapping on it.

"When can I see you again?"

"Ermmm, call me," I said and the taxi drove off.

I would have to tell Emma to let unfamiliar male callers know I had left the country and would never come back. What was Joe thinking? How could he possibly think that Gav and I would ever get on? We sat most of the time in Burger King in complete silence and when he did speak he told me about his fitness regime and how his body is purely muscle. I could only hope that Joe had fixed me up with the wrong Gav or the Gav that he knew had a personality transplant since the last time he saw him.

Two things were for sure, there was no way I was seeing Mr. Gav or Mr. TF (tightfisted as I now liked to call him) again and there was no way that Joe would ever set me up again.

Chapter Twenty Six

There was one good thing that came out the date with Mr. TF and that was Joe and I spent over an hour and a half chatting and laughing about it over the telephone. It was not so funny at the time, but hey in hindsight it was actually quite hilarious.

Joe apologised over and over again once he heard about the disaster the next morning when he called. He couldn't understand how he could have got it so wrong. Apparently, Gav was a babe magnet in his day, so it must have been a different Gav that I went out with last night. I also found out that he was also very thick skinned because he called Joe to let him know that he thought I was great and had tried to call me twice before my phone-call from Joe. The last time Emma acted ignorant and said that she didn't know anyone called Bella and to stop stalking her. I would've loved to have seen his face when she said that.

I felt a bit guilty for not speaking to Gav myself, but I would not have known what to say to him and would probably have agreed to go on a second date with him, something that I really didn't want to do. It would be much easier if I could write him a letter, I'm good with words in letter format.

"My god, you are still so smitten," Emma commented once I got off the phone to Joe.

"I am not!" I said indignantly.

Emma was right though. I had a smile that was making my cheeks ache.

"So when are you and your new best mate Joe meeting up again?" Emma asked.

"Tomorrow for lunch. He wants to make it up to me for the date," I said. "It would be rude to turn him down."

It hadn't occurred to me once that Joe and I were actually going on a date. We had become friends and I was starting to realise that was exactly how Joe saw me. He would pop into the Book Store just to say hello, give me a bell just to see how I was and set me up with so called friends of his.

I reiterated all this to Jody the next morning at work.

"So if you know Joe only sees you as a mate, why are you getting dressed up?" Jody asked.

I leant on the coffee counter and sighed.

"I just like to look nice."

"Bella, your skirt and top are gorgeous, but you normally wear trousers to work and your top is showing cleavage," Jody flicked her eyes to my chest.

"Oooh thank you," I said. "I didn't even realise I was in possession of a cleavage." I have Mr. Wonderbra to thank for that. Anyway take my mind off it."

Jody had big news. She had announced a few weeks back that her and Jez were expecting their first child and she was thrilled. It must be a really exciting prospect. They had so many plans already for their baby girl Katie. They had found out that it was a girl at the scan. I'm not sure if I was in that situation I would be the same. Jody is quite a practical person whereas I like the element of surprise. Jody was ecstatic though and was already starting to show at only sixteen weeks. I didn't want to be the one to tell her she would be the size of the house by full term.

Jody managed to make me forget about Joe for ten whole minutes before I said that work had to be done and went to one of the aisles with the books trolley to do some shelf stacking.

Jody was right. I had made an effort knowing I was meeting Joe for lunch. In fact, the skirt I was wearing was new, a plain black pencil skirt which came just pass my knees and really high black stiletto type heels that I had borrowed from Lin which I couldn't actually walk in. They were so impractical for work. I had to take them off when climbing onto the step ladders and the relief I felt when I sat down for a cup of tea earlier was just immense. At this rate by the time Joe came to see me at lunch I would be hobbling around and that couldn't be classed as attractive. I didn't have to worry about my outfit or my hobbling around after all, as Joe texted me twenty minutes before we due to meet.

"Bell, can't make lunch. Work hectic. Sorry. J."

The disappointment flooded through me and I felt sad that I wouldn't be seeing Joe that day. It was a complete waste of time and pain wearing this outfit and shoes today. I don't know what I'm thinking of. Most of all I was disappointed with myself. I was letting my emotions be ruled by a man. Joe was my friend and that is the way it was going to stay. End of story. I can be quite determined sometimes. Joe was completely forgotten for the rest of the day, as Marie ran into the shop in the afternoon with a huge smile on her face.

"I couldn't wait until later." She grabbed both my hands.

"What's happened?" I held Marie's hands back in an attempt to steady her more than anything else.

"Oh my god, I may burst from happiness mate," Marie started to spin us both.

"What?!" If Marie didn't tell me soon I was going to get dizzy.

"I'm getting married Bell!" Marie shrieked. "I am only blinking getting married!"

"What?!" My voice had just risen a few decibels to match Marie's.

"Baz and I are getting married!"

And with that Marie and I started to scream and hug each other with tears flowing down our cheeks, ignoring the looks we were getting from customers in the store.

Chapter Twenty Seven

I was as good as my word with Joe. It was a self preservation exercise and could only help my little heart get over him once and for all, maybe after this period was over Joe and I could become friends again. The period was called avoidance and that is exactly what I did. When Joe called the flat, I asked Emma to tell him I was out, when he popped in the Book Store I sped to the staff room and stayed there until he had gone and on the one occasion he did see me I got out the step ladder and proceeded to climb to the top to examine books about Physics on the top shelf. Joe did text me a couple of times on my mobile to ask if I fancied meeting for a coffee or a beer but I replied back apologising that I already had plans.

I spotted Joe three times when I was in town on my lunch hour. The first time I dived head first into the nearest open door and proceeded to trip up and fall on my knees in front of three stunned Estate Agents. The second was more dignified, I put my mobile to my ear and had a conversation with myself and pretended I hadn't seen Joe even though we passed each other. It took all my strength not to turn around to see if he had spotted me. The third time I was actually in a shop trying to find a suitable birthday card for Jody when I saw Joe walk past chatting to a petite blonde girl. They were both laughing and seemed enthralled in conversation, obviously me being me had Joe embroiled in a hot new love affair by the time I left the shop. Jealousy is a terrible thing. I would go as far to say jealousy is like a disease that you have no control over, because all I could see in my head was Joe and Blondie chatting and laughing which swiftly moved onto Joe and Blondie kissing and having sex, which made my heart contract with pain and I thought my head would explode.

Six weeks later the telephone calls and the visits to the Book Store had stopped. I would've hoped that Joe would try a little harder. I mean, six weeks is hardly a long time to get over someone is it? Maybe Blondie was keeping him occupied (see there I go again). The bottom line I guess was I missed seeing Joe more than he missed seeing me. I was just doing a very good job of hiding it even from my friends.

They all asked me if I was doing all right for the first few weeks but it had now died off. I felt like Joe and I had been in this huge deep and meaningful relationship and I was trying to get over it.

I was glad my friends didn't know how I was really feeling. It would have stopped Marie gushing and smiling so much about her up and coming wedding although it would have also stopped Richie gushing so much about Craig.

"You can't believe how amazing he is," Richie told us all for the tenth time in the last hour.

"I think we are starting to believe you Rich," Emma rolled her eyes and picked up her coffee.

"Well he is amazing alone for just what he can do with his little finger."

"Stop!" We all cried and Richie chuckled to himself.

I think Richie threw in explicit details just to shock us half the time, that and the fact he loved the attention.

"I have an announcement of my own to make," Marie said. "Although mine is not as interesting as what Craigy can do with his little finger."

"Well nothing can ever be, Lovely," Richie smiled. "We are all ears."

"Baz and I have decided to have a Christmas wedding"

"But that is only a couple of months away!" I said.

"I know. Baz knows the owner of the Royal Berkshire Hotel which has the availability and the rooms for the date we want in December. We're also getting a staff discount and have got our very own wedding planner!" Marie looked round at all of us and we could tell she was waiting for our reactions.

"What's the rush?" Trust Emma to be as tactful as ever.

"Why wait?" Marie answered. I could tell straight away that Emma's comment had annoyed Marie. Marie isn't very vocal when she's annoyed or angry, but what she is feeling is written across her face. She tends to keep things inside and I've told her on more than one occasion that it's not good to do that but it's the way she is. I agreed with Marie that life was too short and it was for living, but I also had my reservations (not as vocal as Emma). Marie and Baz had been dating less than a year and would be married before they hit that milestone. They didn't even live together at the moment. How could you possibly think about marrying someone before living with them? I am sure my Mum would have had second thoughts before marrying my Dad if they had lived together first, for his annoying habit of putting empty containers back in the cupboards and fridge.

"I just don't want you to get hurt," Emma reasoned.

"Why can't you just be happy for me Em?" Marie stood up. "Is that too much to ask from my mate?"

"Don't be like that Marie," Emma said.

"Be like what?!" Marie raised her voice. "I'm fed up with you trying to make me question things that are not even there. I am really happy Em. I want to have ten bloody kids with this man and live happily ever after in the country for goodness sake."

"Steady on Marie," Richie tried to joke. "Start up with a couple of kids and go from there."

"Look, I'm going to go. See you all later," Marie picked up her Gucci handbag, which was a twenty-first present from us all and walked out of the shop.

"That went well," Richie picked up a menu from the table and proceeded to examine it. "I am famished after all that."

Funnily enough neither Emma nor I were very hungry. Emma asked both Richie and I if she did indeed find fault with our plans, even though deep down she knew the answer to this.

I felt sad that Marie felt we were not supporting her

112

enough. It was obvious just from the way her and Baz were together that they were right for each other and the fact Marie just said she wanted ten kids and wanted to live in the country, well Marie had always been a city girl.

"You know what we need to do," Emma said, an hour or so after Richie had demolished his chicken mayonnaise sandwich, jam doughnut and apple turnover.

"I think we need to do something," I agreed.

"We need to plan a hen night for her, make it special," Emma smiled. She had completely redeemed herself in mine and Richie's eyes and would redeem herself in Marie's.

It would be a hen night to remember.

Chapter Twenty Eight

It was certainly that.

The hen weekend was in Brighton, a month before the big day. Emma had really come through for Marie. We were all staying in the Grand Hotel on the seafront, all paid for by Em. There were seven of us in total. Emma, Marie, me, Baz's sister Lou, two of Marie's old school-friends Denise and Caroline, and of course Richie. "Why he is out on a hen night?" Denise asked as soon as we all arrived and met up at the Hotel. "He looks like a man to me."

"I'm all man darling, just with a softer centre so I am more of a lady than you are," Richie answered, leaving Denise opening and closing her mouth like a goldfish. After the initial introductions were over, the hen night really began. Denise kept asking Richie if he was okay and made sure his glass was only full of pink champagne. He lapped up the attention and I didn't have the heart to tell Denise that he was gay. She was going to find that out at the end of the night for herself when she tried to stick her tongue down his throat.

The first evening was quite tame starting with us all sitting in our glad rags with our devil horns (a hen night is not a hen night without them) in the hotel bar sipping pink champagne in flutes and listening to Richard Clayderman (or someone very similar) playing the piano. We all stumbled off to the nearest bar a couple of hours later and after that the nearest club, where we all had our dancing shoes on. We all stayed in the club for three hours with no-one complaining about their shoes hurting until we all walked outside into the fresh air. Why does that happen?

I had to steer Marie back to the hotel as she took her shoes off and kept missing the broken glass on the pavement by centimeters. We all walked into the hotel lobby, laughing, clutching our chips and trying to remember which room numbers we all were in.

It took both Emma and I to get Marie into bed as she continued dancing away in the room, but finally with the veil, handcuffs and plastic whip removed she fell asleep with a smile on her face.

The second evening was not quite so tame. We all started drinking at about six that evening after having a later lunch at one of the seafront restaurants a couple of hours before.

Em thought it would be a good idea to buy us all tequila's, but instead of having just one or two to help us along the way to drunkenness, we had about six each. It's amazing how you can go from being relatively sober to paralytic drunk in an hour.

That is about as much of the evening as I can tell you, because from then on I have a complete memory blank. I think I remember moving onto another bar and going back to the club from the previous night, but thankfully I don't remember Em and Denise having to carry me back to the hotel at the end of the night because I had lost complete use of my legs and I don't remember being sick (with style according to Richie) in the Hotel Foyer, much to the disgust of the reception staff.

I woke the next morning with my head hanging off the bed and a nasty taste in my mouth. I had the hangover from hell. Has anyone in the history of life ever actually died from a hangover? Because I thought I could be the first. Normally the best hangover cure is breakfast but just the thought of bacon, eggs and tomatoes was turning my stomach. I let everyone else go down to brekkie and they came back an hour or so later to let me know we were ready to leave.

The car journey home was one of the worst of my life and I spent most of it with my head hanging out the window like a dog. I felt every bump in the road and every turn Em made in the car.

Even when we dropped Marie off and she thanked the three of us for such a lovely weekend which she would always remember, I couldn't raise a smile.

"Do you want a cuppa?" Em asked as we walked into the flat.

"No thanks," I walked straight for my bedroom. "I'm going to die peacefully in my sleep"

"Ok Bella, see you in the morning"

With that I shut my bedroom door behind me, closed the curtains and crawled into bed.

Chapter Twenty Nine

I had started seeing someone. He was a regular at the Book Store which was a good start as we would have a similar interest (Richie says it makes us both nerds). He is six foot with dark blonde, spiky hair. He's a couple of years older than me, really skinny, great sense of humour and I don't fancy him. He just seemed really nice and he was so easy to talk to, so when Paul asked me out for a drink I thought it would be a good idea.

We had a really nice time on our first, second and third date and even though Paul always gave me a lingering kiss goodbye, I still didn't fancy him. I decided, that physical attraction was not everything and where had it got me in the past? Paul was such a good mate to me. I could tell him about my day and he would listen. Paul could talk to me about his day and I would listen. I deserved this kind of relationship and I deserved to feel special, which Paul did a very good job of. I got flowers every week since our first date and I am not complaining about that at all, although Emma thinks it takes the surprise out of getting flowers when you receive them so often (I think this is also because Em suffers from hay-fever, but I do kind of agree with her).

I introduced Paul to my friends after a month and they liked him, but for all the wrong reasons.

"He's like having a little brother around."

"He will always go to the bar which is a good thing in my book."

"He is easy going."

You would think that easy going would be a good thing and for most people it is but for Paul, well he was far too easy going. Maybe I am just being picky? Paul took me out to dinner after we were together for three months.

"I need to ask you something Bella," Paul said grabbing my

hand across the table.

"Okay," I answered. Oh god the man was going to propose and because I didn't want to hurt his feelings I was going to say yes. I am going to be stuck in a loveless marriage for the rest of my life.

"I think it is time we moved our relationship onto the next level," Paul continued. "This has been a great three months, hasn't it?"

All I could do was nod in agreement. My heart was pounding and the words "Don't ask me! Don't ask me! were spinning continuously around in my head.

"We get on so well, we can talk about everything and I know we're both attracted to each other."

I coughed at this point but Paul didn't seem to notice.

"Anyway," Paul was on a roll. There was no point interrupting him now. "I want us to be more intimate."

This was not the right time for me to have taken a sip of my wine as I ended up spitting it out all over Paul and coughing so much, that he had to get up and start slapping me on the back.

"Are you okay?" Paul's face was full of concern.

Again I just nodded, as I took a sip of the water that the waitress had kindly brought over when she thought I was choking to death.

"So what do you think?" Paul asked, as he sat back down.

I wanted to ask what he meant by intimate but I knew exactly what he meant. He felt it was time we should sleep together and I didn't blame him for mentioning it. Most people in a new relationship would not have waited this long.

"I thought you were happy with taking things slow," I finally said.

"I am," Paul smiled. "If you want to carry on taking things slow, then that's fine. I'm not going to pressure you."

I thanked him but I didn't mean it.

Instead I changed the subject and told Paul about a

customer in the Store earlier that day who tried to bring a book back that had been scribbled on and had so obviously been read as the spine was broken stating it wasn't what he was looking for. Thankfully Paul didn't mention the "intimate" subject again that day, but I knew the subject would come up again. I would deal with it then.

"If you don't want to sleep with the man maybe you are with the wrong man," Emma told me later on that evening.

"I think I am just being cautious that's all," I said.

"Oh right, so deep down you want to tear Paul's clothes off," Emma looked at me and I couldn't meet her eyes.

There was no point talking about the Paul situation anymore. He was a god-send. He never argued with me, always wanted to do the things I wanted to do, was romantic and got on with my friends. Some people never get that in a lifetime. I would just go with the flow from now on and give Paul my all, because he was a nice bloke and he deserved it.

I deserved a good man and I was determined to make this relationship work.

Chapter Thirty

If I'm honest with you now I didn't think wedding planners actually existed. Sure I've seen the film with J-Lo (which is completely unrealistic in the first place) but that's based in the US. America has people that design clothes for your pets for goodness sake. I thought wedding planners were a passing fad. But if you pick up a yellow pages for Central London, there they are listed, about five of them.

Marie had a Wedding Planner. I am pleased to say there was no resemblance to J-Lo at all, which had to be a relief for Marie. How upsetting would it have been for Baz to run off with the Wedding Planner? In fact, the Wedding Planner looked a lot like Dawn French. She was small and round but with a really welcoming pretty face. When I first met her I wondered how this woman was going to take charge of someone's wedding day and make sure it all happened for the Bride and Groom. I completely underestimated the woman.

Dawn's real name was Tinkerbell, yes apparently that is really her name. Her parents must have hated her on sight. Why would you name your defenceless baby daughter after the annoying fairy in Peter Pan? I think there should be a law in this country that names are put forward to a baby names board who approve the name before you can register the birth, otherwise it is just downright child mental cruelty. It would also save the world from less Apple's, Sunshine's and Ryder's (this was actually given to an old school friend's baby girl).

Tinkerbell, quite understandably shortens her name and goes by Tinks, which is nearly just as bad. Tinks is a cat's name! I've never liked cats so was really surprised when I liked Tinks on sight.

Tinks took complete control over the wedding. She organised the flowers, the hotel, the staff, the food, the dress fittings, the suit fittings. My god this woman was Lynda Carter (Wonder Woman) in disguise. I thought I was quite an organised person but with just over a month to go Tinks had organised Marie and Baz's big day. "She's great isn't she?" Marie had asked one day whilst we were out trying on wedding shoes. I hope you understand that I was just trying on the shoes to help Marie make a decision, the same goes for the dresses.

"She is bloody amazing!"

Wherever Tinks went she organised the whole place. Marie and I had visited about six or seven shops on our own trying to match some shoes to her wedding dress. Tinks saw the dress and pointed Marie in the direction of the shop that had the perfect pair to match.

Shopping for Marie's wedding dress was fab. Although Tinks did have to reprimand us for wasting time and money, which I guess was true. It was just really funny selecting the most hideous gowns and getting Marie to try them on. One of them had feathers all the way down the gown and on the head dress, there was also feathers sticking out of the back of the gown which looked like a tail. Why would anyone want to do that to themselves?

"If Baz saw me in this, I don't think there would be a wedding," Marie was bent double from laughing so much.

"Ha ha ha I think a beak would finish that outfit off," I replied.

"Girls!" Tinks clapped her hands and caught our attention. Marie and I looked over at her standing with her hands on her hips next to the shop assistant who was looking at us disdainfully.

"Sorry." We both apologised.

Unfortunately, it was one of those moments where you try your hardest not to laugh but it just bursts out of you even more. I used to get told off all the time at home for this when I was younger. Luckily, a few hours later Tinks saw the funny side but

I think that was only because we had safely ordered the dress and the alterations were currently taking place, in time for the big day.

Tinks was completely focused on Marie's wedding day. I wondered if she only ever had one job at a time, how much she must earn. When Marie told me how much she was paying her I nearly fell off my chair.

"How much?"

"Don't you think it's worth the money?" Marie asked.

"No!" I replied. "I would have organised it for you at half the price mate."

No wonder Tinks only needed one job at a time and always looked completely pristine in her designer suits. The woman must be loaded, she would only need to work six months a year to maintain a good lifestyle.

Even though Tinks did cost a small fortune I think she was probably the best choice for Marie. Marie is not the most organised person in the whole wide world, well universe and if it was left to her the wedding would never happen. With Tinks in charge it was just left to Marie to count down the day, hours, minutes and seconds to her big day. Did you know if you are unmarried they class you as a spinster? It's true. I thought spinsters were women who dressed in black, owned about five cats and lived in a dark and dingy house like Miss Havisham in Great Expectations, but there it was on Marie's wedding licence.

Anyway, I've digressed. Marie was counting down the days, hours, minutes and seconds (understandably so) until she was no longer a spinster but a wife.

Chapter Thirty One

I felt like I was going on a first date which was just ridiculous because none of the people going to be at this "wedding dinner rehearsal" was going to be my date. Marie was milking this wedding for all it was worth and as she was not getting married in a church she wanted a wedding dinner rehearsal (well, Tinks had suggested it) which, as Richie eloquently put it was just a chance for a few of us to meet up, stuff our faces and get pissed.

The reason I had "date" jitters was because it seemed everyone who was going to be at the dinner was paired off. Baz and Marie, Baz's sister and her husband, Emma and Richie (well they were arriving together anyway and only because Craig had to work) so that left Joe and I. I had received a text from Joe once the dinner had been arranged asking if I wanted to share a cab to the little French restaurant situated in the neighbouring town next to the river.

This was not the place that Marie was actually having her wedding dinner but she said that didn't matter and she couldn't just get married without having some sort of do. I realised now was not the time to point out the hen and stag do's.

I hadn't invited Paul to this do because well it wouldn't have felt right. This was a dinner for the "crowd" and Paul wasn't one of us yet. Okay, I realise that sounds childish. The real reason is, I couldn't cope with Paul touching my arm every five minutes through dinner and asking if I was okay.

I telephoned my sister Lin three times before going out asking what I should wear. I had point blankly refused to wear my bridesmaid dress to the rehearsal dinner and Marie agreed, because she didn't want Baz to see her dress until the big day.

"What about the pastel blue top with your jeans?" Lin suggested.

"Shows sweat marks and it gets really warm in restaurants."

"What about your three quarter length boots, brown suede skirt and black Morgan top?"

"Hmmm, too obvious."

"What about your blue shimmery strappy top with jeans?"

"Too much blue."

At this point Lin hung up the telephone on me and refused to answer for a whole ten minutes until I left her a voicemail message apologising and letting her know my life would be worthless without her. This did the trick and the conversation between us carried on in the same vein as above.

I eventually decided on my white halter-neck top, my top-shop jeans and my strappy sandals. I put my hair up then took it down before finally deciding to wear it up, sorry I mean down. The taxi arrived right on time and my heart was beating so fast I thought it was going to shoot straight out of my chest. Emma was meeting me there with Richie as she had been visiting her parents and was just going to Richie's straight from the airport to get showered and changed.

Joe was sitting in the front-seat of the taxi and as it was dark, I couldn't see him very well. I knew he would be able to see me though so I strutted (I think) out of the front entrance and to the waiting cab. I climbed into the back and Joe turned round and smiled at me.

"You look gorgeous Bell," Joe said.

"Thank you. I do try," I answered back.

The taxi journey took approximately ten minutes but it felt like ten seconds. I forgot that I hadn't spoken to Joe in ages and that I was actually ignoring him. The conversation flowed as it always had and I realised that I had missed Joe's company.

"It's on me," Joe said as I attempted to hand him a tenner for the taxi.

"Thank you," I said graciously. This is a very rare thing for me to do. Normally I would have forced the money into Joe's hand and be done with it but it felt nice Joe paying for our cab.

The meal was lovely and on a number of occasions I saw Marie look at all her friends round the table and her eyes would fill with tears. You would think the girl had a terminal disease and we were never going to see her again!

I didn't really get a chance to talk to Joe at the meal because so many of us were chatting together. Marie and Baz held the floor mostly with their chat about the wedding and the funny story about the caterer. This story is funny now, but wasn't when Marie first got the call from them asking if their wedding could be put back a few weeks as the cake wasn't ready. They certainly changed their tune once Tinks had paid them a visit. She wasn't a person to mess with.

Joe looked really well. He also had really nice table manners. Is this important to most women? Joe laid his napkin across his lap before the soup was brought out, offered to fill everyone's glass if they were starting to look empty and didn't talk with his mouth full.

I laughed all evening and thought it had just been the atmosphere, the food and the great company. I felt good, but it wasn't until I stepped outside the restaurant door at the end of the evening that the world began to spin.

Chapter Thirty Two

"Okay, you have to stop the cab!" I shouted.

"Are you going to be sick love?" The worried taxi driver slowed down.

"No you're taxi is spinning," I started to giggle. "Can you make it stop pleesshhhe?"

"She's fine mate," I heard Joe say and I'm sure he was sitting next to me with his arm around my shoulders.

"Where's Em?" I asked

"I'm here mate in the front feeling sick," Emma barely whispered before letting out a loud burp and then apologising.

"What?" I shouted. "Em, I can't hear you!"

The taxi journey home took about four hours, well it felt like that anyway. The blinking car just kept spinning and spinning around. It didn't even help closing my eyes, if anything this made the whole experience worse.

Joe paid the taxi driver again even though I thrust my purse into his pocket telling him to take my money. Luckily for me, Joe refused. He helped both Em and I up to our place.

"I have to sleep!" Em announced and walked straight into her bedroom kicking the door shut behind her.

"I have to go to the bathroom," I announced and desperately tried to walk in a straight line to the bathroom holding onto the walls as I went in case I fell.

I realised I was slurring. I shut and locked the bathroom door behind me and looked in the mirror. This was a complete waste of time because for one I couldn't see straight anyway and two Emma had smashed the bathroom mirror a week ago.

"Oh no," I whispered to myself as I knew what was coming next. That familiar feeling where your mouth suddenly fills with saliva and you know that any second you are going be...

"Urgggghhhhhh," is the only way I can describe the noise I

made as I vomited into the clean, white toilet. I sunk to the floor and actually hugged the bowl.

"Are you okay?" I heard a tap on the door and Joe outside.

"You should go now. I'm fine," I answered back. Please go Joe, I don't want you to see my in this state, please go, please go, please go…

"I'll get you a glass of water," I heard Joe walk back down the hall into the kitchen before I was sick again.

I have never wanted to sober up so much in my life. I was willing myself to stop being sick, for the room to stop spinning and, most of all, for someone out there to invent a device that can make you vomit in silence. There was no disguising what I was doing in the bathroom and I wanted the ground to open up and swallow me whole.

I have no idea how long I was in the bathroom but when I finally emerged (after gargling with mouthwash) Joe was sitting on the floor facing the door with a glass of water beside him.

"Hi," I smiled weakly.

"Hi yourself," Joe said back. "Let me help you"

Joe led me into my bedroom and even through my drunken haze I wanted to shout out "Joe is in my bedroom!!"

I sat down on my bed and Joe sat beside me.

"You're sitting on my bed," I told him. I slapped his leg and then giggled.

"Yes I am," Joe laughed. "Here have some of this"

Joe held the glass up to my lips and I really wish I'd managed to drink it.

Unfortunately it slipped in my hands and went down my top.

"Oops." Again I giggled (what was wrong with me? I felt like I was a ten year old child).

"Your pyjamas are on the chair. I'll go and refill your water. Back in a min," Joe nodded towards my cane chair next to my dresser and left the bedroom.

I had my winter pyjamas on my chair. The fleecy striped ones that keep me really warm and the ones that ooze no sex appeal at all. Maybe I should get out one of my nice bra sets and lay it on the bed so Joe doesn't think I'm a fifty year old woman in the bedroom, maybe I should…

That is the last thing that I remember because I woke the next morning laying on top of my bed wearing my jeans and white halter-neck top. I looked over and saw Joe laying next to me sound asleep wearing his jeans and white shirt. I attempted to lift my head from the pillow but quickly decided against it. My head was no longer spinning but it did now contain boulders and little men working away in there with hammers. A couple of seconds later it all hit me. The whole evening, the night before flashed through my head at a million miles an hour and I wanted to die.

Chapter Thirty Three

Marie looked beautiful. Her dress was white and strapless. It was a very plain straight gown but nothing else would have suited her so perfectly. The buttons at the back of the dress ran all the way up the back of the gown and there were small sequins sewn onto the front, which caught the light perfectly. I can't even compare it to one I've seen a celebrity wear because it was so unique. Marie's dark hair was twisted up onto the top of her head with just a few curls falling down and framing her face. Her eyes were filled with tears.

"Don't cry mate," I said. "You will ruin your makeup." I could hardly talk, my eyes were brimming with tears too.

Marie's make-up was also kept simple because she is the sort of girl you love to hate as she never really needs a lot of make-up, especially today, because she is absolutely glowing.

Marie has come through for me with my bridesmaid dress. It was deep scarlet red and a long straight skirt with a matching strapless bodice. It was lovely. I felt like a princess. I was the only bridesmaid, which I thought was even more touching when Marie told me. She said that she only wanted the special people in her life to be a part of her wedding day, Emma had declined being a bridesmaid (said she was only being asked so we could laugh at her wearing a girly frock). Marie was adamant then that only I would be a bridesmaid, much to Richie's disgust.

I could not believe how quickly time was going by. It had only been a few months since Marie had first announced to me that she was getting married and it only felt like yesterday.

"My hen weekend was such a good send off," Marie said.

I nodded in agreement. The photos had come back to remind and embarrass us all. There was one of me on the second night actually asleep in the karaoke bar I never knew we went to. There were plenty of photos of all the others singing on stage.

Marie had sung her heart out to "Hopelessly devoted to you" with her veil on the top of her head, her L plates swinging behind her and her inflatable ball and chain flapping around by her ankles. I am so sad I missed Richie getting up to sing Britney Spears "Baby one more time." Apparently, Richie actually thought he was Britney swinging his hips and trying to remember the dance routine from her videos.

"Isn't it funny that all our nights out normally end the same way?" Marie smiled and I knew what she meant. They would end with Marie and I with our arms wrapped around each other telling each other that we loved each other so much, whilst we had tears falling down her face. Richie was in his element for the whole night and kept calling the seven of us "his bitches", but it was okay because he meant it in a nice way.

"You look gorgeous mate." I squeezed Marie's hand.

"Thank you." Marie took one last glance in the mirror before nodding to indicate she was ready to go.

Tinks had left for the ceremony after making sure Marie was in her dress and the makeup and hair stylists were en-route. Both of us said we would miss her being around so much.

"Marie it's time." Marie's Dad walked into the room and smiled at his daughter. His eyes filled with tears and I felt a lump in the back of my throat.

"Has Mum gone?" Marie asked.

"Yep just the three of us here and Stan downstairs," her Dad said.

"Stan?" Marie asked. Stan was the one downstairs in charge of the horse and cart. It was a wonderful surprise. Marie's Dad had organised it to take her to the hotel. It was beautiful.

Marie turned back to the mirror one last time. I wondered if she was thinking that this would be the last time she looked at herself as Marie Kemp.

I had such an uncontrollable urge to hug Marie tightly and tell her how much I loved her, but she knew that already and to

130

be honest, I don't think she would appreciate her make-up being smudged on the most important dress of her life. I wondered if Marie would ever let me borrow the dress, just to watch television in or something one evening.

All three of us had tears in our eyes again. Marie walked towards her Dad and took his arm. It was really a poignant moment watching Marie and her Dad walking outside arm in arm. They both looked so similar with their dark hair and dark eyes.

It was going to be an emotional day and even the grey overcast clouds were not going to ruin the occasion.

By the time Marie and I had got to the hotel, no-one but the photographer and Marie's Mum was outside. We only had a few photographs taken outside because it was freezing and goose-bumps are not a good look. Marie looked back at me once before entering the "wedding" room and I wanted to remember that look on her face for as long as I lived. It was the happiest I had ever seen her. She looked so together and so confident as she finally walked towards her groom to the theme of the Mendelssohn Wedding March.

Chapter Thirty Four

I caught a glimpse of Baz's face as he saw Marie for the first time and his eyes lit up. Baz looked extremely handsome and I was surprised I hadn't noticed that in my friend's future husband before. Baz had washed, shaved and spiked up what hair he had at the front. Baz's best-man was Joe. He was wearing the same suit as Baz. A dark, grey suit with scarlet waistcoats, to go with the bride's red roses bouquet and my dress. Joe looked gorgeous and I wasn't sure whether it was just because I hadn't seen him in such a long time (it had been weeks) but I felt a flutter in my stomach.

The room looked beautiful. There were flowers everywhere and I could see no expense had been spared for the wedding. Marie's parents were quite well off and they had put their son through university and not really had to pay out much for Marie. I think this was their way of paying her back.

The ceremony took just over half an hour and it was incredibly romantic. I looked over at Joe as the vows were being taken and occasionally we would catch each others eyes and smile. There was no sign of Blondie, thankfully. Baz looked nervous throughout the whole thing which I found incredibly endearing. He had a handkerchief in his top pocket which he kept dabbing his brow with. It wasn't hot in the wedding room so I could only presume it was down to nerves. It wasn't helped when Baz was asked to repeat one of his vows when he couldn't say the word "impediment." In the end, the vicar just bypassed that part in the vow after seeing how uncomfortable Baz was after his third attempt.

There was a few sniffs from the congregation and I saw Marie's Mum, Tinks and Richie all dabbing their eyes.

"I now pronounce you Man and Wife, you may kiss the bride!"

Baz (real name Barry Jacob) and Marie lent forward and gave each other a soft kiss on the mouth. A snog (as Marie and I had discussed) is not suitable for church. Marie had even practiced a few kisses with Baz (much to his embarrassment) in front of me so we could decide on the best one. The soft kiss was the surefire winner. The congregation applauded and I followed the newlyweds out with my arm firmly in Joe's. It was so romantic.

I wonder if Joe realised that the best-man is always supposed to cop off with the bridesmaid, it's tradition! Ah a girl can hope can't she?

My thoughts were interrupted by Paul coming over and grabbing my arm, which made Joe pull away from me on my other side.

"You look gorgeous," Paul kissed my cheek and I smiled at him, desperately trying to shake off my irritation.

"Thanks," I disentangled myself from Paul's grasp. "Must go and have my photos taken now."

After all the photographs had been taken outside (which felt like hours), we all made our way to the reception in the same hotel. Marie and Baz felt like celebrities. They walked up the aisle and there were flashes going off in their faces, standing next to the horse and carriage and more photos, walking into the reception, constant flashes going off in their faces. But their smiles did not falter. I can honestly say that I have never seen Marie look so happy and it surprised me that even though I was so happy for her, I felt a slight pang of jealously too.

The reception went just as well as the ceremony. Joe looked nervous as he gave his speech and I now understood why he had drunk his last two glasses of wine so fast. They were to give him confidence. The speech was a winner and it made people laugh. I was actually very proud of him, as any friend would be. Marie's Dad made everyone cry with his speech and that was the outcome he seemed to have wanted, so everyone was happy. The wine was flowing, the meal was superb, the tables were cleared and the first dance took place, then more dancing which included Richie's Steps routine with Craig. Before we knew it the day was coming to an end and the DJ told us all that the next song would be the last.

Paul was nowhere to be seen as he had gone outside over an hour ago as he was feeling unwell. He put it down to the dodgy chicken for the wedding meal, I put it down to the fact he wasn't used to drinking so much wine and champagne. But I didn't want to spend my best friends wedding making sure he was okay. Richie had checked up on him twenty minutes ago and apparently he was still sitting next to the urinal in the men's toilets, so I knew he was alive.

"May I?" Joe tapped me on the shoulder and nodded to the dance-floor. "It is tradition for the best-man to cop off with the bridesmaid you know?"

I laughed because I knew he was joking when he winked at me and gave me a cheeky grin. Shame he didn't really believe in tradition.

It was an Elton John song and one of my favourites. I buried my head in his chest and wound my arms around his neck. His hands were around my back and he was singing the song quite loudly in my ear making me smile. Joe smelt gorgeous and I just enjoyed the moment of closeness with him, knowing it wouldn't last for long.

"Glad to see you went steady on the wine tonight Bell," Joe said and laughed.

"Ha ha ha," I answered. "Seriously though. Thanks for looking after me." I didn't want Joe to talk about my drunken night. I still hadn't recovered from the embarrassment. Lucky for me he'd had to shoot off as soon as he had woken up and I pretended to still be asleep so there were no awkward conversations and no apologies from me. Joe had just left a note letting me know he had to shoot off and hoped I was ok.

134

"Hey, what man wouldn't want to be the knight in shining armour and look after such a babe?" Joe pulled back and looked at me. I laughed and gave him a kiss on the cheek.

I looked up and saw Marie dancing with her new husband close by. We both winked at each other. Marie looked shattered. She was off on her honeymoon tomorrow morning.

I realised why I had felt a pang of jealously earlier. I wanted this. I wanted to have my day. I wanted the beautiful white dress and all the attention that went with it. I wanted a man to look at me as I walked up the aisle with tears in his eyes (only in his eyes mind you. I don't want him to be crying his eyes out in the church). I wanted all the presents and to organise everything beforehand with my family and friends. I wanted to be so important to someone that they wanted me as their wife. "Thank you," Joe kissed me on the cheek.

I smiled back knowing that one day I would have my turn, but it wouldn't be with Joe. Why did that feel so wrong?

Chapter Thirty Five

Christmas day arrived five days after Marie and Baz's wedding. As usual, I hoped there would be a fresh sheet of snow on the ground but as usual I was disappointed. I thought of Marie and Baz spending their first Christmas together as man and wife in Italy. I wondered what they would be having for their Christmas dinner. It wouldn't seem right having anything else but turkey on the big day. I popped round my parents in the morning to exchange presents which consisted of my parents giving me cash and Lin giving me a top (which I think was one of mine to begin with). It didn't matter how many times I tried to tell my parents that I didn't want cash and I would prefer a present (something that had been given thought) but every year I got cash. It wasn't a bad thing I suppose. I spent the cash in the January sales and could normally pick up a few bargains. Annie was coming round with Ben and her boyfriend on Boxing Day. They always spent Christmas Day together, even before Ben was on the scene. I think this suited my Dad fine. It meant he only had three or four (dependant on whether Lin had a boyfriend that year) to feed. I left Annie and Ben's presents under the colour co-ordinated Christmas tree (all reds and golds this year). I left after a glass of mulled wine just as Lin was starting to argue with our Dad. It was the same every year. If we all spent more than an hour in each other's company we would start to bicker. We can't be the only family like that.

I was spending my Christmas with Emma, Richie and Craig, much to Paul's dislike. He wanted me to spend Christmas dinner with him and his family, but I couldn't think of anything worse. I had met Paul's Mum by accident, well Paul said she just happened to be in town with him and just happened to pop into the Book Store. She was extremely well spoken and a very over-bearing woman. She reminded me a bit of Hyacinth Bucket from that TV programme. I told Paul that Emma would be extremely upset if I didn't spend her first Christmas in her own home with her and he seemed to buy it (he didn't really have much choice).

Emma was cooking, well she'd bought a "just cook" turkey from Marks & Spencer's and there was plenty of frozen veg, Aunt Bessie's Yorkshires and roast potatoes in the oven. I had made dessert. I had printed out a recipe for a strawberry cheesecake from the internet and made the whole thing from scratch. I was so pleased with myself and even though it was slightly lumpy (they only had cottage cheese in the supermarket and not cream cheese) I still think it was quite nice. Richie, Em and Craig ate it anyway.

After dinner, we all exchanged presents. I had bought Richie and Craig tickets to see the new musical in the West End. Richie loved his musicals and most of his CD collection showed it. Richie and Craig had got me a gorgeous cashmere jumper. It must have cost a fortune. Emma was always difficult to buy for as she was the girl that had everything, so I opted for my usual ensemble of candles arranged in a bowl of pot pourri. Emma bought me a lovely beaded photo frame which contained a photo of me, Marie, Em and Richie on Marie's hen night. I couldn't even remember this picture being taken and from the photo you could tell we were all drunk. All our eyes were bloodshot and it looked like I was shouting at Richie for some reason but it was a great natural shot.

Richie and Craig had sorted the alcohol so by eight o'clock the four of us were feeling very tipsy and tired.

"Hello Bella," Paul was on the phone again for the fourth time that day. I caught both Richie and Emma raising their eyebrows at each other.

"Hi."

"Thought I could pop over," Paul suggested.

"That's really nice of you, but I'm not feeling too good at the moment so will be off to bed soon," I excused.

"I could join you," Paul giggled which just irritated me.

"I will speak to you tomorrow," I replied.

"Okay let me know if you change your mind," Paul said before I hung up. Paul was hinting more and more about us sleeping together and so far, I'd managed to avoid the subject every time. It even annoyed me that he wasn't man enough to ask me what the hell was going on.

Thirty seconds later I had forgotten about Paul as I watched the Christmas Bond film on tele and that's how my Christmas day ended.

It had been a great Christmas and I hoped the year to come would be the year for me.

Chapter Thirty Six

It was official. I could quite easily kill Paul with my bare hands and do you know what for? For being him! He was doing my head in with his niceness and the man thought the sun shone out of my backside for goodness sake. How wrong could he be?

How long do you get for killing someone these days in self defence? The way I see it is my friends would start a petition to free the "Berkshire One" and my face would be emblazoned across the tabloids every single day and in the end the general public would be so hacked off with seeing my ugly mug smiling out at them every day they would sign my petition. Anyway, how bad could prison be, I have seen Bad Girls and as long as I kept out the way of the Shell Dockley's and kept my head down, it would be a breeze.

How had it come to this?!

It had started at Marie's wedding. I was standing and talking to some of Marie's family when Paul came over and just stood next to me with his hand on the base of my spine. Why? It was not comfortable for him to do this and it irritated the hell out of me. Paul might as well have urinated around me and be done with it.

Okay, maybe I am blowing that out of proportion. Another occasion was when we were all talking the other night after we'd been to the cinema.

"It seems like such a long time ago since Ibiza. We must plan another trip soon." Richie clapped his hands enthusiastically.

"Great idea," Marie agreed.

"You sure? You are a married woman now!" Richie laughed as Marie gave him a friendly punch.

"Bella and I won't be able to make it. We'll probably get a cheap and cheerful booking to one of the Greek Islands, so we need to save our energy and pennies for that," Paul said.

That comment pretty much brought the conversation to a standstill, until Richie broke the ice by announcing that he needed pizza, so we all marched into Pizza Hut, which did not please the staff as they were only half an hour away from closing.

"Ermm Paul what is this about the Greek Islands?" I broached the subject with him later when he had walked me back home.

"Don't you think it is a fantastic idea? Just the two of us," Paul grinned.

"Well it's the first I have heard of it actually," I said. "I don't actually take very kindly to being told where I can and can't go either Paul."

"Don't be daft. You can't party like a teenager for the rest of your life," Paul squeezed my hand. Was it just me that found that gesture the most patronising of all? I was in my twenties, not my fifties! I bit my lip so hard before saying good night to Paul that I actually drew blood.

Then there were the Christmas gifts. I had bought Paul a shirt and he had actually welled up when I gave it to him saying he would feel so special wearing it knowing I had thought of him wearing it. What?! Paul on the other hand had gone completely overboard and had bought me some white gold earrings and a necklace which must have cost a small fortune and were really beautiful.

"You can't go on like this Bell," Em said to me later that evening.

"I know," I agreed. "I don't know what I'm doing to be honest."

I didn't. Paul got on my nerves most of the time. He sent me texts every five minutes and if I hadn't replied within sixty seconds then he would call me to make sure I was okay and hadn't been maimed, injured or killed in a horrific accident.

140

We still had not had sex although we had gone further than kissing, but that was Paul pushing it and I just felt like I should go along with it. See, what on earth am I doing?

There was only one thing for it. Paul was a nice enough man and he deserved someone like him (female version of course). This relationship, if you could call it that was not fair on either of us. There was something wrong when I was thinking of making excuses to not see Paul every single minute of the day.

I decided that the following evening would be the day. The day when I would break Paul's heart and I would be the heartless cow. It certainly didn't leave a nice taste in my mouth. I'd never had to do this before. I'd always been the one being dumped. I wonder if any of my past boyfriends had gone through turmoil when they were about to dump me.

I had all the best intentions, as you can see from the above, so how come Paul talked me out of breaking up with him that evening and the one the following week?

"I will have to get Paul to dump me," I announced to Em and Richie, as we sat in Em's front-room watching a repeat of Only Fools and Horses.

"How likely is that to happen?" Em asked.

"What about if I'm really nasty then?" I realised I was clutching at straws.

"You don't have it in your nature Bell," Richie soothed. "Anyway I am sure Paul would find a way to forgive you even if you killed his Mother."

Richie was right.

"So that's it then. I am going to be stuck with my clingy boyfriend forever," I was resigning myself to a miserable life.

"Yep looks that way," Richie winked at me.

"What am I going to do?" I felt sick. I had felt like this for weeks every time I thought about broaching the subject with Paul.

"Bella," Emma continued. "It's time for you to get tough

and if you won't, I will!" Emma was right, I couldn't carry on like this. It was time to get tough for both Paul's and my sake.

Chapter Thirty Seven

I attempted to get tough with Paul four times in the next month and on the last occasion he started to cry and told me that he couldn't live without me. I hugged Paul as he wept on my shoulder I wondered how I had ended up in this situation. Why did these things happen to me?

"So what happened then?" Em asked me later that evening.

"Well he dried his eyes, gulped back a few more sobs and told me he loved me more than anyone in the whole wide world," I frowned.

"Don't do that love," Emma ran her thumb along my forehead. "You'll get wrinkles."

"I think I've gained a face full of wrinkles in the last month," I was wallowing in my own self pity, because after all, I'd got myself into this situation.

"What did you say to him when he said that?" Emma asked.

"I did what I always do when he says that," I sighed. "I kissed his cheek and blessed him."

"So not only is the man using emotional blackmail to keep you with him but he is also so thick skinned he cannot see that you don't feel the same way," Emma shook her head. "I hate seeing you like this mate."

I hated seeing myself like this. I'd even started being really horrible to Paul as well but he always found a way to blame himself and he never had a go at me.

How infuriating is that? I wanted him to shout and scream at me, like any normal man would. I had started to ignore Paul's calls and messages, I'd told him I was going out when I wasn't and made sure he found out. I had gone out when I told him I was having a lazy evening and not told him where I was going. I hated the person I was becoming.

"You're beating yourself up too much Bella," Marie said

after meeting her down the pub one evening, "Any of us would be acting the same."

"What do you mean?" I asked confused.

"Well, if someone lets you walk all over them then you do, it's just human nature. It's what we do. We can't help it. It's more Paul's problems for letting you treat him like this," Marie said, making perfect sense.

I know Marie was biased but I could understand what she meant. I let Pillock treat me badly for years and it was only now I could see why he would not treat me any differently.

"Anyway enough about my problems. How's married life?" I smiled as I watched Marie grin.

"It's really great," Marie said. "I didn't think it would make any difference to Baz and me, but it does. It makes us feel closer. Well we are family."

"I have to say that I've never seen you so happy," I really meant it.

"I have to say that I've never felt so happy."

The rest of the evening was spent drinking more white wine. It had been such a long time since Marie and I had spent an evening with just the two of us and it was really nice.

The taxi was dropping Marie off first so I got out of the car ready to give her a massive hug goodbye. Unfortunately for Marie, the wine had stopped her legs from moving so they stayed in the taxi and the rest of her body flung itself from the car onto the tarmac. Marie landed on the floor with an almighty crash and a loud "ouch", before we both dissolved into tears of laughter, Marie still laying on the pavement and me doubled up beside her with tears running down my cheeks.

"Do you need a hand love?" The taxi man got out of the car and offered his hand to Marie.

"Nope I'm absolutely fine," which just made us both laugh even harder.

The taxi man stood watching us before finally Marie got to

her feet.

"Had a great night mate," Marie gave me a hug.

"Me too," I hugged her back.

I watched as Marie limped into the house she now shared with her husband. The vision of Marie launching herself from the taxi stayed with me for the whole journey home, when I got into bed and into the next morning. So much so that Em came into my room and asked me if I was okay, which just made me laugh all over again.

Things didn't seem so bad today and everything was much clearer. Whoever it was that said laughter was the best cure was spot on.

I knew exactly what I needed to do.

Joe's Story

Chapter One

I had been to my mates Baz's wedding, a few weeks earlier. It still seemed unreal that one of my mates had got married.

I'd known Baz since we were both five years old. We'd hated each other at first sight and would drive our primary school teacher, Miss Snoxall mad, by throwing paints at each other. Baz had actually stopped me getting my head kicked in (well it felt as serious as that when I was seven) in the school playground and from that moment on we were mates. We'd attended the same primary and secondary school and had left school at the same time.

I hadn't really seen Baz a lot lately what with him sorting out his wedding. I always used to be able to pop over to his place after the pub or on my way home from work but now I had to call and check if it was okay.

Baz and Marie did make a perfect couple. It was really nice to see my mate so happy, but in the pit of my stomach sometimes I wanted the old days back. I wanted to go down the pub at midday and stay until eleven at night, move onto the club down the road for a late drink before falling home in the early hours of the morning. I am guessing my Mum likes the fact those days have gone. I still go to the pub most weekends, well when I am not working but it's not the same because the crowd is not the same. There is only so much I can take of Jono anyway.

You could call me a hypocrite really because when Jono's housemate Emma moved out recently, I'd taken her old room. It was about time I moved out of home and had my own independence, although this didn't stop me popping round to my Mums for a Sunday roast every week.

Jono worked long hours, so most of the time I didn't see or hear much of him. There was another girl that shared the house with us, Amy but she tended to keep herself to herself. Amy is the sort of girl that would be perfect for all those American Chick Flicks that my sisters watch, you know the ones I mean where the shy wallflower suddenly turns into a gorgeous supermodel who pulls the best looking bloke in the high school. You could definitely see the potential there but Amy kept herself covered in tent shaped dresses and ill-fitting jeans and she always wore her long brunette hair tied back in a ponytail. I felt I should look after her, like a brother would. Do you know what I mean?

I was off women for a while (I will explain about that later). I decided it would be good to be young, free and single for a while. The last couple of months had been spent with nameless women every weekend. Women that meant nothing to me but didn't seem to mind a grope round the back of the pub, club or in the park on the roundabout (which I wouldn't recommend). Women that I would probably not recognise if I ran into them again, but don't think badly of me, as I said I'm off women for a while and I will explain about that later.

Once I decided that nameless shags was not the way to go, the room at Jono's came free and it was the icing on the cake. I had visions in my head of Men Behaving Badly but the reality was nothing like that. Jono was in fact an old woman.

I had been home from work for about thirty minutes. I'd called out to Jono when I walked in but there was no answer. Bliss, I had the house to myself.

I was sitting down on the faded green sofa in the living room with my eyes closed. I was tired. I always seemed to be tired lately. I thought living with the boys would be a great laugh. We could make as much mess as we liked and do what we liked. Unfortunately, I hadn't bet on Jono being a bird. He left me notes for when I got home from work and for when I got up in the morning.

"Can you use a wooden spoon when using the frying pan as

you're scratching the surface, pal?"

"I've gone through the phone bill. The numbers highlighted are ones I do not recognise so they must be yours. Please can you give me the money in cheque format?"

"I emptied the bins again this week so can you make sure you do it for the next two weeks so we're even? Thanks mate."

The notes were endless and always about something petty. Jono would normally include the words "mate" and "pal" to show he was still a good guy and not just an anal twat.

I had realised after the first fortnight that moving in with Jono was a mistake, but there was nowhere else for me to go. I could go back to my Mum's, but my pride was stopping me from turning up on the doorstep with my tail between my legs.

My dinner tonight would be a pot noodle and some crusty bread whereas when I lived with Mum, I would always have a hot meal ready and waiting for me on the table. I guess I have been spoilt. My sisters reckon it is Mums and their sons, especially if they are the baby of the family. Unfortunately it doesn't help my case that my Mum never made my sisters dinner when they were at home and they had to do their own washing from sixteen years old whereas I have never touched a washing machine in my life. It was an adventure using Jono's machine for the first time. I actually felt quite proud of myself after my first wash that all my pants were still the same colour and a red sock (which thankfully, I don't actually own) had not turned everything pink.

I had to stay put for the time being. Jono was okay sometimes and it was always a good laugh when all the chaps came over after the pub for a drink and a smoke. I found it hard to see Baz so often now, what with him being married to Marie. It was always good to see Baz. He was one of my mates that I could talk to and I could trust. He would always tell me what I wanted to hear as well. Isn't that what real mates do?

My thoughts were interrupted.

"All right mate," Jono called into the living room as he walked through the frontdoor. "It is Pete's birthday tonight. You coming to the pub?"

"Yeah definitely," I called back. What else was there to do? Most weekday evenings I would sit in front of the television or put my headphones on listening to my music. Weekends were normally spent just wasting all my money on booze. "Pete who?" I suddenly thought.

"You know Pete Johnston. A year above us at school?" Jono explained.

"Oh right yeah," I answered. Although I still was no wiser but hey any excuse to go out.

I had a lovely hot shower before getting changed for the pub. I wore my Levi jeans and my blue shirt.

The first person I saw when I got in the pub was Baz.

"All right mate," I slapped him on the back (manly affection).

"You all right?" Baz returned the slap. "Want a beer?"

"What time did you get down here?" I asked as Baz handed me an ice-cold pint of Stella.

"About half an hour ago. I got here with Pete," Baz said.

"Happy birthday mate," I extended my hand to Pete's and shook his hand.

"Thanks. You know my brother Toby don't you?" Pete gestured to the man standing next to him, who looked very similar but had darker hair.

"Yeah of course I do," I extended my hand again and shook Toby's hand. Pete did look familiar but I had no idea who Toby was and if I had ever met him before. Toby hadn't seemed to notice though.

Four and a half hours later I was staggering home, full of Stella and a couple of whiskey shots to help me on the way. This was my life in a nutshell. I couldn't see it changing anytime soon.

Chapter Two

I should tell you a little about my childhood. Where do I start? Well, my Grandad thought I was going to be gay or extremely feminine when I was older. I can still see him now telling my Mum to stop me playing with my sister's dolls and trying to push the big yellow Tonka truck into my hands.

I didn't actually mind playing with my twin sister's dolls. In fact, they used to incorporate my He-Man and Thundercat figures into the family as Barbie and Ken's children. The big yellow Tonka truck that my Grandad gave me was used as the school bus for Barbie and Ken's kids.

My family is tiny compared to some. Baz's Dad was one of seven children and his Mum one of six so he has oodles of aunts, uncles and cousins, most of whom he doesn't even see.

My Grandad was the only male influence in my life and he died when I was eleven years old, which left my Mum and two sisters. My Mum's parents had died just after my Mum got married so I never even knew them but from the photo's I could tell that I really looked like my Mum's Dad. It's quite odd looking at a photo of someone you don't know and someone you will never ever meet, but who you have a remarkable resemblance to. My Mum says I will meet him in good time but I just think she has been seeing her trusted (I use the term loosely) clairvoyant too much.

My Mum didn't worry at all about me being too girly when I was older. I think she could tell from a young age that I knew my own mind. This might have had something to do with me disappearing for three hours when I was five, only to be found asleep under a bush at the bottom of the garden. I had a sandwich beside me (covered in ants) and a torch. Apparently someone at my Play-school had mentioned going camping and I wanted to experience it too. I'm not sure if my Mum recovered from that as she never let me out of her sight again, so my camping experiences were cut short.

My Mum would scold my sisters when she saw that I was dressed in one of their nighties with her makeup covering my face, but not before I saw her giggle at the state of me and take a photo.

We didn't really have a lot of cash growing up, but then again I don't know any family that did. One of the photos that my Mum has up on her mantelpiece is of me on my first day at school wearing a pair of trousers that were too short for me and a jumper that had a hole in the shoulder. Surprisingly none of the other children took the piss, but maybe that is because I had Tas keeping an eye on me. Whereas Maxy would always walk away from an argument or be nice to keep the peace, Tas would stick up for herself, Maxy and me even if it resulted in my Mum coming to the school because Tas had been fighting again. My Mum would always say that Tas should've been a boy.

Mum had a friend at work who would loan us her caravan for one week every Summer so every year for about eight years the three of us would catch a train to Weymouth and spend a mostly cold and rainy time on the beach. Tas and Maxy would freak me out by telling me that if it was really windy there would be a good chance that the caravan could blow out to sea. It's only now I can appreciate what my Mum meant when she said this was quality time. Ah well, I'm not a person who tends to get nostalgic so consider that a brief introduction to the Carey Family.

Chapter Three

I had decided that the money was in office work so I was going to shock everyone and get myself an office job. I would hate it being cooped up inside all day. I loved working outside in the Summer when the sun would be beating down on my back whilst I repaired and painted someone's shed. Okay it's not the most exciting job in the world but it certainly has it perks. My days normally started about six in the morning but I was finished by three or four. Baz paid sixty quid a month to go to an exclusive gym in the area to make sure he kept in shape whereas I didn't need to because I did physical labour everyday. Working in an office would be easy compared to manual work. I could never understand why people got so tired when they sat at a desk all day and the most exertion they had was walking to the coffee machine and back.

I just couldn't live without holiday or sick pay anymore. There was a slight problem with my plan though. I knew nothing about computers, which was a good excuse to see Baz because he has a brand spanking new one with so much RAM (what does that stand for anyway?) and a high speed processor (alien talk to me).

Baz and Marie lived in a two bedroom house about ten minutes from Jono's. It was one of the new estates so it was one of the new houses. It's really handy having my mates living so close. Baz had kept the same theme throughout the house with its wooden floors and neutral walls. It definitely looked more homely since Marie had moved in with its scattering of photos around the place and a couple of well-placed cushions on the cream suede sofa (how do they keep it so clean?).

"Hello darling, how are you?" I greeted Marie at the door kissing her on the cheek.

"Hello Joe," Marie kissed me back and opened the door

wider to let me in. "Baz is in the kitchen, making us some chicken pasta dish I think."

"Should I be worried?" I laughed.

"I am," Marie laughed before walking into the front-room and I walked into the kitchen to greet Baz.

"All right mate, nice apron," I raised my eyebrow at Baz who was stirring a saucepan at the gas stove wearing an apron which had a bra and a pair of knickers on the front.

"I don't want to get sauce all over my shirt," Baz explained. "Beer?"

"Love one," I opened the fridge and took out two ice-cold beers for my friend and I.

"How's things?"

"Same as normal. Jono getting on my tits every five minutes," I admitted.

"I can imagine," Baz sympathised.

"He pretends he has girls in his room and I am sure he just rocks the headboard back and forward against the wall cos I never see these birds." Baz and I started laughing, wondering why and how Jono gets away with it.

As Baz and I caught up on gossip from the pub, Marie continued to lay out the table for our dinner. This is one of the changes I was talking about. Normally, when I went round Baz's for a meal, it would consist of a ready meal from Sainsbury's on a lap-tray in front of the television (have you tried their chicken with mushroom sauce?). In the space of Marie moving in, a square glass-topped table and four black leather stools appeared in the corner of the kitchen. I had to admit it made the place look homely. But a part of me was slightly jealous that there would be no more nights with just the two of us watching some crap on tele eating takeaway curry and talking about the birds we pulled the previous night. I have some great stories to tell you about our nights out although thinking about it now they don't sound that exciting anymore. God, am I getting old? Baz was a babe magnet in his hey-day (before M.A.R.R.I.A.G.E). He was always the one ever since Secondary School, who would get the attention from girls. He was a stereo-typical male with his little black book, but don't get me wrong. He wasn't an arse with it, quite the contrary. Most of the girls he has ever slept with or been out with are all still on good terms when they run into each other.

Dinner was nice and it was good to see that Baz had not changed too much because the chicken pasta sauce was a special from the Homepride range. After dinner, Baz and I decided to tackle the computer. It became clear after only five minutes that this was going to be harder than I thought. I typed like I was a child, when Baz mentioned the mouse to me I started looking on the floor for Jerry and the amount of computer jargon was like a foreign language to me.

It was going to take more than a half hour lesson for me to grasp the concept of modern technology. Luckily for me, Baz is a good mate and also very patient so he said lessons would not be a problem. I was just worried that I would never grasp it all.

I sat downstairs with Baz and Marie enjoying a cup of coffee before my walk home. It was like Marie had always lived here with Baz. She was completely at ease and I knew from Baz that this was one of the things that she was worried about, that moving into Baz's home would never feel like hers.

I had liked Marie as soon as I met her. She was genuine and warm, had one of those faces of someone you could just start speaking to in the supermarket. Do you know what I mean?

I looked at Marie and Baz's wedding photo on the side table next to the sofa. Marie had looked stunning and radiant for the whole day and not once did her smile falter. The photograph was of the bride and groom and a group of their friends on their happy day. There was Jono, Baz's mate from school, Phil, Marie's mates Emma and Richie and next to me on the right hand side was Bella. Bella was one of Marie's best mates and

157

her only bridesmaid. Bella, who had become one of my mates. A mate I could confide in and call on at any time. A mate, who for the past few months had blatantly ignored me, except for two recent occasions and I could only wonder what I had done wrong.

Chapter Four

Have you ever wondered why someone called an orange an orange? I mean, it is not the most inventive name is it? Ah look at the piece of fruit and it's an orange colour, okay we will call it an orange. I think apples are the blandest piece of fruit available in the shops which is why they are called apples. Apples are the most boring fruit of all. It has no taste at all and it goes brown within seconds of taking the first bite. Apple is not the most inventive name. I am sure I could think of a better one if I had more time.....

"Joe are you listening?" Baz interrupted my thoughts. Oh bugger I was supposed to be listening. This was my fourth computer "lesson" and I felt I had come on in leaps and bounds. I could now type with two fingers, although I was probably still no quicker than using one. Does it depend on what keyboard you are using to where the letters are, because if that is true it will be a nightmare for me when I use someone else's Computer? I had also sent my first email on my third lesson, admittedly it had been to my Mum but she had been so impressed phoning me straight away on my mobile asking me if I'd stolen a computer.

"Of course I'm listening." I tried to act indignant.

Baz knew me better than that.

"Okay, what did I say?"

"Something about the main packages for Windows." I crossed my fingers hoping this was the correct answer. After all, I couldn't take the piss with Baz. He was giving up an hour every weekend and had done for the past month to go through this computer stuff with me.

"I have a book for you." Baz reached up on his shelf and brought down a heavyweight paper-back.

"PC's for dummies," I read. "Oh thanks mate."

"It tells you the basics and it is definitely worth a read."

"Okay," I didn't sound convincing.

"What have you to lose?"

Baz had a point. I didn't want this office idea to just be another one of my great plans that I didn't follow through with. One of my ex girlfriends had once told me that I never follow through anything. I come up with these great plans for life but I never follow through and I certainly never finish them. I was insulted by those comments. I had gone for the fireman exam but had failed the mental test so it wasn't my fault they rejected me. As far as I was concerned it was their loss. I had sent off my application to join a Mediterranean Cruise ship but I had been rejected again because I didn't sing, dance, juggle or cook and I couldn't emigrate to Australia after all because I was not a Doctor, Nurse or a well respected Trades person. The only idea I had not followed through on was my policeman idea, but I had decided against that because of the uniform. Can you imagine the amount of stick I would have got?

"What do I owe you for the book mate?" I asked Baz.

"Nothing. Bella lent it to us for you."

"Nice one," I said. "How's she doing? I haven't heard from her in ages."

"Yeah not bad at all. Loving her job and living with Em," Baz said.

"Cool"

I was pleased Bella was doing all right, but the fact that she was ignoring me for no apparent reason was niggling me a bit. Do you think I am being paranoid? Honestly, I'm not. I saw her in town not that long ago and as soon as she clocked me she flew into the nearest shop and I mean flew. When I walked past and looked in the window, she was actually on the floor! What could I have possibly done to make her want to avoid me so much?

I held the "PC's for Dummies" book under my arm on my walk home and tried to think about what Baz and I had gone through today. Once I got home I read the introduction of the book and started to worry. The introduction said "Welcome to PCs for Dummies. This is a book that answers the question, how does a Computer turn a smart person like you into a dummy?" It took me half an hour to work out what the Writer meant by that introduction. It didn't fill me with confidence and I was pretty much giving up hope of ever learning about computers. I didn't have time to get any further than the intro today as I was going out for dinner at a family do. My Mum planned these "do's" every other month to make sure we all got together. It was the only request my Mum made so there was never a no show. The "do" was at the local Steak House that evening. By the time I arrived my Mum, my sisters and one of my sister's boyfriends were already there.

I sat down at the table and my Mum smiled at me.

"How was your day sweetheart?" Mum asked me straight away.

"Good. Not bad at all," I'd decided to keep my office idea a secret until I had sussed the whole computer language and bagged a firm job offer in a top computer company (do you think I am setting my sights too high?).

A glass of red wine was already at my setting and I eagerly took a gulp. Ah, yes I needed that.

"How you two doing?" I asked my sisters.

"Why do you always do that?"

"We are two people you know!"

It must be the time of the month. Normally, neither of my sisters minds me asking how the two of them are, but it was obviously the wrong thing to say today. I give my sister's boyfriend a nod to say hello which just causes Tas to tut loudly.

My family is not an affectionate one. We never have been. I think I remember the last time I kissed my Mum and that was when I was seven years old because she had managed to get me a second hand BMX for my birthday, so it was a very special day for us, well me anyway. My sisters are the same. They never

161

kiss my Mum, each other or me. Is that weird?

I have seen Baz with his parents, for example and he always gives his Mum a peck on the cheek when he sees her. It would seem too weird if I started doing that now.

Anyway, let me introduce my family to you properly.

Tasmine is the elder twin. She has long fair hair which she always wears in some metal clip contraption so her hair is always bundled high on the top of her head. She is the bossy one, always likes to get her own way but is the most organised out of the three of us. Tas is a Nursery School Teacher. If I was four years old and faced with her, she would scare me witless. I feel real pity for her class and wonder how many of the little ones end up in tears every day.

Maxine is my other sister. Again, she has long fair hair but she tends to wear it down or in a ponytail at the nape of her neck. She is the quietest one of the three of us, always goes with the flow and likes an easy life. Maxy works in the same job she got when she was eighteen, a Call Centre. It's easy work and suits Maxy to the ground. She goes in for seven and a half hours a day, with forty-five minutes for lunch and two ten minute breaks and gets her pay-check every month.

Tas and Maxy moved out of home when they were both eighteen years old and jumped on the property ladder at just the right time buying their first flat for a mere sixty grand and selling it six years later for double the amount. They now live in a modest three bedroom house just outside of town.

I always joke that they should have let me rent a room from them, but for some reason, they both think this wouldn't be a good idea.

My Mum. She is a hard working lady. Someone I didn't appreciate when I was younger, but then I don't know anyone who does appreciate their parents then. My Dad died just after I was born, from cancer. My Mum says it was his own fault because he died from lung cancer and he smoked forty cigarettes a day for the whole of his life since he was thirteen and even when he was diagnosed and died within six months at thirty-two. He died with a packet of Marlborough Lights in his pocket (he had made the sacrifice to cut back to light fags a couple of years before that). I carry these cigarettes around with me and have done since my Mum warned me about the dangers of smoking when I was twelve. The fag packet is a constant reminder to me. I've never actually smoked a cigarette in my life and never will and yes I have smoked a few spliffs in my time, always reasoning with myself that it's not the same thing.

Unfortunately, I don't remember my Dad. Tas and Maxy are two years older than me, so they have vague memories, but I don't have any recollection of my him at all.

I think my Dad's death made my Mum stronger. I have never seen her upset and have never seen her falter for a second. She is a tower of strength to the whole family.

It was no hardship attending these "do's" for my Mum every other month. As we worked our way through our fifth bottle of wine I knew that the evening was going to be a success and that made me smile because it meant so much to my Mum.

Chapter Five

I woke the next morning feeling like I had been run over several times by a huge artic lorry. My head was pounding and my mouth felt dry. I opened one of my eyes slowly and realised I hadn't made it up to bed the night before and I was sprawled (one leg on, one leg off) on the sofa. No wonder my body ached.

The second thing I noticed was the half empty whisky bottle next to my hand. Wine and whiskey just did not match. Why did I feel the need to have a drink right up until the last minute before I fell asleep? I could feel the bile rising up in my throat. The third thing I noticed was in my other hand I had the telephone gripped tightly and I couldn't remember why.

The only saving grace I had was the fact today was a Sunday and I had no work. Actually it didn't really matter that today was a Sunday because even if it had been a weekday I would have called in sick. I needed today to let my head recover.

It was still early, about 9 in the morning and I felt I could fall straight back asleep and wake again at 9 that evening.

"Morning mate." Jono walked into the living-room and surveyed the mess that I'd made the night before and shook his head. He picked up the whisky bottle from the floor and proceeded to put it on the table.

"I'll clean up in a bit man," I told him. Jono just gave me a nod which meant he did not believe a word I had just said.

"No problems mate, fancy a fry-up?" Jono asked. Thank god he wasn't making a big deal about the mess of the place. I was inclined to give him a punch just for the sake of it. I'm not really one for violence either to be honest. I had a few scraps at school and had to punch a bouncer once a couple of years back but it was called for. The dirty old man (fifty year old with a long grey ponytail) groped my girlfriend at the time blatantly in front of my face. That was a question of pride.

"A fry-up would be great," I sat up on the sofa and held my head in my hands.

"Anything up?" Jono had walked into the kitchen but was now shouting back through the hallway.

"Nah mate just a bit worse for wear," I answered. Even if there was something up, Jono was not to be trusted. He would not be able to keep a secret and even if you told him one he would be so opinionated that it would make you feel like going the opposite way.

Jono seemed to be making a point of showing he was in a great mood this morning, which could only mean one thing. He'd pulled last night and was dying for me to ask. I felt like I should humour the man. After all he was making me breakfast.

"So why the good mood this morning?" I asked.

Jono walked back into the front-room rubbing his hands together with a huge grin on his face. Here he goes, I thought.

"I only pulled Vicky Wallace last night!"

"Really? Good on you mate," I smiled at Jono as he walked back into the kitchen. "Let me make us brekkie and I'll tell you all about it. Mate, she was practically begging for it."

I shook my head. There is no way in a million years that Jono would have been able to pull a bird like Vicky Wallace.

Vicky Wallace is a girl that used to be in our year at school. Beautiful looking and really popular. Vicky and I had always been mates although we had not seen each other for a while. Vicky was definitely out of Jono's league. Everyone understands how leagues work right? A league is how you rate yourself really, but you just don't tell people for fear of setting your sights too high or appearing arrogant. I don't know why Jono feels the need to lie but he does. His mates and I included just humour him and none of us have ever turned round and asked him why he has lied. He once made a stupid rumour up about Marie saying that they had a thing going on for a while before Baz met her. Of course we all knew it was lies. Marie is the only one who said anything to Jono about it though and she did it in spectacular fashion.

"Jon, we have never gone out have we?" Marie had asked as we all stood in a group.

"Ermmmm well… nope," Jono had to admit, in front of the mates he had told earlier that Marie had rode him all night long.

"Oh, good, glad we cleared that one up," Marie had taken a sip of her drink then added. "Don't ever use me for your lies again, understand?"

Jono had been gobsmacked. He had made his excuses and left early.

Jono did make a fantastic breakfast. The best cure ever for a stomping hangover was eggs, bacon, beans and tomatoes. The only thing that ruined it was the fact I had to listen to his "made-up" night of passion with Vicky in the back of her flash new car (bearing in mind I know that Vicky doesn't drive!).

"Anyway mate, she wants to see me again but I think it would ruin a good friendship," Jono was continuing on, slurping at his tea and chewing on his bacon.

"Good point," I agreed.

"Ah well, it was a good night. One I won't forget in a hurry anyway." Jono put his plate down and sunk back into the armchair. "I needed that."

"I know what you mean." I put my plate on the floor and lay back on the sofa closing my eyes. I was starting to feel more human again, could start to think more clearly and didn't feel like my head was going to spin off my shoulders.

"Oh, by the way Joe…"

I opened one eye and looked up at Jono.

"I got a voicemail from Baz this morning."

Why did I think it wasn't going to be good news?

"Baz, me, Maxine and Bella all got drunken phone-calls from you late last night mate."

My day had just got worse.

166

Chapter Six

"Yes! Yes! Yes!"

Sue and I had been out on a couple of dates. That was obviously all that was needed to get Sue up against the wall outside Jono's house and agreeing with me so fiercely (I don't know why we didn't wait until we were inside).

This was a quickie. I knew it was going to be. I was drunk, it was a bit cold outside, and to be honest, I didn't want this to take any longer than necessary. I just wanted the relief at the end (oh come on that is a nice way of putting it).

"That was great Joseph." Sue stroked my hair.

I pulled away from her at this point. I don't know why she kept calling me Joseph. She did it to everyone. Jono was Jonathan and Baz was Barry. I hadn't introduced Sue to the boys. They had been down the pub when I'd pulled her. I had tried taking her out of the back of the pub that night but she pretended to be shocked saying that she was not that kind of girl. She obviously was because why else would it have taken two dates later (one of those includes the night I pulled her).

"Shall we go inside?" Sue asked as I zipped my flies back up and she pulled her skirt back up and adjusted her knickers.

"Ermm yep cool," I unlocked the door and showed Sue the front-room where she could wait whilst I took a "slash." I never said I was classy.

"Fuck!" I muttered to myself as I watched my piss flow into the toilet bowl. I did not want Sue to stay but she obviously thought that is what happened next. I had not let any girl stay overnight with me since, well since my ex girlfriend.

If Sue stayed over would it ruin the memory do you think? For God's sake what is the matter with me? I'm acting and behaving like a girl. Yes that is right, it's you girls that need the love and affection. Us boys are happy with a couple of shags and perhaps a blowjob every now and then. Yes I know, who am I trying to kid right?! There was a knock on the door which brought my thoughts back to my current situation.

"You all right in there Joseph?" Sue asked.

"Yep," I opened the door.

Sue is not a bad looking girl at all. She has short dark hair and really lovely blue eyes. It was her eyes and her lips (I don't need to tell you why) that caught my attention.

"I was feeling a bit lonely in there," Sue smiled. "Maybe you can make me feel better." Sue walked closer towards me until our faces were nearly touching and she pulled her top over her head. Her breasts were fantastic, ones that Jordan would have been proud of and I felt myself stiffen again. I took Sue by the hand and led her into my bedroom, never taking my eyes from her breasts heaving up and down. I kicked the bedroom door behind me. The decision was made. Sue was staying the night, after all it would have been rude to not let her, right? It had been a fortnight since I had spoken to Baz, Jono, Maxy and Bella in my drunken stupor. I had spoken to Baz, Jono and Maxy apologising for declaring my undying love to them. I had no idea if I had said the same thing to Bella because I only got her mobile voicemail.

"Hi Bella. Sorry about my drunken phone-call yesterday. I must have dialed every number in my phone…"

Okay, I know this is a slight exaggeration.

"Anyway, sorry mate. Maybe we can catch up again soon. See ya."

I doubted I would be catching up with Bella again but hey I was waking up in bed with another woman for the first time in a really long while and it wasn't a bad thing.

Chapter Seven

Ok why is it when women put mascara on, their mouths immediately fall open? What is that all about?! Sue looks like a bloody goldfish when she puts the stuff on and she puts enough blusher on to give Aunt Sally a run for her money (for those of you that don't know... Worzel Gummidge).

Sue and I had been seeing each other for a month now. A whole month and it was the longest month I had ever experienced. The sex was great and when you are seeing someone sex is on tap, so that's a point in Sue's favour. Don't get me wrong I haven't started writing a list marking Sue's good and bad points, well only in my head. She also has a great body, so yes another good point. But she does have massive toes. Sue is apparently a size seven shoe (I reckon it's more like nines), if that is the case then her feet must be crying out every time she squeezes those babies into a pair of her narrow shoes. That is a point against her.

The mascara thing is not really a bad point. It just fascinates me and it bothers me that I can't remember if my ex (I will get on to her later) did the same thing or if she even wore mascara. Should I know this? The blusher thing is also a habit I could live with and I guess it does give Sue a "healthy" glow.

Why does Sue feel the need to leave something behind every time she stays? I have got into the habit of scanning my bedroom as soon as she has walked out of the door and chasing after her down the street with her toothbrush or her "compact." I called this her silvery round thing. Sue says she is just forgetful. I am more of a cynic than that and think she is trying to get her size sevens over the doorstep. Am I being paranoid? This is a bad point in Sue's favour because it drives me mad.

Sue stays over a couple of nights a week. We don't tend to go to her house because she shares with two of her girly friends and to be honest I don't want to be introduced. What would I be introduced as? I know what Sue would introduce me as and I don't feel entirely comfortable with that yet. Sue and I have not really gone out since we started seeing each other. I prefer for her to come round and for us to go to bed. If this is a problem for her, she would say. It obviously suits her down to the ground too. Another plus point is Sue likes to go on top (saves me doing all the work).

Sue is very helpful and likes to tidy up. After we have shagged I leave her in my room to get us some drinks and by the time I come back all my clothes are hung up in my wardrobe and my socks paired up and put in the drawer. That is a plus point. I could never be arsed with that domestic chore. I wonder how my Mum put up with me for so long.

I am going with the flow with Sue. Who knows, by knowing her I might meet the love of my life. Oh, who believes in all that crap anyway!

One of the points that I do like about Sue is the fact she takes real pride in her appearance, although I did wonder why my white pillow was brown after she stayed one night. Amy (you remember my house-mate) told me this was fake tan, so every day is a school day.

Sue did want to come round this evening but I had made Wednesday my studying day. The day when I would read my dummies book and try and make sense of it all. Baz could actually leave me on my own with his computer now without worrying that he was going to come back to a wiped hard drive (I actually know what that means now).

Baz said it was about time I signed up to one of the agencies in town, so after finishing work and a quick shower I ventured into town.

The girl at reception looked me up and down as soon as I walked in the door.

"How can I help you today?"

"I'm here to register."

"Take a seat and I'll get one of our representatives to help you." The girl gestured to an empty seat in the reception area.

"Cheers." I smiled and sat down. I'd done it. I had made the first move. Who said I didn't follow through on things?

An hour and a half later I left feeling dejected and pessimistic. I had a chat with one of the representatives first and I answered no to all her questions which was not a good start.

"Do you have any office experience?"

"Have you used any of these Software Packages listed before?"

"Have you had any experience using any telephone system?"

If that wasn't bad enough when I was asked by Jill (well, that was on her name badge) why I wanted to transition across and work in an office, I said nothing and my mind went blank for about thirty seconds before I blurted out.

"Money."

Luckily Jill smiled at my answer and decided to set me up on a couple of standard agency tests. I had never been into one of these agencies before so I had no idea what sort of test I was being asked to do. Should I have brought my trainers?

I didn't need my trainers. I had a spelling test, a typing test and an arithmetic test. I passed my spelling and arithmetic test with just a couple of wrong answers and I felt myself puff my chest out when Jill seemed impressed and congratulated me on high scores.

I got fifteen words a minute on my typing test with six mistakes which from Jill's facial expression was not so good. However, she advised me that she now had all my details on file and if a suitable job came up then she would contact me straight away.

I didn't hold out much hope on that.

Chapter Eight

Sue immediately decided we should celebrate by going out to dinner. I couldn't be bothered to be honest, but I hardly made an effort with Sue as it was and felt bad by saying no this time. Anyway I know how much Sue liked to doll herself up.

I didn't really see any point in celebrating a Call Centre role which I had only got because Maxy had recommended me to her Manager, which I'm sure she would regret once I started typing fifteen words a minute, with six mistakes every time.

Sue disagreed, said that all my hard work had finally paid off and I would now be able to spend more time with her and not spend it with my head hidden in a computer book. Great.

Sue had driven us to a lovely restaurant about twenty minutes away from home. It was a family run Italian and as soon as you walked in you could feel the atmosphere. The service was amazing, the food was superb and the wine flowed. The only downside was the company.

"I went past the Travel Agents today. They had a great deal in there for a week in Greece. I think we should go," Sue looked at me expectantly.

"I'm about to start a new job Sue."

"Everyone is allowed a holiday. It's the law!"

"Yeah that is true. Well get some brochures and we can take a look," I smiled at Sue and she grinned back.

I knew that the very next day Sue would turn up at my house with a bagful of brochures wanting to book a romantic break away that very minute. Was it me or was the restaurant air suddenly very thin and constricting?

Give someone an inch and they will take a mile. I've heard that expression before and it really does suit Sue to the ground. I was worried that she was going to turn up round Jono's one day with her suitcase packed. Sue is not a bunny boiler by any means. She has a great circle of friends (who I still haven't met) and a great social life, but I know that Sue wants to settle down pretty quickly and have babies. I don't think she even cares who it is with.

Sue continued to chat on about the latest holiday deals she had seen and how lovely it will be for us to be away together alone when I saw her.

She looked gorgeous but then she always did. She was wearing a pair of well-fitting jeans and a white boob tube which showed off her great colouring. She had quite a bit of make-up on, well for her anyway and her hair was as shiny as normal. She looked fabulous.

She spotted me a few seconds later and she smiled. She turned to her companion who I had only just noticed and whispered something which caused him to look over.

He looked a bit like Ben Affleck, so if you like that normal boring look then you could probably say this man was good looking. I didn't feel he was her type at all.

Ben Affleck was definitely an office boy. You could tell by his soft clean hands. I looked down at mine and noticed the chipped nails and hard skin.

They were walking over and Sue noticed that she no longer had my attention as the couple appeared at our table.

"Joe, how are you?" She smiled.

"Really good, you?"

"Yeah, not bad at all."

I noticed Ben Affleck was holding her hand tightly and definitely checking me out like I was the competition.

"Ermmm Joe are you going to introduce us?" Sue suddenly interrupted and I saw the same expression on Sue's face as I just had on Ben's.

"Yeah, of course," I smirked. "Sue, it's my pleasure to introduce you to Sally." I had never mentioned Sally to Sue and it showed on her face.

I think it is about time I introduced Sally to you all as well.

Chapter Nine

Sally is my ex girlfriend.

It still seems weird calling Sal my ex. Do you know what I mean? When you get so used to someone being there and all of a sudden they're not anymore.

Sally and I are complete opposites but we really hit it off straight away. I'd met Sally at Marc Antoni hairdressers in the town centre. I obviously wouldn't pay their prices for a haircut but my sister would. The only reason I was in town with Tas was because it was our Mums birthday and Tas said it was about time I made an effort to get a gift rather than give her the cash which I had done for the past fifteen years or so.

Anyway I walked into the hair salon with Tas and watched as some bloke, (who was quite obviously gay) took her coat and showed her to her leather hairdressing chair. At this point, I picked up one of the hair magazines from the table and flicked through, not taking much notice of anything on each page because none of the hairstyles were realistic. For example, one woman had blonde spiky hair that was styled in a way so it was over her eyes. How would this style suit a normal, every-day woman? It just wouldn't! The Accident and Emergency department would be inundated with cases of people walking into lamp-posts and knocking themselves out.

"Can I get you a tea or coffee whilst you wait?" I looked up and there she was.

She was the smallest adult I had ever seen in my life. I'm sure I could have picked her up with one hand and put her in my pocket. She must have been about five foot give or take a couple of inches and she had red shoulder length hair. She was gorgeous.

"No I'm fine thanks," I finally managed to answer.

"How about a cold drink?" Sally asked.

"A water would be good," I answered. I didn't actually want a water, but I wanted Sally to come back over and talk to me.

"Coming right up," Sally answered and I watched as she walked away from me. She was wearing her work uniform which was black trousers and a black shirt.

At this moment Sally reminded me of Smurfette. Do you know who I mean? The only female Smurf. Well anyway, she reminded me of her but she didn't have a blue face.

Sally walked back over with my glass of water and I watched her approach. As she leant down to hand me my drink, I caught a glimpse of the black bra she was wearing beneath her shirt.

"Thirsty work shopping." I took a gulp of water, desperately racking my brain trying to think of something wittier to say than "thirsty work shopping."

"Not many men would go shopping with their girlfriends on a Saturday," Sally nodded her head to Tas, who was in the process of having her hair clipped up in various places on her head.

"She's not my girlfriend!" I exclaimed in horror. "She's my sister."

"Oh right," Sally nodded. "I'm Sally."

"I'm Joe." I introduced and extended my hand to her. Sally's hand was as smooth as a baby's bum (although I haven't touched many babies' bums, but that's how the saying goes). One of the other things I remembered about her was her cute nails. Each nail was perfectly manicured and finished with a different colour nail varnish and a star on the tip.

"Well it is really good to meet you Joe," Sally said and walked away but not before turning around and smiling at me.

The rest is history.

I left the hair salon that day with Sally's number in my jeans pocket much to Tas's disgust.

"You can't sleep with the woman who works in my hair salon."

175

I didn't realise there was a rule about these kind of things but decided to ignore Tas's advice on this occasion (actually I ignore her advice on all occasions). How could I take advice from a woman that had just spent an hour in a hair salon, paid over eighty quid and come out with her hair looking exactly the same?!

I waited a whole twenty four hours before I finally caved in and called her. I was smitten.

Chapter Ten

I knew the questions would start as soon as Sally and Ben Affleck walked away from the table. Sally did introduce me to her new man but I wasn't paying much attention. He could have been the real Ben Affleck for all I cared. Although if he was I might have asked him what J-Lo was really like.

"Ex girlfriend?" Sue had asked as soon as Sally was out of ear-shot.

"Uh huh," I answered.

"Serious was it?" I could tell by Sue's snippy tone of voice that she was not happy.

"Not really."

"Broke up quite recently then?"

"A while ago."

"Is that her new man?"

"Looks like it."

"He looks really nice. They look really good together."

The conversation went on like that until our coffee had been drunk and our bill had been brought over and paid. I helped Sue on with her coat, which one of the waiters had brought over and we walked to the door. I caught Sally's eye and winked. Sue saw all this and I knew as soon as we walked outside in the cool night air the line of questioning was going to change tack.

"Do you still love her?"

"Nope."

"Do you fancy her?"

"Nope."

"Do you think she is prettier than me?"

"Nope."

By this time I was giving standard answers. As it happens, Sally and I were never a serious item but we really had some fun together. We had the same sense of humour. You know the childish sense of humour where if someone farts in a crowded room you snigger or if someone trips up you have to stifle a giggle? I just never loved Sally the way she wanted me to. However, I do still fancy her and I do think she's prettier than Sue.

"I'm going to go home tonight Sue," I said as we walked to the taxi rank.

"Oh good, we can have a lovely lazy morning tomorrow," Sue linked her arm into mine.

"No, I want to stay at mine on my own tonight. I just feel knackered." I felt Sue stiffen next to me.

"Fine!" was all she said but it was so obviously far from being fine. I'd heard that word on many occasions from the three other females in my life to know when a woman says "fine" like that then you need to be on-guard immediately.

Sue stopped walking just as we got to the taxi rank and looked at me.

"This is about her isn't it?" Sue asked. Her face was looking at me expectantly and I so wanted to give her the right answer. The one she wanted to hear.

"About who?" I played dumb instead.

"Sally," Sue said in a really childish voice which I think she realised because I saw her face redden.

"Don't be ridiculous." I kissed Sue on the nose.

"Oh right so now I'm ridiculous. I'm betting perfect Sally was never ridiculous!" Sue's voice was getting higher causing the people in front of us to turn round.

"Sue, I'm just knackered and want to get some sleep. No man would ever get to sleep with you next to them."

It was the right thing to say. Sue smiled and gave me a huge hug before getting into the waiting cab.

I watched as the taxi drove round the corner before deciding to walk home. The walk would do me good, clear my head a bit.

I am not sure if Sue had believed me but I had lied. This

178

was about Sally. It had shocked me to see her. The saying is spot on, out of sight, out of mind because I hadn't thought about Sal in a quite a while. She also looked fabulous and happy. I mean, she really looked happy. Happier than I could ever make her which I think was the whole problem. I just didn't love Sal the way she wanted me to. She was approaching thirty years old although she still had the face and boobs of a seventeen year old. She wanted the works, marriage, kids and a house that we could do up like the DIY programmes you see on television every time you switch it on.

Unfortunately, it wasn't what I wanted. That was the last difference that finally broke the camel's back. Sally and I were like Chalk and Cheese. She liked staying in and watching a video with a pizza and I liked going to the pub until closing and getting a curry on my way home. Sally smoked like a trooper and I despised it.

Sally was great with money, would always put a quarter of her salary in a savings account for a "rainy day" whereas I would be lucky to have a few quid left after pay day. Sally had real ambition, she wanted to get somewhere with her life and dreamt of owning her own hair salon one day whereas I was content enough to just stick at my dead-end job and earn enough to buy myself a few pints at the end of the week.

Sally and I both ignored these differences, neither one of us broaching the subject or wanting to have a "talk." I think we both realised our visions were completely different and so far from each other they couldn't even be classed as opposites, but we just put it to the back of our mind.

It was a really sad day because, as I picked up my toothbrush from Sal's bathroom and my spare pair of boxers I kept in her drawer, I realised that I would miss laughing with her and that someone somewhere out there would be really lucky to find this Smurfette, because as you now know there is only one. I wish it hadn't ended the way it had, but as the saying goes "if it doesn't end badly, it doesn't end…"

Most of all, I realised that I was losing one of my mates and tonight she had looked so happy that I wondered if I would ever make someone glow like that. I found the whole situation very difficult to swallow.

Chapter Eleven

Sue and I broke up. I guess you knew that was going to happen right?

We broke up for all the right reasons and for none of the wrong ones. I toyed with idea of sending Sue a text message or even writing her a letter, but knew this was a cowardly thing to do and I doubt she would have understood a word in my scrawly handwriting anyway. Have any of you ever been in the situation where you have had to dump someone knowing that they really care about you? I was dreading it. I had lain awake the night before wondering how I could let Sue down gently, but knowing deep down that it was best to just tell her the truth because she would be hurt either way. She might appreciate my honesty.

"I don't feel we should see each other anymore," I said as soon as I sat down on Sue's sofa. She looked shocked and just stared at me.

"Why?" she had asked without looking at me.

"I just don't think this, us, is going anywhere," I said. Sue asked me why a further four times before she realised that I was serious and wouldn't be changing my mind. After that she politely asked me to leave and that was that. It was easier than I thought it would be and without sounding patronising I was proud that Sue had enough self respect to accept my decision and ask me to leave. Baz once went out with a girl at college who wouldn't accept it was over when he told her and ended up refusing to leave his house. In the end Baz had to call her Mum to come and get her. My god she must be so embarrassed by that now.

The next morning it felt like a weight had been lifted from my shoulders. I wanted to share this moment with one of my friends so I decided to call on Bella (I mentioned her before) in the Book Store she manages.

I saw Bella before she saw me. She was wearing her black trousers with pink shirt, I thought you girls reading this would like the level of detail. She had her back to me and was talking to some bloke, probably a customer.

It became clear that it wasn't a customer though, as I approached. The bloke who was quite slim kept touching Bella on the arm and shoulder and I actually saw her flinch. I was wondering whether I should go over and check if she was okay when all of a sudden the bloke enveloped her in a huge bear hug and she seemed to fall straight into it. He looked vaguely familiar. Oh yes this must be her new bloke. He was at Baz's wedding although I only saw him briefly after the ceremony. I remember Baz and Marie mentioning something about him… dammit what was it they said about him?

I walked away without Bella seeing me and I turned around one last time before leaving the historical aisle, to see Mr. Muscle (you know like in the adverts?) kiss Bella on the head. Funny he really didn't seem to be Bella's type. Although I didn't actually know what Bella's type was. I hadn't seen her with anyone since I'd known her. She had mentioned some pillock she had been out with on and off for a few years, but apart from that there didn't appear to be anyone special. Maybe this man was the one?

I didn't really like the thought. This was probably because Bella could do so much better. I mean, Bella could have beaten that bloke up with one finger or breathed on him and he would have fallen over. Oh who am I to judge? Bella deserves to be happy and maybe this is the bloke to do it for her.

I wanted the best for her, like I would for any of my mates. That's only natural right? Anyway I should change the subject. The job.

Ha ha the job. I have been in my Call Centre role now for three days, three hours and twenty-five minutes and it felt like forever. The building I walked into was three floors high and

182

grey. I felt depressed just looking at the place but the décor inside was different. It was an open-plan office with bright lighting and beige carpeting throughout. I couldn't type, fifteen words a minute is something a four year old would be able to achieve. I also felt like a robot asking the same question over and over to different people on the telephone.

"Hello Joseph speaking, please may I take your name and serial number of the product please?"

Apparently I couldn't call myself Joe on the telephone because it sounded like I was being over familiar with the customers which was ridiculous. One of the Call Centre girls was christened Kate but the Manager had decided this was quite familiar too and she now wore a name badge saying "Katherine"!

The customers on the telephone weren't the brightest sparks either which just made me laugh at first but after the second day I had lost all patience.

"And where is your equipment located?" I had asked, fingers poised ready to type away as fast as my two fingers would take me.

"It's on the cabinet next to my record player," the customer answered. This type of answer and information would certainly help our Engineers find the equipment on the London A to Z. Another customer had tried to clean their Printer by inserting a tea towel and wondered how they could now retrieve it from the roller assembly.

I had never been in an office environment in my life and I didn't expect this. I had regular tea breaks (ten fifteen and three thirty) and my lunch was from twelve to twelve-forty-five. There are only two other blokes in the Call Centre and the other eight are women ranging from about eighteen to fifty-five years of age.

This would be my starting block. This was the office experience I needed and I had to stick it out. The money was good, nine pounds and fifty pence an hour which gets paid into my bank account every week without fail. I like being paid weekly as I am less likely to be short again the following weekend.

The office where I work is right next door to the town centre so I spent my forty-five minutes walking aimlessly about munching on a mayonnaise filled BLT. At least it gave me something to do although it wasn't helping me save my hard earned nine pounds fifty an hour. I'd managed to buy two CD's, a DVD and a book in the last three days. I had to knock that on the head for a start. For one, I didn't even read books but I had felt obliged to buy one the other day when one of the Assistants in the Book Store had caught me staring at Bella and her man so I picked up the nearest book to me which was about World War II. Oh well, I would wrap it up for my Mum. She liked books like that.

One of the highlights of work was my sister. Maxy worked in the same Call Centre and had managed to wangle the same tea breaks as me so we spent the fifteen minutes standing outside the building chatting and taking the piss out of the Boss. It was like being back at school, which I guess suited me down to the ground. I was the joker at school. It was never about learning for me and one of my proudest moments was reading another pupil's funniest moments on Friends Reunited which mentions the time I soaked the whole class with the fire extinguisher. I got a month's detention for that stunt but it was worth it.

Friday finally came and I was so proud of my achievement. I had managed to last a whole week in the Call Centre. This was cause for celebration (as I have mentioned before, any excuse).

I asked Maxy what she had planned for her weekend at our last three-thirty tea break on Friday afternoon.

"Having a quiet one," Maxy replied.

"Don't be daft. We need to celebrate."

"I am trying to save for Lucy's wedding," Maxy said.

Lucy was Maxy's best friend and so like her which is why they had been friends since school.

"Where's she having it?" I asked, suddenly realising that Maxy and I would need to find something else to do on our tea-breaks because it was bloody freezing.

"St Lucia," Maxy said. "Hey, maybe she's going to the same resort that you did."

I smiled as I was suddenly transported back to what felt like years ago but was only about six months.

Chapter Twelve

Sally and I booked our first holiday away together a few days ago. A last minute week in St Lucia. Sally had persuaded me to go telling me what a good laugh it would be and how we both deserved a break from our normal lives. Both cases were true. I knew we would have a laugh and I did need a break, a bit of sun because the British Summers can be a bit of washout, literally.

It was easy to be persuaded to go to St Lucia. The pictures in the brochure just showed clear blue seas, beautiful lush green areas and the daily temperatures reaching over 85 degrees Fahrenheit every day, which just sealed the deal for me. Sally was an important person in my life. She made me smile and laugh. She's the sort of person that everyone knows and I really like that about her. I was right about the sex with Sal too.... Wow! Although, if I am going to be honest it did take a few attempts to get it perfect. We were so nervous the first time that it was bound to end in tears or an apology (which it certainly did). Our first time was on our second date (well what is the point in waiting?) I would have done it on our first date but I didn't want to rush Sally. Anyway, it just made me want her more, like a child being told he cannot have any more sweets.

We arrived in St Lucia with the late afternoon sun still in the sky. Even when Sal and I were at the airport in England I really didn't believe I was going on holiday with my girlfriend. I had never been on holiday anywhere with a girl before in my life (well apart from my sisters).

We pulled up outside our apartment block, which was painted salmon pink (which funnily enough was not off-putting). I could see the pool area and the bar from the reception. I couldn't wait to jump into the pool and have a refreshing ice-cold beer. I looked at Sal and smiled. We obviously had just thought of the same thing. It took us half an hour to get our keys, drop off our luggage, change and jump into the pool. Sal got changed into a bikini but then covered her behind with a sarong to only take it off again before jumping into the pool. Yet again, I will never understand women.

We did have a great holiday. It was perfect. I didn't want it to end not only because I would have to go back to reality and work, but I would not be waking up with Sal every morning. I felt like I should make an effort you know? Well, most of my friends, would never put me down as being romantic at all, but I wanted to show Sal I could have my moments. I wasn't one for big gestures but I did book us on a night dinner cruise as a surprise. It was obviously the right thing to do because Sal shrieked like a girl. That should've been my most romantic evening, but it wasn't. We ate our dinner by candlelight as we watched the sun setting in the distance (it sounds like a film doesn't it?). After the meal, we watched the cabaret show and later we were dancing to the music… Well, I was showing off and kept showing Sal my moonwalk until she started to yawn. We were too drunk by that point to really notice though.

Most of our days were spent by the pool or on the beach and if it rained we went to the bar and drank. It was a really relaxing break and exactly what I needed. We arrived back in England on a cold and wet rainy day. It reflected our moods perfectly.

Sal had mountains of photos from the holiday. Photos of me asleep, in the pool, on the beach, drinking and the odd one every now and again of us together. Sal bored all our friends and families with the pictures. It's just not the same if you haven't been yourself.

I'd seen other couples on that holiday staring into each others eyes and holding hands constantly, so I knew this holiday should've been the most romantic experience of my life. Apart from the sex (I'm only human) Sal and I were mates, so we returned knowing that the end was imminent but what a fun ride it had been.

Unfortunately, the memory was tainted by the fact that I caught Sal sleeping with someone else a few days later. The end was sooner than we thought it would be.

Chapter Thirteen

Do you have a picture in your head of me yet? Do I sound like someone you could be mates with?

I am three inches under six foot which is not very tall for a bloke these days. Baz is over 6 foot and both my sisters are taller than me which is just downright embarrassing. Luckily Jono is smaller than me, actually a lot smaller than me. Jono reckons good things come in small packages so he must be happy with his two inches over five foot.

I am quite fair, although if I don't wash my hair for a few days it can look quite dark, like today for example. When I worked outside I didn't shave all week and Friday evening became my shave day which was bloody marvellous. Shaving is such a hassle. Unfortunately, now I work in a Call Centre I have to shave every day. The dress code itself is smart casual which also means I can wear my nice jeans (no rips, holes or frayed bits) but not a tee-shirt. Does that make any sense to you at all? I mean I speak to customers all day but how can they tell from the tone of my voice that I am wearing an old pair of jeans and my Pulp tee-shirt.

I am quite stocky but never tuck my shirts in as I am constantly trying to hide my beer belly. It was easy to shift when I was doing manual work but sitting at a desk all day is now taking its toll.

I have a Celtic tattoo round the top of my arm as well. I had it done when I was eighteen years old and it seemed like a good idea at the time. Baz was with me but he chickened out of getting the dragon on his back (which in hindsight is probably a good move). I'm starting to think when I reach eighty years old my tattoo won't look as good. However, I do like it at the moment and there is not much I can do about it now anyway.

Monday morning arrived again and my alarm woke me

with the sound of ringing. My Mum always asked me if I would like a radio instead so I could awaken to the dulcet tones of Kylie or The Corrs instead of the constant ringing, but the music would never get me out of bed. I would be more likely to fall asleep rather than jump out of bed to hit my alarm every morning. I actually put my alarm on the other side of my room just in case I did turn it off by accident and went back to sleep. Believe me this has happened on more that one occasion.

It occurred to me that yesterday was the first Sunday in a really long time I hadn't gone to the pub and yesterday it hadn't even occurred me to that I wasn't going. I'd got out of bed (with a hangover), ate crap all day (fry-up, toast, chocolate hobnobs and a Chinese takeaway for dinner) and eventually fell asleep at nine. I'd been in work for ten minutes when my Manager Hugh came up to me.

"Joseph," he said. "Could I have a word please?"

"Yeah course." I took off my headset (like the one Madonna wore in her video Vogue) and set my phone to off.

I followed Hugh out of the Call Centre making sure I closed the door behind me. The noise outside the Call Centre could provide a distraction to the Operatives on the telephone apparently. Normally when a Manager or my old boss wanted a word with me I knew what I was about to get bollocked about. This time I had no clue, unless they were completely unimpressed with my fifteen words a minute. Hugh walked into one of the vacant meeting rooms down the corridor and held the door open until I walked in and sat down.

"We believe you have real potential Joseph," was the first thing Hugh said.

"Eh?" I am sure you can appreciate why that is the only response I could make.

"We already know that you are a likeable member of the team," Hugh continued. "We like to reward new members of our team."

Excellent, I could do with some more money.

"Therefore we would like to send you on a course," Hugh smiled. It was not a nice smile, more of a patronising, business-like smile. Do you know the ones I mean? It would probably help if I told you that Hugh wore pin-stripe suits to work every day, had slicked back hair, was in his forties and spoke a lot like Basil Fawlty.

"Eh?" My responses were not changing and I was slightly concerned that Hugh was going to notice I had lost the power of speech.

"There is a three day course the week after next on telephone and communication skills at our Scotland office. We would like you to be one of the attendees." Hugh passed me a folder. "In this contains all the flight, accommodation and travel arrangements. All your food and beverages are of course covered by the company, although within reason."

Good job Hugh added that onto the end.

"Okay," I managed to say taking the folder from Hugh's hands. "Thanks."

I didn't manage to look through the folder details until my tea-break where Maxy and I looked through the details. Maxy had been offered the chance to go on this course as well about three times but all three times she had refused, because as I said before Maxy is only interested in working her hours and getting her money. That is the way she lives.

The flight left two weeks on Tuesday evening with me, my supervisor Helen and two other colleagues Eleanor (Ellie) and Samuel (Sam). We were all going to be staying in a Travel Lodge, with all our meals included at the restaurant next door and the Training Centre was about ten minutes up the road.

I read the course description over and over again and I couldn't quite work out what they could fit into three days to teach us all how to talk on the telephone and communicate with people. After all I'd been communicating in some way with people ever since the day I had been born.

But hey this is the new me. I am all for learning new things and this might help me move onto something better one day. If all else fails I always have the option to treat this three day course as a skive from the office and a bit of a jolly. After all three days away from work is still a holiday in my book.

"It should be a good laugh," I told Maxy. "I'm actually looking forward to it."

Maxy just shook her head and smiled. Her knowing smile as if to say "I know something you don't but I'm going to let you find that out for yourself."

Chapter Fourteen

We were in the middle of nowhere. The Travel Lodge place and the restaurant next door were the only places for miles. The Training Centre ten minutes away was extremely popular for companies as it gave them the chance to make sure their employees had no distractions and could focus on the job at hand.

We didn't arrive on Tuesday at the Travel lodge until nearly Midnight and I found myself sharing a room with Sam. This was actually the first time I had ever actually spoken to him, because a head nod every morning at work is not the same thing.

Sam was a really reserved man. He was in his late thirties at least I would say and he spoke so quietly that I wondered on many occasions how he'd ever got a job in a Call Centre.

We were given our alarm call at seven the next morning for breakfast.

Helen and Ellie were already at the table when Sam and I strolled over from our room.

"Morning," Helen smiled. I liked Helen. She was always really friendly, took no stick from anyone and gushed when she talked about her two kids.

"Morning ladies." I pulled out my chair and sat down.

"Morning," Ellie returned the greeting. Ellie and I had only ever exchanged pleasantries at work and I wondered why. Ellie was probably the same age as me, of average height and really slim with brown hair.

The course kicked off at nine and it was harder than I thought. The four of us were not the only people on the course. Two other companies had sent three members of their staff as well. The Tutor, Hazel, seemed all right although a bit tough looking, you know the sort of person you wouldn't want to mess with. A bit like Fatima Whitbread, but with long hair.

We all had to introduce ourselves in the first ten minutes with a list of criteria issued by Hazel.

"Hi, I'm Joe. I am a Call Centre Operative and have worked there for nearly a month. I hope to gain an understanding of this course from the three days and I support Portsmouth."

I felt like a wally. How was I supposed to know what I was going to gain from the course in the first ten minutes? Hazel had asked us to tell something personal about ourselves so the first thing that came into my head was Portsmouth Football Club, which seemed a bit lame now especially when other responses included travelling around India for three months and sky diving in Australia. How dull did I sound?

Role play is something I thought only actors did on stage, like in musicals. Role playing is in actual fact pretending to talk to someone who isn't who they really are.

I was in a role play with Helen. Helen was the aggressive, non-understanding customer and I had to show the group (oh yes I had to stand up in front of all ten of them and embarrass myself) how I would handle the call. Afterwards Hazel tore me apart. I couldn't remember being this embarrassed since my Mum turned up at my Junior School with my forgotten packed lunch, letting me know she had put a twix in for a treat.

"You should never argue with a customer. Just empathise with them."

"Never raise your voice even if it is to be heard."

"Never forget to call them Sir or Madam to show respect."

"Always end the call with is there anything else I can do for you?"

I was ready to give up and the day didn't get any better. We swapped partners all day and read our "new role" descriptions. I liked it better when I was the aggressive customer but only when Hazel was on the other end of the telephone. I didn't want to be nasty to Sam, Ellie and Helen. They were good guys and Ellie looked like she might cry at one stage.

Lunch was brought in for us all so this was a good chance to chat to everyone on the course. The other groups were swats and I haven't used that word since I was at school. They were reading up on Hazel's notes whilst eating their sandwiches and holding their apples. My group (easier than saying their names) chatted amongst ourselves and I was pleased to find that we were all finding the course a bit tough at the moment.

Hazel was almost human over lunch. She chatted with us all, asked about our jobs and our lives, but as soon as it hit one o' clock again then she turned into Fatima Whitbread again.

I was pleased when the day was over. It had been a long old day. By the time we got back to our rooms, it was almost six and we were meeting at seven for dinner. I could quite easily skip dinner and go to sleep, which as you know by now, is a big deal for me.

Dinner was okay, it was typical pub grub but the restaurant itself was actually quite cozy so you felt like you could be sitting at a dining table in someone's house. It had wooden floors and beams throughout with really soft lighting. The bar was at the end of the room and scattered around were a few pine wooden tables with chairs.

I didn't think I was that hungry but I managed to finish my beef ale pie and chips. Thankfully I stopped myself from licking the plate, realising that I wasn't at my Mums now.

We were all safely tucked up in bed by ten which was not my idea of a holiday, but I had to agree with the rest of them. We were knackered and none of us knew what tomorrow would bring. It was a survival tactic and by sleeping now would mean we would have all our senses about us tomorrow. How funny! Who would have thought a Communication and Telephone course could be so tough?

How was I supposed to know that was just the beginning?

Chapter Fifteen

"I've got to do a test!" I shouted down the telephone to Baz on our last evening.

"It'll be fine mate," Baz chuckled.

"Yeah right. When was the last time I did any sort of test?"

"Your agency tests the other week?" Baz questioned.

"They don't count. I wasn't prepared for them," I answered. This was completely different.

"Look, if they're going to be multiple choice, it should be easy mate," Baz reassured.

"When's the last time you did a test?" I asked.

"Probably my GCSE's at school mate," Baz answered and I heard Marie laugh in the background.

"You and your wife are not helping with the nerves," I said. "I had better go. Dinner is in ten minutes. Catch up with you and Marie at the weekend okay?"

"Yeah, cool."

A test! I am a couple of years off being thirty years old and haven't been asked to do a test in years. The last exams I had ever done were also my GCSE's at Secondary school. I loved using my hands at school so I actually excelled in Pottery, IT and Computer Design Technology, but I flunked in everything else. Embarrassingly enough, I didn't even get graded for my English and French exam. I wondered if the examiners just had a laugh at my papers the day they marked them, they could have just decided to not grade a pupil for a laugh. Hey, it happens. I read the tabloids. One of the subjects I also passed, if you are interested was Math's which was as much a surprise to me as it was to my Mum. I got a B which is a bloody good grade in my book. Tas and Maxy both excelled at school so I was the dunce in the family. Tas actually cried because she got a B grade as all the rest were straight A's. She even wrote a letter to the examining board asking for their reasons for the B grade. Funnily enough they never replied.

I was now going to have a twenty questions test and do a role play (again) and be assessed. I felt under pressure. Hazel assured us all the test itself would be easy enough as the answers were multiple choice, but was easy for her to say as she had been doing the job for a hundred years. I was so nervous I didn't even have a beer with my meal on the Thursday evening. I was offered wine or an alternative alcoholic beverage, but I stuck to coke for the whole two hours. I just had to get through the next morning. I felt I had something to prove to myself. I am unsure of what at this stage.

The assessment of the role play wasn't too bad. It could've gone a lot worse. Ellie was my customer and even though she was supposed to be aggressive she was more like a pussy cat and I could handle that after going through my paces with Hazel/ Fatima. I even got a clap at the end of it, well actually everyone did but I felt like I was standing at a podium at the Olympic games winning a bronze medal (obviously winning a gold would mean I was just getting carried away).

The multiple choice questions were quite easy and a sigh of relief actually left my body because I knew it would be okay.

Two hours later and the course was over. We had all passed which was great news. Unfortunately we couldn't celebrate together due to the fact our plane was leaving in three hours although we all managed to have a quick pint at the airport before boarding the plane. I felt like I could sleep for a week.

When I worked outside I always wondered why people in the comfortable air conditioned offices got so tired sitting at a computer screen all day, practically doing nothing? I mean the most strenuous part of their day was walking to the toilet and back but this was different. I actually felt like I had used my brain over the last three days and I was mentally tired. I didn't even know what that was until now.

197

I would grab Jono when I got home, perhaps give Baz a bell and hopefully all end up at the pub this evening. Well, completing this course was a reason to celebrate and it would be good to be home, with local amenities nearby.

As you probably know by now, things never go according to plan. I will never know why but when I got dropped off by the taxi that evening I decided to pop to my Mums. I never pop to my Mums on a Friday evening but thought she would appreciate me dropping in for a cuppa before my mammoth pub session. I also wanted to brag about my achievements on the course.

My Mum's house is a semi- detached three bedroom place right at the end of an Estate. She has lived there forever and had refused to move even when Tas, Maxy and I were falling over each other as kids, because of the lack of space available. The house didn't have that much space, but Mum said that too much was a waste. She said her and my Dad had fallen in love with the place because of the garden. Our garden was huge and it was the second big love of my Mum's life. She would spend hours outside pruning, weeding and digging. You would actually see her puff up with pride when someone complimented her on a flower or the onions she was cooking smelling of real homegrown aroma.

It hadn't bothered me too much about the space due to the fact I had my own room. Tas and Maxy shared which couldn't have been a bad thing, bearing in mind they both now own a house together. I couldn't imagine my Mum living anywhere else. Neither could she. This was the house she moved into with my Dad, where she brought her children home from hospital and where, one day, she would die.

The front-door was ajar when I got there which was not unusual in itself as my Mum always left the door ajar so her next-door neighbour Sylvia could pop in whenever she felt like it. Tas was always on at my Mum to just give Sylvia a key rather than leave the door open.

Mum was sitting in her usual place. The green flowered arm-chair at the back of the front-room. I knew something was wrong as soon as I walked in the room. For one the lights were dimmed down so much they were almost out. I turned the dimmer switch up and as soon as I set eyes on her I felt my heart leap to my chest. My Mum's body somehow looked smaller than normal and her head was in her hands. She looked up as soon as she saw me and I noticed that her eyes were red. I have never seen my Mum cry before and even though she wasn't crying now, I knew she had been.

"Mum," I managed to say. God my throat felt tight.

"Oh Joe," Mum got up from the chair and flung her arms around me.

"What's happened?" I asked, growing increasingly worried by the second.

That is when I noticed the man sitting on the sofa at the other end of the room. It took a couple of seconds to register this man was in a uniform and even less time to figure out this man was a policeman. He was looking sympathetically at me.

You know the head cocked kind of look. I disentangled myself from my Mother and sat her back down in her chair. She slumped back into the same hunch-backed position but she still held my hand tightly. There was only word that I could use to describe her and that was "shocked".

The last time I had held my Mum's hand was when she took me to school when I was five years old. That was the one and only time I could remember because after that I told her constantly that I was a big boy now and didn't need my Mum to hold my hand. Well that and the fact the other kids were taking the mick out of me.

I will never know where I found the strength from, but a confident voice suddenly came from my mouth directed at the policeman.

"Just tell me."

Chapter Sixteen

"Your sister was involved in a motorbike accident," the policeman had told me.

"Don't be ridiculous," was the first thing I said back to him. Unfortunately, though, it was true. Tasmine had been involved in a motorbike accident. She had been riding pillion with her boyfriend and had come off on the motorway. I thought my sister had more sense to get on a motorbike. Didn't she read the papers?

Motorbike accidents, on motorways especially, happened every single day. I was disappointed in her. I mean, what sort of example is she setting to the kids at her school? There are adverts about the dangers in every interval for Corrie for goodness sake, so Tas had no excuse because she wouldn't miss an episode of Corrie for no-one.

"Your sister is stable but I'm afraid Mr. Steven Wright died from massive head injuries."

I wish I'd thought about my response before replying back to the policeman then but I didn't have much time to think.

"Thank god!"

It was the first thought that entered my brain. Tas was okay. The policeman just raised his eyebrow and asked if my Mother and I would like a lift to the hospital.

Mum and I got in the backseat of the Police Car as he drove us to the nearby hospital. The Policeman had not been able to provide details of Tas's condition to us at the house, but I didn't care I just knew she was okay.

Mum was in a state of shock. Her face was so pale and when she tried to speak the words seemed to get lost.

A lorry (another bloody dangerous vehicle in my opinion) had jackknifed on the M25, knocking the motorbike from its wheels. Steven had died instantly from his head injuries but Tas was stable. What did stable actually mean? It meant she was breathing right? Did it mean she had lost the use of her legs or she was now severely brain damaged? I am not sure if thinking of the worst case scenarios was helping me, but I was hoping that I would be pleasantly surprised with the nicer outcome. I had always thought that way.

Hope. I could actually feel a bubble of hope in my chest. I was in danger of choking from it. I still held my Mum's hand tightly and it felt so cold. Mum was looking out of the window and I could see from the street lighting that her face was distraught but she was holding it together, I think she was holding it together for me. I knew there was no point telling her there was no need.

The journey took forever and neither my Mum nor I said a word to each other. The weather outside was cold, miserable and wet. It felt dark and gloomy, which was apt for this occasion. I wanted to shout at the Policeman to put his sirens on and his foot down when we got to junctions and traffic lights. It felt like we were travelling in slow motion.

We eventually arrived twenty minutes later. Would you believe that is our nearest accident and emergency department? I am only glad that Tas was on a motorway junction that got her here sooner.

The policeman opened the door for my Mum and I got out the other side. My Mum and I had to let go of our hands and suddenly I felt lost.

"Would you like me to come up with you Mrs. Carey?" the Policeman asked.

"No thank you," my Mum said. "Thank you for the lift Officer."

The Policeman nodded and got back into the car. He didn't start the engine until we were almost at the reception area entrance.

"Maxine?" I asked Mum. I had forgotten to ask if Maxine

knew. What was the matter with me? I was the man of the family. I had to pull myself together and had forgotten one of the most important people to Tasmine.

"She knows Joe," my Mum told me. "She should be here already."

Apparently, the hospital had been trying to get hold of Mum all day to tell her about the accident but there was no answer. Mum had been out all day and it wasn't until she got home from work that she found a police car parked outside the house. Fifteen minutes later I had turned up.

The big glass doors opened as soon as we walked towards them and I remember thinking that this place had obviously been done up since I was last here. When I was eight years old I had opened a can of custard and caught the top with my finger. There had been so much blood over the kitchen that my Mum had initially thought I'd lost a finger at one stage, but a quick visit to the hospital and a few stitches later had sorted me out. I never ate custard again though. The doors back then were old, red and wooden.

I walked up to the reception desk not even noticing who the person was behind it. "Tasmine Carey please?"

"One minute Sir," the voice answered. Even now I cannot remember what that person looked like that I spoke to for a few seconds.

I saw her first. Maxine sitting in one of the waiting room chairs. Her face completely white and her hair wet from the rain clinging to her neck.

"Maxy." I walked over to where Maxy sat and she looked up. Mum was next to me.

"Oh Mum!" Maxy jumped up and threw her arms around Mums neck whilst she smoothed her hair back and soothed her.

"It's okay darling," Mum whispered into Maxy's hair.

How could Mum say that? How could she know? Was it okay or was my sister lying in this hospital somewhere in a vegetable state?

All we could do was sit and wait. Mum sat with Maxy curled up next to her stroking her hair with Maxy's head on her shoulder whilst she placed her hand on my leg, which I found extremely comforting.

It's funny the things you think of and remember when you have time on your hands. My Mum got burgled once, about a year or so ago when she was sleeping upstairs. They took the video recorder, some cash from the jar and a packet of hobnob biscuits. I remember Tas being so worried about Mum after that, well we all were, but Tas really made sure Mum was okay. She would pop round after work, phone before going to bed, phone before going to work until Mum told her one day that it had to stop. The burglars, or the "bastards" as my Mum called them didn't change a thing. She said it would mean the bastards had won if she did. Mum still kept the back-door open most of the time and the front-door ajar when she was expecting company. Tas takes after our Mum a lot.

It must have been a couple of minutes before I suddenly saw a Doctor walking towards us. I am trying hard now to think of the words to describe to you what I am feeling now, but all I can think of is scared and afraid.

"Mrs. Carey?" The Doctor shook my Mum's hand, who remained sitting down. I don't think she trusted herself to stand. Six expectant eyes looked at the Doctor as he began to speak.

"Your daughter Tasmine suffered massive head injuries so we had to operate to relieve the pressure on her brain. She is stable at the moment but we have to make you aware that the next twenty-four hours are crucial."

Did this mean there was a chance that Tas, my sister could ermmm well die?!

I could hear wailing and I looked behind me before I suddenly realised the wailing was coming from my sister Maxine. She had sunk to the floor and was curled up on the pale pink carpet in the hospital waiting room.

I felt helpless as I watched my Mum go to her daughter and gently pick her up from the floor. There was nothing we could do but wait, hope and pray.

Chapter Seventeen

The next twenty-four hours were crucial. We all knew what that meant. Maxy, my Mum and I didn't leave Tas's side. We were allowed to sit with her and the Doctor even encouraged us to talk to her.

I could hardly see Tas's face through all the tubes and machines that seemed to surround her. Tas was in intensive care. It was a really nice ward full of nurses that smiled and asked us constantly if we would like tea or a sandwich from the canteen. None of us took them up on the offer. The only downside was it smelt like a hospital. My Dad had hated hospitals. Apparently he had lost his own Mother when he was thirteen and from then on until the day he died he would try to avoid them at all costs. Ironic really that he died in one.

"Exactly like your Dad's room in hospital," my Mum had muttered when she thought I wasn't listening.

The room that Tas was in had a window but it was covered with a clear, cream blind, which was pulled down. It had two chairs on one side and another that had been brought in especially for me. I hardly sat in it. I paced the room, peeking every now and then out of the blind to check on the weather.

Every so often, a nurse would quietly walk into the room, check my Sister's vital signs and leave again, without saying a word. We never heard her coming because of the rubber-soled pumps she wore but if we had turned round we would see her through the glass panel in the door looking at us all first before she entered the room. The three of us would look expectantly at her but she always just smiled and cocked her head to one side, sympathetically.

It was the longest night of my life. I watched as Mum did her usual and kept it together for us, like I saw her do all those years ago when we lost Grandad. Her face showed every single emotion she was feeling and I thought I would cry when I saw how distraught and tired she looked. Her eyes were so sad that they looked like they might drown in tears. Maxy would chat away to Tas for a while then would realise all over again that she wasn't answering back and break down. I thought I would always hear the sound of beeping and sobbing. Things would never be the same again.

Mum and Maxy knew exactly what to talk about to Tas. I didn't need to say a word. Mum talked to Tas about the state of the house (why would she want to know that?) and she wanted to know whether Tas wanted to come on a shopping trip with her to Lakeside soon because she needed some new jumpers. Maxy managed to jabber on about her day, who she had spoken to and more importantly (according to Maxy), who had called the night before to ask for a date.

I could just imagine Tas listening to Mum's and Maxy's inane chitchat and shaking her head like she always did and then saying, "You two do go on," laughing and then launching into a bigger and better story of her own. God, I would miss Tas's laugh if...

"Right we are going to get some tea," Mum said. This was the first time in about five hours since my Mum and Maxy had left the room. Mum had to pretty much drag Maxy from the room, who didn't avert her tear-filled eyes from her twin once. "Watch your sister."

I was in the room alone with Tas. It seemed strange Tas being so quiet. She was the noisiest out of the three of us, she would be the one who was always telling Maxy and I what to do and when to do it. Funnily enough we always listened. Does that happen in all families? Is one of the siblings always the leader and is it always the eldest?

It was my chance now to talk to Tas. To tell her the things I never got the chance to tell her and things that she may never ever remember. Why am I so bad at this stuff?

"I can't cope with Mum and Maxy on my own Tas." I sat down next to her and placed my hand over hers gently. "You know what we're like. We need you to organise us all. Mum can't do it on her own."

Her hand was lifeless and felt cold.

"Do you remember when we were younger and you and Maxy used to make me play Barbie's and Sindy's?" I carried on. "You would always want some major drama in Ken and Barbie's life and Maxy would always want them to live happily ever after?"

No response.

"You know the way you would always make Ken have an affair with Sindy and then they would have a big custody hearing for the twins?"

No response.

"I was always on your side with that. Did you know that Tas?"

No response.

"Life is all about dramas isn't it?" I carried on. "It's all about families coming together and through the worst possible times to make them stronger and closer. I think this is what this is all about Tas."

I looked round and saw Maxy and Mum walking back up the corridor towards the room. I got up, lent forward and whispered in Tas's ear.

"Because of this Tas, because of you we will all get through this and we will be a stronger family. No-one will ever be able to touch us Tas. Can you hear me Tas? This was supposed to happen. We will be an even closer family and we will all have you to thank for it. It's all because of you."

Chapter Eighteen

It was three days before Tas finally opened her eyes and I wasn't there to see it. Thankfully my Mum and Maxy were. I had been sent to get some clean clothes for both Mum and Maxy who refused to leave the hospital site.

It was weird going to Maxy's without her or Tas there. I sat on the edge of Tas's bed and stared at the photo of her and Maxy she had on the chest of drawers, before finally composing myself enough to grab Maxy's clothes and leave.

I, on the other hand had to leave although it was never for more than twenty minutes. The antiseptic smell and the white walls at the hospital closed in on me every single day, so I took fifteen minutes to walk around the building and breathe in fresh air, well traffic fumes, but who cares.

The Doctor was extremely pleased with Tas's progress, said her vital signs were looking good and all was positive. Maxy took this as Tas being able to come home by next week. Mum and I took it with a pinch of salt, because after all, anything could happen. Although the glimmer of hope the Doctor gave us was held onto tightly but put to the back of our minds, just in case.

Apparently, it is normal for head injury victims to not wake up for days after a major operation but I just couldn't see past Tas never waking up. I wanted to see her open her eyes again.

We were also firmly told that the news about Steven was not to be shared with Tas until she was firmly on the mend. I had been quite selfish where Steven was concerned, if I am entirely honest. I just hadn't given him much thought in the past few days. Mum had. She had bought a condolence card from the hospital shop and asked me to put it in his parents door when I popped back to Mum's one day. Steven's parents lived in the next street to Mum. His parents and Mum had always exchanged pleasantries at the local shops.

"I don't even know their names!" Mum exclaimed, as she wrote out her sympathies for them losing their son.

"I don't even think they will notice their names are not on the card," I said, as I took the sealed envelope from Mum.

Tas had met Steven as he was picking his nephew up from Primary School. He had smiled at her and she had smiled at him. They had been a couple for about eighteen months until now.

I thought about Steven more now because I realised what this news would do to Tas. If the bike accident hadn't killed her, then maybe this news would. I have no idea how serious Tas and Steven were, but it had to be quite serious to last eighteen months, right?

I felt guilty because I hardly knew Steven at all. This was the man who had dated my sister for the last year and a half and I hardly made any effort at all to get to know him.

Steven was a quiet man; he had hardly said a word when I had met him or when he was out for dinner with us all. I guess he wouldn't get a word in edgeways with Tas around anyway. That's probably why they complimented each other. I didn't even know Steven had a motorbike. If I had known, would I have warned him about the dangers and would he have listened?

How would we break the news to Tas? Who would break the news to Tas?

"How's she doing?" Baz asked over the telephone.

"Still not awake," I said. "That's normal though."

"Are you okay mate?" Baz asked.

"Yep I'm doing all right," I answered. "Thanks."

"If there is anything Marie or I can do…"

"I know," I said. "Thanks mate. I do appreciate it. Speak to you soon."

The saying about finding out who your real friends are in times of trouble is true. I switched my mobile phone back off and walked back into the hospital room to see Mum and Maxy crying. Mum wasn't crying through sadness because her smile was wide across her face. Her face was showing pure joy.

"Oh my darling, you're awake at last," Mum was stroking Tas's hand. Maxy was on the other side kissing Tas's hand over and over again whilst crying.

"What's happened?" I asked and then I saw her.

Tas had her eyes half open and was blinking rapidly trying to focus on her surroundings and the people around her.

"You're awake!" I said.

"She has been for about ten minutes now," Mum continued looking at her daughter. "She's come back to us."

Tas attempted to lick her dry cracked lips before wincing slightly and closing her eyes. The Doctor said this was normal and she would drift in and out of consciousness for a while and sleep was the best cure.

I felt like all my birthdays and Christmas's had come at once. I had taken so much for granted. This was a new start for me because as long as Mum, Tas, Maxy and I were all ok then what else could go wrong?

For the first time in four nights, I was going home that evening to sleep in my bed. It felt weird. It felt like I should be staying at the hospital with my family, but the Doctor had insisted we all go and let Tas sleep.

I'm not sure if any of us would actually be getting any sleep that night but because it was in the best interests of Tas we all agreed with the Doctor and said our goodbyes, not knowing if she could hear us or not.

"Do you want the cab to drop you off on the way Joe?" Maxy asked as she hailed a cab outside the hospital. "I'm staying at Mum's tonight."

"No I'm going to walk," I said. "See you two tomorrow."

For the first time I can remember Maxy walked up to me and hugged me. I hugged her back and do you know what? It did feel a bit awkward but it was bloody nice.

"Come on Maxine." Mum opened the taxi door. Maxy let

go of me and smiled before getting into the car. Mum winked at me before getting in and closing the door. I waved them off before starting my stroll home.

I switched my phone back on and it beeped five seconds later to show I had a voicemail message.

"Hi Joe, I've only just heard the news. God I hope your sister is okay. I don't know what hospital she's in because I could come and sit with you, or not. Whatever you like really. Anyway you know my number, well I think you do. It's 77456 at the end. I'm here if you want to talk or just have a beer with. Hope to speak to you soon, Joe."

It was Bella.

Chapter Nineteen

"Joe?" Bella answered the phone on the first ring.

"Hello you," I smiled. It was really good to hear her voice.

"Are you okay? Is Tasmine okay?" Bella asked.

"Where are you?" I asked.

"The Book Store. Working late."

"Can you leave now?"

"No probs at all. Where do you want to meet?"

"The Blue Lion."

"See you there in twenty minutes."

"See you soon."

Bella was as good as her word and twenty minutes later we were sitting in the pub sipping our beer. I realised I had actually missed her, her company and just her being around.

I told Bella all about the accident, about Tas, about Steven, about Mum… It felt good to finally talk to someone. An outsider from it all. A person I didn't have to worry about telling the truth to.

"How do you feel?" Bella asked.

God that was like the million dollar question.

"It's been really hard you know," I gulped back another mouthful of beer. "I thought Tas would you know…"

"I know," Bella reached over the table and placed her hand on mine. Her hand was really soft and her fingernails had parts of burgundy coloured nail-varnish on. I could only imagine that Bella had bitten the rest off.

"It feels weird not being there you know?" I said. "I feel guilty about being here." I shook my head. I felt like I wasn't making any sense.

"You have pretty much lived and breathed the hospital for the past few days. It's only natural to feel like that," Bella assured me. "When are you going to tell Tas about Steven?"

"I really don't know," I said, looking at Bella. "How is she going to cope with it?"

"She will cope with it okay. She's got you, Maxine and your Mum hasn't she?"

"Yeah of course"

Bella removed her hand from mine and it suddenly felt cold. We drank the rest of our beers in silence but it wasn't uncomfortable. I felt that it was okay not to say anything but just sit here and soak up the atmosphere. Bella left the table to order us a couple more beers and I smiled. That's what I liked about her. She didn't have to ask. She knew me well enough already.

"It's good to see you Bell," I said.

"You too," Bella smiled.

"Tell me what's been happening with you. The Book Store?"

"That is still great. I'm pretty much running things now as Stella is never there, which is fine by me. The place is doing so well. I think people really like the ambience of the place you know?"

"Yeah, I do," I actually did. Bella's eyes lit up as she spoke about her work. How many people could say that about their jobs?

"How's the crew?" I asked.

Bella laughed and gave me the update on all her friends. Bella's friends were her family. She didn't always see eye to eye with her biological family so Em and Marie were her sisters and I guess Richie is the brother she never had.

Bella made me smile as she told me the latest idea of Richie's was to get married and have a gay parade in his honour through London City Centre. Richie and his boyfriend Craig were obviously getting on like a house on fire if they were thinking of getting married. It seemed they were more than thinking about it because they had enquired at a place in London that offered civil ceremonies for gay couples. Richie just had to persuade Craig to be his Groom and Bella to be his Best Woman.

Emma seemed to be loving the single life and having her own place to come home to. Bella never saw much of her in the evenings because she had always popped out for dinner or a few drinks with some people from work.

"So I have the place to myself most of the time. It's not a hard life, snuggled up on the sofa with my tele viewing lined up, with a pizza on its way," Bella said.

Marie was the same as Baz. They both seemed to love married life and it just seemed to have cemented their relationship.

"It's quite sickening really," Bella said. I could tell she didn't mean it. Bella was the most genuine person I know. She was ecstatic for her friend.

"I think it's about time I went home." I looked at my watch. The watch my sisters had got me when I was twenty-one years old, so quite a few years ago. It had a chunky metal strap and a blue face. Tas and Maxy had told me it was "something that I could keep."

"I need to sleep."

I suddenly felt exhausted and knew if I didn't get to my bed soon, I would fall asleep where I sat. It was as if the last few days had finally caught up with me. I guess there is only so much sleep depravation and emotional stress that one person can take. As I have mentioned before my Mum is a rock.

"Let's go." Bella downed the last of her beer before grabbing her coat. I watched her as she buttoned her black coat up.

"You look like Paddington Bear," I smiled as she took a friendly swipe at my face and missed.

Bella and I walked back to her flat. I stopped as she got to her front-door.

"Thanks Bell," I said. "I really needed tonight."

"That's what friends are for right?" Bella faced me as she rummaged around in her pocket for the key. She then turned to put the key in the lock and held the door ajar, before turning to me. There was a silence as I just looked at Bella and for some reason I was stuck for words for about ten seconds (although it felt like minutes).

"See you soon," I said.

"Bye Joe," Bella replied and walked into her entrance, closing the door behind her. I walked back up the path and continued on my short walk home.

What the hell had happened there?! I realised that if Bella hadn't turned round to unlock her door when she did I might have kissed her. What was that all about? I looked at Bella's lovely face and I wanted to kiss her. I shook my head. Bella was my mate, what on earth was I thinking? The last few days and the beers had just muddled my brain. I was obviously after some comfort of my own and that was not the best way to go about getting it.

Chapter Twenty

Tas was told about Steve a week after she opened her eyes. Maxy was the one who broke the news to her, Mum and I weren't there.

Maxy told me that it took about half an hour before the news actually sunk in, then apparently Tas just started to cry and she didn't stop for about two weeks.

It was a double edged sword. I was so happy to see my sister alive and getting better every day, so much so that I could actually see the colour flowing back into her face. But it was awful to see her look so unhappy. Her face was just so sad and I knew there was nothing I could say or do to make her feel better. Steve's Mum came to visit Tas one afternoon in the hospital and Maxy waited outside. She could see Tas and Steve's Mum holding hands and crying before his Mum finally left an hour later. Tas had requested that all her photo albums were brought into the hospital and it pained me to see her lingering on each picture of Steven knowing she was never going to see him again.

It really seemed weird going back to work, being back at work seemed somewhat surreal. I'd been off for nearly two weeks and I still didn't feel that I should be going back when my sister was still in hospital, but I couldn't afford not to go in. Maxy, on the other hand, said that she was going nowhere until Tas was out of hospital and on the mend. It was odd being back in the Call Centre and realising that whilst my family was praying for my sister's life, the world was still carrying on as normal. I felt like I should have made more of an effort to let everyone know that working and watching television, the normal everyday things you do, didn't matter when something like this happened.

I had learnt a lot from the experience.

It had also showed me who my real mates were. Baz,

Marie, Jono and Bella had been absolute stars and I would've been lost without them.

"It's just going to take time," Marie said, handing me my plate. This was the third time in a week I had popped round Baz and Marie's for dinner.

"I just wish there was something I could do," I said. "The food looks good as always."

Marie was a legend in the kitchen, could concoct a meal in minutes that would make Gordon Ramsay jealous with just a few ingredients she happened to find in a cupboard.

"You are doing something," Marie sat down opposite me. "You can only be there for her."

Marie was right. There was nothing I could do but be there.

"Thanks," I said and Marie smiled. I could see why my friend married Marie. She was one of the most thoughtful people I knew (that and a good chef).

I helped myself to potatoes, veg and some chicken cooked in a coconut style sauce. It smelt good.

"How was Tasmine today?" Baz asked, as he spooned in a forkful of chicken.

"The same," I shook my head. "It is still early days though. She's bound to be in this black hole for a while yet."

Baz and Marie both nodded in agreement. I didn't know what the timescales were to get over something like this. Would she ever get over something like this? I mean Steve could have been the man she married? Did Tas believe in "The One"?

I met up with Bella after dinner at the local pub and asked her the same question.

"I don't know if she does," Bella said.

"Do you?"

Bella paused and looked directly at me, in a kind of funny sort of way. She had her head cocked, her cheeks were flushed and she had a smirk at the corner of her mouth.

"Yes I do Joe," Bella replied.

"Oh right," I was lost for words and I had no idea why. Bella believed in the one. Most girls did right? Well from my vast experience girls did, my Mum and Marie.

My Mum had always said that once my Dad died there would be no-one else for her and there hadn't been. I'm not sure how I would have coped if there had been another man in my Mum's life.

"I am not sure I believe in that," I finally replied to Bella.

"You are not sure about the one?" Bella asked

"It's too idealistic isn't it? There being only one perfect match out there for you. I mean, there are billions of people in the world and there is only one perfect match for you," I just couldn't get my head round it.

Bella looked thoughtful and she started to pick the pink nail varnish from her nails, which I had come to realise meant she was nervous or thinking about something. It was the latter.

"I think that you're bound to meet some half matches on the way. These half matches make you into the person you are today," Bella continued. "I mean I was meant to go out with Pillock to make me the stronger person that I am today because when I meet The One, my strength will be a quality he admires in a girl."

"Well put. My god Bella you nearly had me crying there!" I started to laugh and Bella gave me a friendly punch in the arm. Well I think it was friendly, it didn't hurt anyway. Bella laughed but I think she knew that I understood where she was coming from.

As I walked back to my place later that evening my head was spinning with thoughts about "The One", which is slightly worrying for many reasons. The first being that I am a blokey bloke. You know a bloke that doesn't cry at Titanic, can handle stubbing his toe on the bedroom cabinet and could quite easily hit a pigeon accidentally with the car and not think anything of it. The second being that I had never thought about all of this

218

before. I decided that the emotional trek I had been on in the last few weeks had taken its toll, either that or I was turning into a woman!

Chapter Twenty One

Tas quit her job, said there was no point in returning to work. The whole point of work was to save money so that she and Steve could get their own place. This was worrying as Tas loved her job. I mean, rather her than me, but she did love her job. She loved teaching the kids, even the horrible little brats that never said please or thank you. You know the ones that really just need a clip round the ear to put them straight?

Tas had really struggled to get her dream job. She had studied and worked for years. Whilst I was out wasting my school years drinking and playing truant, Tas was studying making sure she could get the best grades possible because her motto in life was "if a job's worth doing, then it's worth doing well." It was such a waste for her to jack it all in now. I remember her face when she told me she got the job at the school. You would've thought she'd won the lottery.

Mum was worried sick that Tas was losing her mind. Maxy decided that Tas had just lost the will to live life to the full. I guess losing someone you love will send you either way. It will either make you realise that life really is too short and that each moment should be appreciated for what it is or it could make you feel that life is too short so what is the point in bothering anyway.

I would like to think that if I had lost Tas (it makes me shudder thinking about what could've been) then I would have lived life to the full because that's what Tas would've wanted from me. I am sure that Steve would've wanted the same, so he didn't die in vain.

I had attempted to talk to Tas about it all yesterday evening. It hadn't gone according to plan.

"Do you think Steve would want to see you like this?" Nothing like taking the bull by the horns.

"Steve is dead," Tas replied. Tas was sitting on her sofa wearing her pale blue patterned pyjamas. In fact, Maxy said that Tas hadn't actually changed out of them in over a week. She was also wearing a cap on her head to cover her scars and the bald patches on her head where she had the operation.

"But Tas?" I asked, well in fact I pleaded.

"I'm not interested Joe," and that was the end of the conversation.

I spent the rest of the evening with Tas watching television and making cups of tea.

Maxy got home at ten-ish and that's when I left. Maxy's face fell when she saw Tas in exactly the same position she had left her that morning and in exactly the same clothes.

"So did she listen?" Maxy asked as she showed me to the door. Her face looked at me expectantly.

"Not a word," I kissed my sister on the cheek (one of the new things we all did since Tas's accident) and said goodbye.

On the walk home I realised that I am hopeless in these situations and always had been. One of my mates at school had lost his sister to a rare blood disease and do you know what I did? I avoided him when he came back to school because I didn't know what to say. Sorry just didn't seem to cut it. Luckily for me, my friend didn't think I was a complete arse and came up to me to tell me that he understood. It's a shame I lost touch with him. He was a good mate.

I didn't know how to help Tas or what to do for the best. Fortunately, I didn't have to ponder that thought for too long as the next day Maxy called me to tell me that Tas had agreed to go to a grief counsellor. To this very day I don't know how Maxy persuaded my stubborn sister to do this, but the following week Tas started attending counselling sessions and attended every week. I have no idea what the counsellor and Tas talked about, and I never will but I could see from the fourth session that it was helping.

For example, Tas had refused to go to Steve's funeral. She said that Steve had hated funerals and she was not ready to say goodbye yet. My Mum, Maxy and I all tried to make her see sense, that she had no choice. This was her time to say goodbye but she missed it anyway. Mum and I attended in Tas's place, whilst she sat at home all day with Maxy watching television not saying a word.

There's not much to tell you about the funeral. It wasn't a happy affair. A young man taken in the prime of his life, the son of two loving parents and the brother of a younger sibling. Steve's Mum and Dad looked wrecked. Their faces looked ravaged (it's the only word I could think of) by grief and I wondered if they would ever get over it.

The church was full of people and again I realised I didn't know Steve at all and I felt guilty. Were all these people his friends? People he worked with? His family? I had no idea, but it showed he was a popular man.

Mum approached Steve's parents at the end of the service to offer her apologies and they just nodded in acknowledgement. They didn't mention Tas but I think they understood why she wasn't there. Steve's Mum had visited Tas on a couple of occasions since she had got home from the hospital.

Since the counselling, Tas had visited Steve's grave. She had insisted she go alone and even though Maxy was worried sick that she would hang herself at the church or something, Tas came back two hours later with a tear-stained face and a smile on her face.

"The head-stone is perfect," was all Tas said about her first visit. But since that day she visited Steve more often. I was all for it. It really seemed to help.

I didn't want to count my chickens, but things were looking up, and would you believe it but in more ways than one?!

Chapter Twenty Two

"Eh?" is the not the best reaction when your Manager has just told you that he wants to promote you within the team.

"As you know Joseph, one of the Team Leaders has left so there is a spare vacancy. I feel this could be something that may be of interest to you," Hugh and my Deputy Manager just looked at me waiting for my reaction.

The Deputy Manager is a funny looking man. He's short for a bloke (about fivefive), with a full head of brown hair and spectacles that sat on the front of his nose. He wouldn't be out of place wearing a school uniform complete with cap and grey shorts or he could play a grown up Harry Potter.

"What do I need to do?" I finally asked.

"Excellent!" Hugh smiled and clapped his hands together, already under the assumption I had agreed to whatever was necessary. He then proceeded to explain what that actually was.

It didn't sound very easy. I had to attend an interview for the job. I'm not very good at interviews or exams for that matter. I didn't even have to go for an interview for the job I am in now, just managed to scrape through on Maxy's recommendation. No-one thought to ask if Maxy's recommendation might be slightly biased, seeing as I'm her younger brother.

I told my Manager that I would think it over and let him know. I spoke to Marie and Baz about it, who thought it was a great opportunity for me to do more and improve my skills (I reckon my typing was up to seventeen and half words per minute now). Maxy was the one that persuaded me that I had nothing to lose. If I got the Team Leader role, my money would go up by about two grand a year! I would be just plain daft to turn that down.

"Why on earth didn't you go for the role then?" I asked Maxy.

"What for? I'm happy doing what I'm doing, earning the money I am so why would I want to change it."

Fair enough.

My interview was set for a week later. Hugh and his Manager would be interviewing me and I was up against two other candidates. One of them was Ellie who had been on the course with me and another was someone from outside the Call Centre, someone who wanted a change of direction. I was determined their change of direction wouldn't be at this company.

I enjoyed preparing for my interview. I realise that I sound quite geeky saying that but I did.

Maxy ran through all the possible questions that I could get and we both had to work hard on my answers.

"Why do you want this promotion?"

"The money is so much better."

Apparently this is not a response that would win over my interviewers, neither is the response "something to do."

Bella called me the night before my interview to wish me luck. It had actually been a few days since I had last spoken to her and that was again just a quick phone call and she had phoned me.

I just didn't seem to have the time at the moment. My life had been a hectic mess for the past few months, what with Tas and her accident and now the job. It was just one of those things.

"Let me know how you get on," Bella asked as we ended our phone call that night. "Yeah course," I replied. "Thanks for phoning."

Okay, I admit I went into the interview with the wrong attitude. I thought the whole process would be a "piece of piss" but in fact it was harder than I thought. When you are actually in the small air-conditioned office with two people in suits firing questions at you, it's a completely different ball-game to Maxy asking me questions sitting in her living room, with a cup of tea and some chocolate hob-nobs and us spending up to ten minutes thinking of the best answers.

The frustrating thing was the questions that I was being asked were exactly the same ones that Maxy and I had run through, but for the life of me I couldn't remember what I was supposed to say.

"What would you say your five top strengths are?" was one of the questions.

"I can cook a mean curry," It's a fact. I actually said that, obviously I only meant that as a joke (although I can actually cook a mean curry), but for some reason the two interviewers did not find that funny. My Manager's Manager just raised one of his large bushy eyebrows which not only freaked me out but made my nervousness worse.

"What would you say your weaknesses are?"

"Women and booze," I laughed.

It was like I was digging a hole for myself and I couldn't get out of it. There was no stopping me now. I was on a roll.

"Where do you see yourself in five years time?"

"On a desert island."

The interview lasted less than an hour, but I was so relieved when Hugh finally said. "Thank you very much for your time Joseph. We will let you know the outcome in a few days."

I was angry with myself. I had completely lost the plot in the interview, answering questions with the first answer that came into my head. I didn't need for them to tell me the outcome. I closed the office door behind me and gave Ellie a wink as I walked past.

"It's all yours mate."

A few days later the outcome was announced. The best woman got the job and that was Ellie. She even came up to me to make sure I was all right about it which I appreciated and I didn't have any bad feelings towards her at all. I buggered up the interview all on my own. I was actually really pleased for Ellie and I could tell that this was something she really wanted. Hey, maybe I was turning into a nice person after all.

Chapter Twenty Three

I had decided to get fit. My body had been a completely different shape when I was doing manual work. I never realised how much exercise I actually got.

Nowadays, the majority of my exercise is getting up from my chair and getting a coffee from the machine which is approximately 200 yards away from my desk, so not exactly strenuous.

Don't get me wrong. I didn't used to look like Arnold Schwarnegger but at least I could see my feet. It hit home to me the other day when I raced upstairs to get my mobile phone which I had left in my bedroom and the caller (my Mum) hung up because she thought she had the wrong number. I couldn't utter a word as I just heavy breathed down the phone trying to catch my breath.

Marie had told me that Bella had just joined a local gym so I should give her a shout if I wanted company. I certainly didn't want to attend one of these places on my own, so I gave her a call.

"I joined about a fortnight ago," Bella advised me over the phone.

"How is it?" I asked apprehensively.

"Hard."

"What do you mean hard?" I was getting worried.

"For your first few visits one of the trainers spends an hour with you to run through the equipment and make sure you are training correctly," Bella explained. "It's not as easy as I thought it would be."

It turned out Bella was on my wavelength. She wanted to pay a monthly fee and go to a gym two or three times a week, sit on an exercise bike whilst watching MTV (Bella informed me of this) and then go home and eat some pizza for a treat.

"I'll get you an introductory appointment with one of the nice ones," Bella said.

"Can't I just go along with you one day?" I asked.

"No!" Bella replied very quickly and very shrilly. "You are ermm.. much better off with a trainer."

"Okay," I resigned myself to the fact I was going to have to go to the gym on my own after all. "Thanks."

Bella was as good as her word. One of the trainers Becki (not Becky, which she clearly pointed out to me over the phone) would see me that weekend.

"How about nine a.m?" Becki asked on the phone.

"On a Saturday!?"

"No pain no gain," Becki replied. I was starting to think this was a bad idea.

That is how I found myself sitting in the reception of a quite posh gym on a Saturday morning just before nine a.m. whereas normally I would be fast asleep. I thought Jono was going to die from laughter when I told him that I couldn't go for a few beers on the Friday night because I had a gym induction. Who could blame him right? It was all right for Jono. He had hollow legs and arms. There was not one ounce of fat on him, although I would always rather look like me. He was too skinny for my liking.

I had arrived at the gym fully prepared, wearing a pair of tracksuit bottoms, an old grey t-shirt and a black hooded fleece.

My first impression of the gym was a good one. The reception was really bright and had one of those really long wooden curved tables. The two people that manned the desk had impeccable manners (my Mum would've been impressed) and looked immaculate. I looked down at my worn addidas trainers and felt slightly embarrassed, but hey you have to start somewhere, right? My first point of call after this induction would be to get some new trainers.

"Morning Joe," Becki came striding into reception and I

rose out of my wicker chair to shake her hand. Becki was slim (naturally) with really long dark hair which swung behind her in a ponytail. She was also wearing mountains of make-up because no-one's eyelashes could be that long and no-one's face could be that orange. Her make-up couldn't disguise her real age though, she must be in her mid forties at least.

"Let me show you around," Becki smiled. She had really white teeth and it was on the tip of my tongue to ask her how she got them that white, but I stopped myself.

Maxy had told me that some celebs bleach their teeth to get them so white, so maybe Becki did that too and she wouldn't appreciate me bringing attention to it. We walked through the double wooden doors and were in a long corridor. Becki pointed out the men's and ladies changing areas, the door which led the swimming pool and at the end was the door that led to my pain.

The gym itself was absolutely massive, you know the ones you see on television? There were rows of exercise bikes, rows of treadmills, rows of some climbing contraptions and rows of rowers with televisions positioned at the front although no sound. The only noise was the hum of the machines and the low volume dancey type music playing in the background.

Once Becki had shown me around the rest of the gym including the "studio room" which was used for step and aerobic classes, it was time to get me started. I had no inclination of doing one of those classes ever in my life. I wouldn't wear a leotard for anyone.

I was sitting on one of the exercise bikes. Becki had provided me with a complimentary pair of headphones so I was actually watching "soccer am" on Sky. I couldn't really concentrate on it because Becki kept coming back every thirty seconds to check I was keeping my speed on the bike up. After ten minutes my legs felt like jelly and I realised how unfit I actually was.

Becki hadn't finished with me yet, she got me on the rower

229

and the treadmill before she finally said that would be enough for today. She wanted to leave the "versaclimber" (whatever that is) for another day and we could work on the weights later. Becki seemed to think I had already signed up for my gym membership when in actual fact I was starting to think it was a really bad idea.

"Do you want to change before we run through the membership forms?" Becki asked.

"Yeah that would be good." She had obviously noticed my sweat-marks on my grey t-shirt (mental note to oneself not to wear a light coloured top to the gym). I took a quick shower in the changing area and was really impressed with the facility. They even had a sauna area in there and hook's for your towels whilst you showered. Someone had obviously given this place a lot of thought. The wooden theme throughout was really welcoming and warm and the tiled floors made it clean and fresh.

It was obvious that some people who came to the gym took the whole thing too seriously. I mean there was one bloke out there that looked like he was lifting his own bodyweight in dumbbells. He actually had muscles on top of his muscles. I would be worried my face would stay in that grimaced look. There was also the professional people, you know the ones in all the right clobber? And, why were there some women out there cycling away wearing a full face of make-up? Doesn't that defeat the purpose?

Oh well, each to their own.

I knew I was going to ache tomorrow. My legs felt stiff and that was the decider for me. The thing that made me sign on the dotted line and make Becki smile wider (she was obviously on commission).

It was official. I had joined a gym. Wonders would never cease.

Chapter Twenty Four

It was really odd. I had been a fully fledged member of the gym for just under a month now and had started to get really into it, well I had been attending three times a week which is pretty good in my book. That is nearly 12 times in a month and I'm sure I can tell the difference already, especially when I suck in my stomach.

Anyway, that isn't the odd thing. The odd thing is in all that time I had only ever seen Bella once and she didn't look at all pleased to see me. She was wearing a pair of three quarter length sporty trousers, with a vest top and her hair was scrapped back in a ponytail. It was actually quite refreshing to see that Bella didn't have one scrape of make-up on either.

"Hiya Bella," I had walked up beside her as she was running on the treadmill, which thinking about it now might not have been the best time.

"Joe!" she replied and then I am not sure what happened next but it resulted in Bella ending up in a heap at the bottom of the treadmill with her headphones still attached to her head.

Bella was embarrassed. That much was obvious (I have never seen anyone go so red). She did try to laugh it off and I did try to help her up and do the gentlemanly thing, but in vain.

"Ermmm well sorry about that. Got to go," Bella had said, after picking herself and her water bottle up from the floor and she had shot off. That had been about two weeks ago and I hadn't seen her since.

I had checked with Marie and apparently she wasn't sick and was still a member. I hoped she wasn't still embarrassed by the fall which was probably my fault anyway from interrupting her momentum so I left her a voicemail but after leaving it I realised that was probably not the best thing to do to make someone forget about an embarrassing incident either.

"Hi Bella. Hope you are ok and not lying broken somewhere after your recent fall from the contraption they call the treadmill. Anyway see you soon. Oh it's Joe by the way."

I did mean well, but I'm presuming that Bella wouldn't see it that way. It bothered me that she might be trying to avoid me again, it was probably best that I left her to it for a while. Time to get her pride back or something.

Anyway, I was coming on in leaps and bounds at this gym lark. Becki was thrilled (her words) not mine by my progress and was "proud" that I was pushing myself. Bloody right I was going to push myself. I was paying just over forty quid for this membership. Forty quid, which I sweated out for an hour three times a week.

I actually had a mountain of respect for Becki. Firstly the woman didn't sweat (which is a good job because her entire face would fall off). I had seen her through the window teaching a stationary bike class and there were about seven people in this class all huffing and puffing, but Becki still had this huge smile on her face, her make-up still intact and not one drop of sweat. She did take a towel and dab her face but that was obviously just for effect.

Secondly, the woman had an amazing ponytail. It swung behind her as if it was independent from her body. I had never noticed before but Becki had really long hair. Her ponytail alone nearly reached the bottom of her back. She could so easily do one of those hair care adverts, you know the ones with all the girls with the glossy hair (only me and you know it's because they have about twenty lights shining directly onto their heads).

I never attended the gym at weekends. The one and only time that happened was my introductory session. The rest of the time would be weekday evenings which suited me fine. I felt so lazy after leaving work. It's actually hard work sitting on your arse all day staring at a computer screen. My body was crying out for something to do. Becki told me that it took real discipline

232

as well to make myself attend after work, because that's when most people just want to go home and chill out.

I was pleased with my progress and pleased that Becki thought I was doing extremely well too. I have to admit though, this is my first gym experience and it's like a kiddie in a sweetie shop. I was just waiting for the novelty to wear off. I just wasn't prepared to face Becki's wrath just yet, so for the time being three times a week it was.

Chapter Twenty Five

The English Summer was crap this year. It had to be said. There had been a couple of days of really glorious hot weather (which had occurred when I was stuck in an office or at the gym) and the rest of it had been cloudy and even rainy. I couldn't believe we were reaching September already.

The break was Baz and Marie's idea. I was a bit hesitant at first for a number of reasons.

1. Would I really know anyone else?
2. My belly was fat.
3. Wasn't I supposed to be saving money?

I finally decided that I needed a break and agreed with Baz and Marie's plans. Jono had actually persuaded me to because he was concerned he wouldn't know anyone else and at least this way we could share a room together and neither of us would have to pay single occupancy. I felt a bit guilty that I had spent no time at all with Jono lately. I mean I lived with the man but I could count on one hand the number of times I had actually had a conversation with him in the last few months. This is what swayed me in the end. After all, you get out of friendships what you put in.

I knew there was no point in trying to persuade my sisters to go. Maxy would have loved a break from the town we lived in and the people we worked with at the moment but wouldn't even think about going without Tas. Tas, on the other hand refused straight away. It was too soon for her to be going away after Steve (she had only ventured to the supermarket for the first time a few weeks back) and she also had to think about returning to work. It was all well and good for Tas to give up her job, but now she realised that she couldn't survive just sitting on the sofa for the rest of her life and there was no way that Maxy could or would keep paying the entire mortgage on her salary and savings.

The break was booked for a month later. We all decided on the main ingredients we were looking for from this break.

1. Drinking (we all agreed).
2. Dancing (Richie and his boyfriend).
3. Relaxation (we all agreed).

I was a little bit disappointed when I found out we were going to the coast for a long weekend, a Friday to Monday booking. I had hopes of somewhere the weather would be guaranteed and you had to get on the plane to travel to. Is it just me that never feels like I'm about to go on holiday until I am sat on a plane?

Anyway going to the coast would actually work in my favour. I would save money by not going abroad and the weather forecast was looking promising for next weekend.

I decided that if I was going away I should try and shed the extra weight that I had put on around my middle. It was obviously just booze because I didn't tend to pig out and would often come home and make myself a pot noodle. I mean, how fattening are they? One kebab a week surely can't be that bad for you either?

I had actually stood in front of the mirror last night wearing just my boxers and checked myself out. How vain had I become? Not at all if you could see what I looked like. Maybe my boxers were just a little too small as I noticed the red marks around my waistband. Yeah right, who am I trying to kid?

How long was it meant to take before this gym lark took effect?

There was a holiday meeting tonight. No, I don't know what a holiday meeting is either, but apparently Baz and Marie wanted to discuss what was happening, who was sharing with who and how we were getting to the coast. To be honest, I thought it was good idea. I had no idea who else was going, other than the four of us. Marie was cooking as well, so it was no hardship to go round there.

I was wrong about that.

When I got round there Richie was standing in the dining room with a flip-chart and a marker pen. Honestly! Jono and I just looked at him with our mouths open, I caught Baz's eye who just smiled and I sat down to what was obviously going to be a long night.

There was quite a few of us crammed into Baz's dining room, around his relatively small table. It turned out that Richie and his bloke, Craig had organised the break so in their capacity as "holiday organisers" (which they gave themselves), they wanted to make sure we had it perfectly, well organised.

Marie was a star as normal and supplied us all with Mexican food which we helped ourselves to throughout the night. After my third chicken fajita, a bowl of nachos and my second beef chilli taco I decided that I might have to start going to the gym four or five times week.

Richie started the evening (on his flip chart) by detailing the reasons why we were all going on holiday which seemed a bit pointless but saw there was no point in arguing with him.

Baz & Marie – skint and need a cheap and cheerful holiday (apparently their honeymoon was just a distant memory now).

Jono – wants to pull (he admitted to that).

Richie & Craig – first romantic holiday.

Emma – stressed from work.

Joe – gone with the flow.

Bella – to get away from psychotic bunny boiler.

I caught Bella's eye and she just looked into her lap. She looked a bit uncomfortable with her reason being spelt out like that in front of everyone. How come I didn't know about this psychotic bunny boiler but everyone else in the room bar Jono seemed to?

Once Richie had gone through who was sharing with who (we had already sorted that but we didn't want to burst Richie's bubble) and how we were getting to the coast (lifts and trains) then the overall summary of the reason was simple. Everyone just needed a break and I wanted to know about the bunny boiler. Roll on the holiday!

Chapter Twenty Six

Are all men emotional cripples? I felt like one because I travelled down to Bournemouth with Bella, Emma, Marie and Baz in his car. I was sat next to Bella for the whole journey which wasn't entirely comfortable considering Baz had a Nissan Micra and there were three grown adults in the back. It didn't make sense to me why Marie was sat in the front as she was one of the smallest but who was I to argue. I didn't think broaching the subject about Bunny Boiler would be appropriate in a car full of people, I thought having a few drinks would loosen Bella up as we sat in the bar at the hotel waiting for the others to come downstairs so I left the subject then. I didn't want to put her off her food whilst we ate the restaurant and I felt like I would ruin her evening if I mentioned it when we were all chatting and having a laugh at the bar afterwards. It seemed there was every reason not to mention it, but I was dying to know. I mean Bella is my mate, so why has she not mentioned this to me before?

Friday night ended with us dancing at a gay club. I have never been in a gay club in my life and I don't think I would ever go in one again. I am the sort of person that would rather be kept in the dark about this sort of thing. Half naked men were all over the place, dancing, kissing and Emma came back from the toilets and told us all she had to actually step over one couple. Richie and Craig were in their element and I could see why they loved it here. This was a place they could be theirselves and be a couple. It was only now I noticed that in public they are reserved and you wouldn't actually know they are a couple.

Jono had gone back to the hotel a few hours before complaining he had a headache when in actual fact he had drunk far too many whiskey shots. Emma and Marie were in the middle of the dance floor strutting their stuff. Bella was talking to both Baz and me, letting us know that she thought Baz was great and she loved him so much for being a great husband to her bessstttest mate.

An hour later and after a few more spirit shots Baz, Bella and I were on the dance floor too and I would like you to keep this information to yourself. As I was with Baz, people presumed he must be my boyfriend so we were left alone which was fine by me, but not by Baz.

"All I'm saying is that it would be nice to be approached that's all. I mean am I good looking?" Baz slurred and shouted at Bella and I.

"Gorgeous Baz!" Bella shouted.

"Well, it would just be nice to get some attention that's all I'm saying," Baz looked around him.

"You're heterosexual though mate and married," I touched Baz's shoulder to reassure him.

"It's always good to have options," With that Bella and I started to laugh. Bella gave Baz a hug and whispered something in his ear which caused him to smile and more importantly shut up. I was getting slightly concerned at my mate wishing for male attention.

We all left the club together in the early hours of the morning. It was a short walk from the club to the hotel so we all decided to walk it. It wasn't too cold so it wouldn't be a hardship although I hadn't counted on the girls moaning about their shoes. Why do you wear such uncomfortable shoes if they cause you so much pain?

"Cos they look good!" Marie, Bella and Emma all shouted at me when I asked the question.

I shook my head and swore again that I would never understand women. Marie and Emma had now taken their shoes off and were swinging them around as they walked. I'm sure their outfits would look just as good with a pair of black pumps, but now wasn't the time to suggest that to them all.

"I need to sit down for a minute," Bella said and plonked

herself down on the bench in the park we were walking through.

"Oh Bell!" Emma said. "I need to sleep."

"You all go on. I'll catch you up," Bella had her head in her hands.

"Don't be daft," I sat down next to Bella. "You all go on. I'll make sure we get back."

There were no further arguments to that as the rest of the group walked back to the hotel. I watched as they disappeared into the distance.

"You could've gone on Joe," Bella looked at me and smiled. From the street-light next to the bench I could see that her eyes were blood-shot and she looked drunk and tired.

"I'll wait for you mate," I squeezed her hand.

"Mate mate mate," Bella said and put her head back in her hands.

"Hey, what's up?" I couldn't understand why Bella now seemed sad.

"Joe, tell me about Sally," Bella suddenly said. "Tell me how it ended."

It was weird really. I had never spoken or told anyone of the moment when Sally and I ended even though everyone knew why we had. I told myself that I would never talk about it with anyone and I found myself sitting with Bella on a park bench in Bournemouth listening to the sound of the waves nearby, telling her exactly what happened.

Chapter Twenty Seven

I decided that I would pop into Sally's on my way home from work. I didn't do this normally and I had no plans to see her that evening, but I thought it would be nice to stop off, have a cuppa and then go home to have a restful evening. Sally was always telling me to be more spontaneous.

I got my boss to drop me off at the end of Sally's road. She lived with a couple of her mates in a rented house about fifteen minutes away from me. For the past month I had stopped knocking on the door and always used the back-gate. Every house in the street had a back-gate which I noticed most of them kept unlocked. I had tried to call Sally a couple of times on her mobile but there was no answer. I knew she had been having a tough time at work recently. Her boss was trying to get her to work more hours and take on more clients and Sally was already maxed out. I knew her shift had finished about an hour before so I thought she might be asleep.

It's so obvious where this story is going right?

Anyway, I walked in the back door and there was not a sound in the house. I knew Sally's other housemates would still be at work. It was then that I heard a sound from above and that was Sally's room, so I knew she was in. I stood in her relatively untidy kitchen for about five minutes, oblivious to what was going on upstairs as I made a cup of tea and took it upstairs. It was then that I heard the groaning. Sally was always quite vocal when we had sex so she was either having fun with her vibrator or there was someone else there. Unfortunately for me, there was someone else there.

I should've turned and walked away as soon as I heard her groaning but curiosity got the better of me and I turned the handle and walked into the room. Sally was laying flat on her back with her legs wide open with a man on top of her, completely naked. I couldn't see what he looked like as his arse was the only part of his body facing me. Funnily enough (although not very funny at the time) Sally and her bloke hadn't noticed me until I coughed, so I watched him pumping away at my girlfriend for about ten seconds before Sally finally realised I was there.

"Shit Joe!" was Sally's first reaction.

The man on top swung round and climbed off her. I didn't know him and had never seen him before in my life. Sally pulled the bed clothes up to cover them both which I thought was a bit odd because I must've seen Sally naked a hundred times and she had never been the sort of person to be shy about being naked.

It was only then that I noticed that I had dropped Sally's tea. The cup was in pieces on her bare wooden floor and the brown milky liquid was creeping slowly under her bed.

I always thought that if I was in that situation I would want to kill both the girl and bloke with my bare hands. I always thought I would turn the air blue with obscenities. Instead I just stood there feeling humiliated and completely hurt by Sally. The man was insignificant. I realised that there was nothing to say.

I looked at her one last time, before leaving the room and even closed the door behind me. Sally and I knew it was over. This was just the kick I needed to move on. I walked home, took some headache pills and went to bed. I didn't wake up until the next morning when Sally was knocking on my door to collect her stuff. She had tried to get back together with me a few weeks after that.

But once a relationship is over, should you ever go back? If you are honest with yourself are things really different or do you fall back into the same routine? Okay, I did actually think about getting back together with Sally. I had a million thoughts flying through my mind and I knew the right answer. God, deep down I knew the answer.

The same routine would happen without you actually

realising. Before Baz had got together with Marie he had attempted to get back together with an ex girlfriend. He stayed with her for a further four months because he didn't want to admit to himself or her that they had failed at it again and there would be people out there who would not be able to stop themselves from saying "I told you so."

I knew Sally and I would fail at this. For one, the trust had completely gone. I would never trust her again. But on the other hand, I wanted it to work to prove to myself, to Sally, to friends and family that you can make it work. Actually, to be honest, I have never cared what my friends and family have thought about my relationships and believe me both my sisters have been very vocal about that in the past.

When Baz and his ex first got back together, he thought that it would work. He appreciated every single moment and he promised himself that he wouldn't take her for granted again. It took Baz a long time to get over that as he felt like he had broken a promise to himself.

Sally knew as soon as I sighed on the other end of the phone that my answer was no and it always would be. The relationship was over, dead and buried.

Chapter Twenty Eight

I couldn't believe I had talked so much. Bella had just listened as I told her everything about catching Sally with another man. Every now and then she would pipe in with a "bitch" or "slag" and it would make me smile. I felt like she was fighting my corner, although it was a fight that was over a long time ago.

Bella and I got up later than everyone else the next day, probably due to the fact we didn't go to bed until three hours later. By the time we woke everyone else had gone out. Emma had left Bella a note asking her to call her when we woke up. Instead, Bella knocked on my door and we decided to have a wander around together.

We were walking around aimlessly, in no particular direction and poking our noses in a shop every now and then. We walked to the end of the street we were on and noticed a bar on the corner, called The Bar.

The reason I have called this place a bar and not just because it is called The Bar (very ingenious and unique of the owners to name it that by the way) but because this was a bar and not a pub. Have you ever noticed the difference? I have some time to kill so let me tell you.

A pub is somewhere where the décor is old, a little bit yellow round the edges and has a carpet on the floor that is normally the same one in your grand-parents front room. A pub is somewhere where the boys go and have a pint sitting on a few bar stools, with the one pound juke box next to them (no doubt playing a few golden oldies like the Beatles or the Stones). A pub is somewhere where you know people as soon as you walk in and is mostly full of blokes smoking and drinking, getting louder as the day and night continue.

A bar is somewhere where the décor is light and airy. The floors are wooden throughout and there are retro pictures on the wall. There are comfortable sofas around round tables and no jukebox in sight, only a quiet lull of background music which is a bit jazzy. A bar is somewhere where no-one knows anyone and it is full of women, catching up on gossip with their handbags sat nicely on the table next to their cosmopolitans.

"A pint and a half of lager mate," I say to the barman, as we entered.

"We only serve wine here Sir," the barman replies.

See what I mean?! Firstly, what "bar" doesn't serve beer or lager and secondly, I don't want to be called Sir when I go for a drink. The only person that can call me Sir is my Bank Manager and I would be hard pushed to get that out of him, taking into account my current bank balance or should I say overdraft.

"Two glasses of wine then please," I am now at the stage where I don't mind what I drink. I just need something to do.

"Red or White?"

"White."

"Dry or Medium?"

"Dry will do."

"Large or small glass?"

"Large."

"Would you like your complimentary peanuts with that Sir?"

What is this, the Spanish inquisition? We just wanted a drink! I manage a nod at the barman and he serves me two large glasses of dry white wine with a pack of cashew nuts. We should have come in here earlier. This barman could easily have passed the day for us. I look over at Bella who is struggling to hoist herself on one the steel stools situated around the Bar.

"Nine pounds ten please Sir," the barman instructs.

I reluctantly hand over the money. I have no fight left to dispute the astronomical cost of the drinks. I actually want to ask if I have been charged for my complimentary cashew nuts by mistake but I decide to leave it. After all, I need to learn some perspective.

I sit down at one of the uncomfortable stools in the corner with Bella and our wine in front of us. As it turns out not a sip of wine really touches our lips until almost an hour later. It turns out Bella and I have lots to talk about.

"How are you feeling?" Bella asks and touches my knee. I'd never realised how thoughtful Bella was before. I can understand why she is asking me and she is asking quite shyly which is even more touching.

"Yeah all right cheers," I answer.

Bella shakes her head and smiles. She starts to run her finger along the top of her wine glass watching it intently.

I don't really want to talk about last night. I mean how many blokes do you know put all their feelings on a plate like that? I have managed all my life to keep feelings to myself and I didn't want to start changing the habit of a lifetime now. It would be like a can of worms being opened. I appreciated Bella being there though and asking. I also know I could trust her and everything I had told her wouldn't go any further, but that is because Bella is such a great mate.

"You look tired mate," I change the subject.

"That's what four hours sleep will do for you," Bella smiles.

"Well you look bloody great on it."

It's true. I look like crap. I haven't had a shave today so I feel a bit like Grizzly Adams (ok maybe I am exaggerating slightly). My facial hair does seem to grow a whole lot faster than other people's. I shave in the morning for work and if I am going out in the evening I would have to shave again. I didn't manage to have a shower this morning so I'm starting to feel a bit grubby. I am also aware that I probably reek of alcohol but I'm hoping Bella won't notice that considering she put a fair few beers away last night herself.

Bella, on the other hand, has her hair scrapped back into a

ponytail and she looks fresh faced except for the bags under her eyes. Mine are like suitcases. She is wearing a black shirt with her Top Shop jeans (the only reason I know this is because Maxy owns a pair). The outfit which I have seen before suits her and I feel slightly ashamed that I didn't make more of an effort when changing this morning. I'm actually wearing the same boxers as last night, is that too much information to share with you?

"How come you only had four hours sleep?" I suddenly realise that Bella and I got back to the hotel about five but Bella didn't wake me until eleven so that's a least five and a half hours.

"Long story," Bella sighs and carries on looking intently into her glass.

"Bella," I lean forward and place my finger under her chin tilting her face up towards me. "I'm all ears."

Chapter Twenty Nine

I finally found out about Bunny Boiler.

Bunny (as I nicknamed him) was actually called Paul and he was a bloke that Bella had met through the Book Store.

"Tall slim chap?" I asked.

"Yes," Bella confirmed. "How did you know?"

"Oh, think Baz mentioned it before," I lied. "Carry on."

It was the bloke I had seen her hugging that time in the Book Store. I was quite surprised that he and Bella had a thing going because he didn't really seem to be Bella's type. Bunny looked like a young lad, not a man of twenty-nine which apparently he was.

"Did you see his passport to prove this?" I asked.

"Joe!" Bella raised her eyebrows at me signaling me to stop interrupting.

"Sorry," I mumbled. I thought it was a fair question. I mean if I was trying to pull a twenty something woman and I was only sixteen (okay, maybe I am being a bit harsh) then I would probably lie about my age as well.

It turned out that Bella had actually ended with Paul three months ago and before that three and a half months ago and before that four months ago, but no she had been extremely assertive and determined that when she told Paul it was over three months prior that would be it.

"I had to be brutally honest with him in the end," Bella said.

"How?" I asked.

"I told him that I would never have any real important feelings for him and I didn't find him attractive," Bella blushed.

I couldn't imagine Bella saying anything like that to anyone, so I'm guessing that Bunny had really pushed her to the limits.

"What did he do?" I was intrigued to know what these limits were.

"Phoning me constantly, sending me presents, crying when I wasn't with him. The list is endless," Bella started to wiggle one of the buttons that was coming loose on her shirt. "So I told him it was over"

"Then what?"

This is when Bunny really did turn into a male version of Glenn Close. He had started turning up at the Book Store every day just to say hello, even though Bella knew it was out of his way. He would turn up when Bella was out for the evening. He even tried to start a fight with some bloke that Bella was talking to at the bar. Fortunately the bloke (who was actually her sister Lin's new boyfriend) found it very funny and laughed it off, but it could've gone so horribly wrong. Bella started getting gifts attached to her car. Flowers, chocolates (which had half of them missing by the time Bella got to her car in the morning), a teddy bear, cards declaring their undying love.

It sounded like a nightmare. One which I thought could easily be resolved.

"Shall I go and have a word with him?"

"No!" Bella was obviously adamant about that.

"What happened last night?" I asked. "When I got back to my room I had five missed calls on my mobile and three answer-phone messages," Bella said.

"Saying what?"

"Listen for yourself," Bella retrieved her mobile from her small pink rucksack beside her stool and dialled in her voicemail number before handing me the phone.

A deep voice, which surprised me because I expected it be squeaky, was on the other end of the phone.

"Bella, where are you? This is the third time I've tried. Call me."

"Bell, I've been round to your place but no-one is in. You

249

are worrying me now. Call me."

"Bella. I'm not sure whether to call the police. It's now two o' clock in the morning and I haven't heard from you. I'm going to stay outside your place just in case you or Emma come back. Just making sure you are ok."

"Bloody hell!" was all I could say.

"I know," Bella agreed.

"So for all you know Bunny could still be parked outside your place waiting," I said.

"Yep could be," for some reason this tickled me and I started to laugh. It was infectious because Bella started to laugh as well.

"Poor bloke must be cold," Bella said which made us laugh even harder.

"Maybe he thought ahead and brought a tent and sleeping bag with him."

It was ten minutes or so before Bella and I managed to stop laughing.

"Seriously though Bell. We need to do something," I said.

Bella looked at me thoughtfully.

"Yes Joe," she said. "We do."

Chapter Thirty

"So did you get your leg over then?" Jono asked me as soon as we walked back in our front-door.

I dropped my bag and looked at him.

"With who?" I asked.

"Oh come on mate," Jono walked into the kitchen. "Tea?"

"Yeah would love one," I answered. "Who are you talking about? I was with Bella most of the weekend."

"Bingo!" Jono says as he switches the kettle on.

"Bella is my mate Jono," I try to explain.

"Course she is mate," Jono says. I'm finding this conversation extremely annoying and just a little patronising.

"So you don't have any girls you would class as your mates?" Ask a stupid question.

"Can't say that I have," Jono says. "None as fit as Bella anyway."

Ten minutes later I am laying on my bed staring at the cracked ceiling. The bedroom I have at Jono's is actually Emma's old room so it's actually really nicely decorated. The walls are neutral beige and there's a cream carpet which could pass for new if it wasn't for some make-up stains near the door.

I'm turning into a girl. That's what my problem is. When had I ever stopped drinking for a weekend to pour my heart out and offer a shoulder to cry on? I was getting in touch with my feminine side and to be honest, I didn't like the thought of having one. God forbid if my Mum and Sisters found out, they wouldn't stop laughing.

Jono was different to me. He had never had a girl he could call his friend in his life. Maybe that's because he lies about all women, including his sister. I don't really know Jono's sister very well, but I know she has been married for the last five years bringing up two kids under the age of four so I am ninety-nine percent sure that she didn't travel to Australia and Far East Asia in the last six months. I saw her in Tescos last week for goodness sake.

"Baz, do you think I'm turning into a bird?" I rang Baz who I knew would tell me the truth.

"Eh what?"

I proceeded to explain the Baz about my chats with Bella without going into detail and the amount of time I've spent with her.

"I don't think you are a bird mate," Baz continued. "But I do think that you like Bella."

"Of course I like Bella. She's a top girl," I was confused.

"No mate. I agree with Jono. I think you really like her," Baz said. There was a long silence before I finally spoke.

"Bella is my friend. Why would I want to jeopardise that?" I asked.

"Cos it could be a good thing," Baz said.

I quickly changed the subject, asked after Marie before telling Baz I had to go and replaced the receiver.

I called him back two minutes later.

"You don't think Bella thinks that I fancy her do you?"

"No Joe I don't think she does," Baz said very positively.

"Oh okay. Good. I don't want her to think I'm being a letch," I was relieved.

"She wouldn't think that mate," Baz said. "Funny how you're worried what she thinks eh?"

"See ya Baz," I replaced the received again.

"Fuck!"

It hit me. Bella must have told Marie who must have told Baz that I was coming on a bit too strong. It was just what she didn't need at the moment what with dealing with Bunny. I didn't want Bell to get the wrong idea and I didn't want to suffocate her. I would help her out with the Bunny problem and then I would leave her be, give the girl some space. I wanted to smack myself hard on the head. How could I have not seen what I was doing?

Bella was far too polite to tell me the score and I hated the thought of her being in that awkward position, because of me being me.

I was as good as my word. I helped Bella cut Bunny from her life as best as she could in the hope he would start to leave her alone. Our first stop was changing her mobile number which she did over the phone with me making encouraging noises. The second stop was to start returning all Bunny's unopened cards to his address in a large brown envelope stating "return to sender." Our third step was to collect all the presents Bella has accumulated in the last few months and drop them off at the local charity shop. The presents must have cost Bunny a fortune. He could actually start his own cuddly toy shop. Bella and I took the three black bin-liners to the local charity shop who must have thought that Christmas had come early. The fourth step Bella could only do on her own and that was to start ignoring Bunny. As Bunny had no other means of communication available to him now he had started to show up on her doorstep. Bella phoned me after the first time. Her voice was filled with complete joy.

"I did it!"

"You did?" I asked.

"I walked past him as he kept shouting my name and I just ignored him," Bella shrieked down the phone. "I think after this he finally may get the hint."

It took six more times for Bella to ignore Bunny when he turned up at her home and place of work but finally it stopped. There were no more cards, no more presents and no more unwelcome visits.

"Thank you Joe," Bella said to me on the phone when she reached a fortnight with no contact.

"What are you thanking me for?" I asked.

253

"Helping, silly," Bella laughed. "We need to celebrate."

I felt it would be rude of me not to accept Bella's invitation to celebrate. After all she did deserve it. I would celebrate Bella's breakthrough and then I would distance myself from her. I was sure of it.

Chapter Thirty One

"Earth calling to Joe"

"Joe, are you listening?"

"Joe!"

The last, rather loud shout of my name brought me back to the real world and I looked up to see Maxy looking at me worriedly. We were sat in her living room on a Sunday afternoon. We had just had a massive roast chicken dinner with all the trimmings which both myself, Maxy and Tas had enjoyed. Maxy could cook a great roast. I felt like I couldn't move. Tas had disappeared after dinner for her weekly visit to Steve's grave, which gave Maxy a chance to tell me her news.

"Are you okay?" Maxy asked.

"Yep fine, just a bit tired that's all," I excused. "So tell me again about your new man?"

Maxy was really excited about this new man she had started seeing. I could see it from her face. He also sounded too good to be true but I kept that information to myself, after all that was just me being cynical. Unfortunately, Maxy felt like she couldn't talk about him in front of Tas who was still grieving for her dead boyfriend. This was the first time ever that I had known Maxy to keep anything from our sister and I could see that she hated it. Tas had come a long way in the last few months. She actually looked forward to her trips to the grave so she could tell Steven all her news and everyone else's for that matter (a gossip through and through). Tas would also smile when she spoke about Steven and even though she had a long way to go yet, I knew she was on the road to recovery. I was sure that Tas would be pleased with Maxy's news, but Maxy begged to differ and asked me to keep it a secret for now. I didn't want to be there when Tas did find out that Maxy had kept this from her though but, hey, that's not my decision. It was a big deal for Maxy to find a man and to actually talk about him positively. Maxy didn't just date anyone and those she did, she didn't mention or they had a long list of faults.

"Too tall."

"Too short."

"Weird feet."

"Nostril hair."

I guess you could say that my sister is quite picky with men but as she spoke about James, I was starting to feel decidedly inadequate.

"Great sense of humour, good looking, really intelligent, great job, lovely home…"

The list was endless.

As Maxy continued to talk about the perfect James I found myself drifting off to my previous evening with Bella.

It was a really good evening. The pub we had gone to had a really good atmosphere. It was just outside of town so I had borrowed Jono's car (I hadn't managed to get myself a replacement to the banger that I had crashed into a tree about three years ago) and had taken us there.

The pub itself was a really old building and apparently years and years ago it used to be the village school, although you wouldn't be able to tell that now. It was a pub that you would go to not for a good drinking session, but for a chilled out and relaxing evening. The beams and large wooden doors with the old fashioned locks gave the whole place an "Olde Worlde" feel. Do you know what I mean?

Anyway I am digressing. This was the place that I took Bella and she liked it as much as I did. She had never really ventured this way outside of town before so I mentally gave myself a brownie point for choosing a new place.

Yesterday evening was slightly odd for me because I had known Bella for quite a while now and I have to admit I think she's fantastic. She has a great sense of humour and we get on really well.

256

I can also admit that she is a great looking girl, but the oddest thing happened. When I got to Bella's I beeped my horn to let her know I was there. She walked out of her place and was walking up the path towards me in the car with her usual great smile on her face and do you know what happened? My breath got caught in my throat and I couldn't avert my eyes from her. This has never happened to me before. I am reluctant to say it, but as I have been honest with you all so far, she physically took my breath away!

Chapter Thirty Two

Maxy gave up trying to talk to me about James. She could see I wasn't listening from the glazed look I had across my face. She kept asking me what was wrong, but I couldn't really pinpoint it to be honest so what could I say?

"I thought one of my mates looked fit last night."

or perhaps…

"I think I'm turning into a perv and my mate will hate me for it."

Maxy wouldn't see this as a problem. I knew already what her advice would be and that would be to go and speak to Bella about it. I couldn't do that for a number of reasons.

Again what would I say? I didn't know what it meant. I mean how could that subject be broached?

"Bella, by the way I was really perving over you yesterday evening, shall we talk about it?"

Okay, I wasn't exactly perving last night but I was noticing a lot more than I usually do which I am finding extremely unsettling. For example, when Bella drinks a glass of wine she cocks her little finger out and there is a tendril of hair that constantly falls in her face. I noticed what she was wearing yesterday. I noticed that she was wearing a really nice perfume and I wanted to know if it was the perfume she always wore, I noticed that her hair was still just slightly damp on the ends when we arrived at the pub so I knew she had a shower before meeting me.

I understand this is probably my mind playing tricks on me because I hadn't had sex for quite a while. Was the last person Sue? No that can't be right she was donkey years ago. If it was Sue, this was probably why I wanted to rip my mate's clothes off and have sex with her. Do you think if I suggested it she would be up for it? That would probably help me get it out of my system. I laughed to myself at my ludicrous idea.

I don't know any men that are open with their feelings. They wear their hearts extremely close to their chest and don't really talk about serious matters like life and death.

However, this was not a normal situation for me and I need to talk to someone. Someone who would understand that I was like a dog on heat at the moment. Okay maybe not for just anyone and just focused on one person, but there had to be a simple explanation.

Luck was on my side. I gave Baz a call as I was leaving Maxy's. Marie was out round Bella and Emma's for a girly Sunday evening.

"What exactly is a girly evening mate?" I asked, as Baz led me through to the living room with two cups of tea in his hand.

"I never really liked to ask," Baz admitted. "Think they talk about boys and stuff with face masks on."

"You've been watching too many of Marie's girly films," I laughed.

"Yeah that could be true. She has bloody hundreds of them," Baz pointed at the nearby cupboard which contained the majority of the films. At a quick glance, I could see the girly classics like Titanic, Sleepless in Seattle, Notting Hill ... Yep it seemed Marie had them all.

"So how you been?" I asked Baz who had sat on the opposite sofa to me.

"Pretty good at the moment as it goes," Baz smiled. "Marie and I are getting on really well. This married lark is easy peasy. You should try it."

"Ha ha ha, yeah right," I replied. "Who with?"

Baz raised his eyebrows and now was the time to tell my best mate all. I knew what Baz was thinking and he hadn't even said a word.

"I think I'm turning into a perv," I admitted and pretended to be really interested in the liquid swirling around in my mug.

"You're not a perv. In all the time I've known you I could only accuse you of being a pervert once," Baz said.

"With who?!"

"Remember Janet at Primary School. You used to give her your apple everyday in exchange for a kiss on the cheek and for the rest of the time you would stare longingly at her across the dinner hall," Baz laughed.

"My god I'd forgotten all about Janet," I laughed. "She was an angel with her long hair and bright blue eyes. Wonder what she's up to now?"

"Probably married with four kids," Baz replied. "Now what's this about you being a perv. I think you had better start from the beginning."

So I did. I told Baz it all about Bella being such a good mate and how we got on really well, how I could confide in her about anything and knew it wouldn't go any further. That was an important trait in my book. Baz knew that. I told him about the night before. How Bella looked gorgeous and all night I had to fight the urge to keep my hands from her. How when I dropped her off I couldn't even look at her for fear of embarrassing myself and moving in for the kill. I also mentioned how I hadn't had sex in a while and this was probably the reason why I felt like this.

Baz didn't say anything for a while after I had finished. He looked at his carpet, scratching his chin and I could tell he was thinking. I valued Baz's opinion, so I let him have his think knowing he would probably give me some good sound advice.

"You need to talk to her man," Baz finally said.

Hmmm okay maybe not.

"To say what?!" I asked. Maybe Baz had lost his touch with offering sound advice.

"Joe, come on," Baz cocked his head and looked at me.

"Didn't you hear what I said? It's cos I haven't had sex in a while right?" I explained.

"Joe, you need to talk to her, to tell her," Baz said again.

"To tell her what?" I asked. Baz was starting to irritate me and here I was hoping he would help.

"I am going to tell you it straight now mate," Baz warned and I knew I wasn't going to like what he was about to say. "You need to tell her that you want to be more than her friend and that you fancy the pants off her."

Chapter Thirty Three

It took me three weeks and two days to finally admit that Baz was right and I was as shocked as I am sure you all are. I hadn't seen this coming at all. First of all, I had ignored Baz's advice, had left his house that evening and gone home thinking my mate had gone bloody mad. I could only put that down to him being a married man. I had quickly changed the subject after Baz had offered me his advice and even though he knew I had done it, he allowed it and we had a good evening catching up. It was good to see my mate so happy. Marie was a god-send.

I had ignored Bella in those three weeks and two days. Yeah I know, extremely grown up of me but I didn't know what else to do. If I met up with her or talked to her I might have done or said something that I might regret and then I could lose Bella from my life completely. I just needed to get my head straight before speaking to or seeing her again, which was fair enough. I felt bad though when I got messages from her, well two in fact. She had left me two messages in twenty-three days.

The first one was a few days after I had gone round Baz's.

"Hi Joe. It's me. Just thought I'd phone and say hello. Thanks again for a really nice evening on Saturday. Had a great time. Anyway must go. Catch up with you soon."

I didn't need to phone her back for that message right? She hadn't asked me to and she was just thanking me and saying hello.

The second message was a week after that.

"Hello Joe. Hope you are okay. Haven't heard from you in a little while. Anyway, as you probably know there is a bit of a get together at Baz and Marie's at the weekend so hopefully see you then."

I didn't go to Baz and Marie's get together. Baz understood. Marie just thought I was being aloof and I knew

Bella would think I was being weird with her.

Instead I went out of town for the night. If I didn't there was a good chance I would find myself popping round Baz's house for the get-together and I couldn't risk it. My head was still not right so I jumped on the train and went to the next town which had a lot more nightlife than my home town.

I wore my jeans and new salmon pink shirt, yeah I'm not sure about it either but my Mum got it for my birthday and she reckons it looks good on me. Maxy thinks pink shirts on men are a no-no. Mums know best though. My birthday was actually a few days before but I had let the event slip slowly by with no celebration. I was now on the wrong side of thirty and who wanted to celebrate that? I never thought about the fact I was actually going out for a night out on my own. Blokes just don't. It's girls that have to plan days in advance and know exactly what time they're all meeting etc. Maxy and Tas used to drive Mum mad with the phone-bills and most of the time they would just be confirming dates and times with their friends.

Anyway, the town was heaving, which of course I knew it would be on a Saturday night. I sat on one of the spare stools in All Bar One with my pint and took in the atmosphere. Two hours and five pints later I met Jessica.

Chapter Thirty Four

Jessica was tall for a woman. She was really tall and it wasn't just because I was sitting down when she came over to me. She had long dark straight hair and was wearing a top which left little to the imagination. It was one of those backless tops that had a butterfly thingy on the front. Anyway this butterfly thingy only just covered up Jessica's boobs. Her jeans were also skin tight and she had an ample arse which I watched as she went to the bar and got us some drinks. Jessica was out with a few of her work friends, but when they left to go somewhere else she stayed with me and I knew where the evening was heading. Presumptuous? maybe. Wrong? no.

Jessica and I stayed in the bar until we were kicked out in the early hours of Sunday morning. She had done most of the talking last night. She worked nearby, loved her job (earned a fortune by all accounts) and owned her own home. By the time we left the bar, I was not as drunk as I would like but did feel quite lightheaded. Jessica lived just round the corner and asked if I wanted to come with her for "coffee." She certainly knew her own mind and I like that about women.

Jessica lived on one of the new estates about five minutes away from town. She spoke animatedly about her own first place.

Jessica and I started to kiss as soon as she closed her front door. It was nice and had been a while since I had kissed a woman like this so it was no hardship. The only problem was twenty minutes later we were still kissing (although we had moved to her living-room and were now lying on the sofa).

"Would you like to go upstairs?" Jessica asked in between kisses. I looked down at her and for the first time noticed her. She wasn't a bad looking woman at all. She had a fantastic body and I could see her boobs straining to get out of the top. All it would take would be one single hand movement and I could free those babies but my hands seemed to be stuck to Jessica's side.

"Ermm Joe, are you okay?" Jessica asked.

I realised I hadn't said anything for a while and was probably freaking her out by just looking at her.

"Yeah just feel a bit drunk that's all," I answered.

"Ah, right, "Jessica smiled. "It happens sometimes." Jessica moved her arms and I sat back so she could move off the sofa. "Would you like some coffee?"

"Nah I'd better be going," I said. It felt odd. Here I was saying goodbye to a woman I hardly knew in her house.

"You might as well stay," Jessica said. "Sleep on the sofa. I'll get you a blanket." Jessica left the room and came back ten minutes later with a steaming mug of coffee and a blanket.

"Night Joe," Jessica bent down and kissed me on the lips.

"Night," I answered back and watched as the ample arse walked away from me. What on earth had bloody just happened?!! I hardly slept that night.

I left Jessica's early that morning before she had even got up. I had folded the blanket, washed my coffee mug (in her spotless kitchen) and left a note which simply said "thanks."

Jessica in my opinion was too trusting. I could have been a thief or even an axe-murderer for all she knew. She could've woken up this morning to find her tele, DVD player and possessions gone. I hoped my sisters had more common sense than that but then again I wouldn't want to know about my sisters picking up strange men in bars for one night stands in the first place.

I had got home to Jono asking me a hundred million questions (okay maybe a slight exaggeration) about the night before. I was more interested in finding out about Baz's do last night.

"Yeah, it was all right," Jono had answered nonchantly when I asked.

"Who was there?" I asked casually (or at least I tried).

"Usual crowd."

"Any gossip?"

"Nah not really."

I had to hold my breath and count to ten in case I smacked Jono in the mouth for being so thick skinned. I wanted to know if Bella was there, if she was by herself and what she was wearing (although I am pushing it for Jono to remember that). Instead I let Jono think I had got lucky last night, he called me a dirty dog and that was it. The rest of our day was spent chilling, watching MTV and getting a takeaway later that evening. Jono was good company. He chatted about his life, his women (most of them made up) and his job (he was a landscape gardener and he loved it). Jono's inane chit-chat took my mind off Bella and the night before with Jessica.

Work on Monday and Tuesday dragged slowly. I sat at my desk in robot mode, asking strangers on the phone for their names, addresses and computer details. I could do this job standing on my head even with my poor typing skills (I was sure they would improve eventually). I went to bed early on both nights, which worried Jono no end who thought I must be really sick especially when I turned down his offer to pop to the pub and instead made myself a hot chocolate before going to sleep.

It was three days after my night with Jessica before it hit me and I realised what had happened. I knew what I didn't want.

I didn't want anyone else. I didn't want Bella as my friend. I didn't want to make my life so difficult anymore.

I knew what I did want.

I wanted Bella.

It was time to tell her.

Chapter Thirty Five

I felt like I was turning into Bella's new stalker. I watched her as she took the new books from her trolley and stacked them on the shelf. She hadn't seen me yet. I watched as Bella took one of the new hardbacks, lifted it to her face and smelt the cover before smiling and placing it on the shelf. I smiled to myself. Bella looked great. She was wearing a pair of plain black straight leg trousers with black shoes and a pink roll-neck jumper. Her hair was tied back in a ponytail and she had a pen mark across her face which she had obviously not noticed.

The Book-Store was busy today. I'd popped in on my lunch hour so it was always going to be. I watched as a customer walked up to Bella, asked her something and she smiled. She then led them away from where I could see them.

"Can I help you Sir?" A girl walked up next to me and asked.

"Ermm nope, haven't found what I am looking for. Thanks anyway," and with that I left.

Okay, that could've been embarrassing. Had the other Assistant in the Book Store seen me staring at Bella and if so had she got a good enough description to let her know it was me.

What could I have said to Bella anyway, whilst she was working?

I'm not sure how people coped without mobile phones. I sent Bella a text message. It was a casual message I think…

"Hi Bell. Hope you're okay. Fancy meeting up later? Nothing important. Just fancy getting together but no probs if not. Anyway not important. Just would be nice to see you and all that stuff. Ermm bye"

Was that breezy?

It was sixty three minutes before Bella replied and I was just in the middle of a phone call with a customer at work when my phone vibrated to let me know I had a message. I have to say I completely lost concentration.

"Okay, thank you for the information. An engineer will be with you shortly," I said to the customer on the phone.

"That would be a miracle seeing as you don't have my address," The customer replied.

Once I took the customers address I finished up my phone call and set my phone to an offline status so no more calls would come through on my line. I didn't really care that at this moment in time the board at the front of the room was telling me that eight calls were currently waiting. I'm sure they wouldn't mind waiting a few seconds more.

I had one new message. It was from Bella.

"Hello. Nice to hear from you. I can't make tonight Joe. Sorry. Some other time. See you soon."

What was she doing tonight that was so important? Was she seeing someone new? None of the answers to those questions mattered because I knew I had just received the brush off and I felt absolutely gutted.

Chapter Thirty Six

It was two weeks before I saw Bella again and this time there was no getting out it. For one Baz said he would kick my arse if I didn't come out and second I knew I had to get over the bloody woman (yes I had resorted to calling Bella that Bloody Woman).

It was Marie's birthday. We were all going out for a meal at the local curry house so no big deal and I could sit at the opposite end of the table to Bella. I was a grown up for goodness sake. I'm sure I could be civil to Bella for one evening and her new man. Okay so no-one had actually told me that Bella had a new man, but I was sure of it. Baz was being quiet about the whole thing so I took that as a sure sign.

I arrived at the curry house ten minutes late on purpose. I didn't want to be sat there with just Bella and her new geeky bloke (well he had to be a geek didn't he?) for company. By the time I got there everyone was seated although there was no sign of Bella. Ten minutes later I had actually given up hope of seeing her when I spotted her walking out of the ladies loo chatting to Emma. She was laughing and her cheeks were flushed, which meant she had a glass of wine or two already.

She gave me a little wave when she saw me and I smiled back. There was no sign of a man as Bella took her seat next to Marie and Richie.

The table was long so as Bella was sat at the other end I didn't really get a chance to talk or look at her because she was on the same side as me. There were nine people sat at the table with the pristine white tablecloth. I must be turning into a woman to have noticed something like that. The usual crowd was there as well as a couple of people from Marie's work.

Everyone, but me gave their gifts, just as the poppadoms were delivered to the table so we all continued to munch away whilst the excited Marie ooed and aahed at her gifts. I was embarrassed for not getting her a present. I hadn't thought. I left my seat and gave Marie my card and a peck on the cheek hoping no-one else would notice I didn't hand over a present at all. Bella smiled at me when I caught her eye and I tried to say something smart to make her laugh but all I ended up doing was clicking my fingers and pointing them at her. I'm not sure why I did that and as I shuffled back to my seat I wanted the evening to be over.

Bella looked good. She had her hair piled on the top of her head which made me realise that her hair had grown so that she could get it all up now (again I think I am turning into a woman). She was wearing her Topshop jeans (Bella always called them her trusty top shop jeans) and a cream low-cut top. When I gave Marie her card I could see that Bella was wearing a cream lacy bra.

I made polite conversation to the people I was sat near, Marie's workmates, who were both really nice although quite quiet, and Baz. Every now and then I would hear Bella laugh and wonder what she was laughing at. I also got caught not listening to my companions at dinner because I was straining to hear what Bella was saying.

Dinner was nice. The food was great (I haven't been to an Indian restaurant yet that had disappointed me), the Tiger beer was spot on and most of all Marie looked like she was enjoying herself. A little too much because after the meal and her fifth flaming sambucca Marie told Baz rather loudly that he was to take her home that minute and ravish her.

I was glad the evening was over when we finally paid and left the restaurant together. Marie's workmates shot off to their car, but the rest of us waited for Marie to get into her coat before Baz told us he had better take her home before she falls down. Marie gave us all massive cuddles and kisses before Baz finally grabbed her arm and led her off down the road.

"Who wants to come to mine for a nightcap?" Richie asked.

270

I liked Richie. He was down-to-earth and what you saw was what you got with him.

"Great idea!" Emma said. "Let's go." Emma linked arms with both Richie and Craig.

"I'm going home mate," Bella said. "I'm knackered."

"We will walk you home first then," Richie announced.

"I will walk Bella home," The words had come out of my mouth before I could stop them. It was probably the first full sentence I had said all night.

"Are you sure Joe?" Bella looked at me.

"Positive," I had never more sure of anything in my entire life.

"Cool. See you later," Richie said.

Richie, Craig and Emma walked off down the road waving goodbye and laughing which left Bella and I alone (at last).

Finally, I was going to have my moment and there was no going back.

Chapter Thirty Seven

The evening was chilly. The sky was completely clear and there was no sign of a cloud which meant the cold was closing in.

"Do you want my coat?" I asked Bella. She was shivering in her knee length cream coat as we walked down the road to her flat.

"You'll freeze!" Bella laughed. "No I'm fine. We could walk faster which would warm me up."

I didn't want to walk faster. I needed time to think about what I was going to say to Bella.

"You been busy?" I asked.

"Yeah, I have lately. The book store had a really famous author in the other evening and I had to prepare for it. I got completely star struck when I saw him. I mean, his books are so fantastic and this comes from his amazing mind," Bella said. "Boring, eh?"

"Not at all," I replied. I never found the way that Bella talked about her work boring. My god, I sound as smitten as I used to be about Primary School Janet.

"What about you?" Bella asked.

"Not really. Plodding along," I answered.

Ten minutes later we arrived at Bella's. It only felt like ten seconds.

"Thanks for walking me back Joe," Bella turned to walk towards her door.

Now Joe. Now Joe. Now Joe was going around in my head.

"Wait!" I shouted causing Bella to turn around with concern in her eyes.

"You okay?" Bella walked back up towards me.

"Bella I.. ermm I need to .... I need to....," I stuttered leaving Bella looking concerned and now confused.

"Joe are you ok?" Bella asked me again.

It was now or never so I took Bella's hand and moved towards her. I lent down towards her expectant face and I did what I had wanted to do for months and months but had never realised it. I kissed her. The kiss didn't leave me disappointed, especially because Bella kissed me back. As I pulled away I wanted to kiss her again. Her face was flushed and her nose was cold. I couldn't tell from her expression what she was thinking. Had I misread everything? Would Bella regret the kiss? Would she be angry with me?

The silence seemed to be never ending even though it must have only been seconds before Bella spoke. "Joe," she said very quietly.

"It's about time" and then she kissed me.

The End.